PEACE of OURSELVES

JOHN,
HOPE YOU ENJOY THE ADVENTURE.

ALL MY BESTS,

KENN

KENN VISSER

NEWMAN SPRINGS PUBLISHING
320 Broad Street
Red Bank, NJ 07701

First originally published by Newman Springs Publishing 2019

Peace of Ourselves is a work of fiction. Although the book is inspired by a true story and historical events, with the exception of public figures named in the book, any resemblance to actual persons, living or dead, is purely coincidental. Other than the historical events cited, incidents, events, places, and locales are the products of the author's imagination or used in a fictitious manner.

The Vietnam War and the estimated 40,000 young Americans that sought sanctuary in Canada, however, are very real. Recognized by the Canadian government as immigrants instead of refugees, an archived report on the Canadian Citizenship and Immigration website indicates that most of the American immigrants stayed in Canada after the war, "making up the largest, best educated group of immigrants this country ever received."

ISBN 978-1-64096-669-7 (Paperback)
ISBN 978-1-64096-670-3 (Digital)

Printed in the United States of America

To Pierre Elliott Trudeau, whose courageous pursuit and defense of multicultural democracy significantly influenced the shining light of freedom that Canada has become.

Well, I'm livin' in a foreign country but I'm bound to cross the line
Beauty walks a razor's edge, someday I'll make it mine
If I could only turn back the clock to when God and she were born
"Come in," she said, "I'll give you shelter from the storm."
—Bob Dylan

Introduction

The Okanagan is a land of casual extremes, a false front for the True North that trades the real deal for the day-to-day. Within a few short months, this partly imagined oasis presents a disguise of heat strong enough to sustain a lingering image of the season. A half-truth that makes winter bearable, it offers the potential for the sun's warmth to peek-a-boo through during spring and fall, extending the hot flash of summer.

Chapter 1

November 22, 1963

On the Friday morning of the day that President Kennedy was assassinated, Kevin Pederson Fischer had two of his teeth pulled in preparation for new braces that his parents hoped would tame the very buckteeth he was born with. Still high on the residue of the sodium pentothal he had been anesthetized with, Kevin was drinking a fresh banana milkshake his mother made while watching *I Love Lucy* reruns when the program was interrupted with the first bulletin about President Kennedy being shot in Dallas. It seemed in his partial dream state that what he was hearing on TV was as unreal as so much of his day had been waking up from oral surgery.

The nurses told him before they put the needle in his arm that sodium pentothal was the truth serum the Nazis had used to extract information unwillingly from their victims and that, most likely, the Russians were using the same or worse now. He wasn't sure why they told him that or what the relevance was, but in Kevin's mind, that was often the case with adults.

When the needle was in and they were ready to take him under, Kevin was instructed to count backward from ten. Maybe he made it to the micro-moment between eight and seven before the black velvet darkness took him to a place too deep to dream, or at least to remember dreaming. He certainly didn't remember anything about the surgery except for a vague sense of something he felt unsettled about.

Kevin's first impression of consciousness was the twilight between the deep black sleep and the distant call of awareness. It was like straddling two worlds, but with one foot on a ledge two feet lower than the other, forcing him to teeter and fall back into the pool of darkness, making it more difficult to find his way to the light at the surface. Each time he became more conscious of being awake, he also became increasingly aware that pain was a part of his experience. In spite of this pain throbbing in his head and radiating from his jaw, he was jolted by another awareness—his full-on erection. The nursing gown he was wearing was far more open at the back than usual and now seemed to have a tent pole. All the while, he was mumbling on about how beautiful the nurses were and that they looked like the angels he had just been with.

It was both puzzling and confusing trying to mesh the idea of a boner and angels, and why, in all of his pain, he had a stiffy in the first place. Unfortunately, a boner that was not hiding from anyone. Was it possible that the sodium pentothal revealed his most private secrets and brought truth to his urgings, as well as any questions that might be asked? In all of that mental meandering, he was still being seduced back to the dark pool where his erection could go on without him and to where he had no concept of feeling guilty for what he was feeling so strongly about, its underlying cause still undetermined.

His mother never mentioned his erection on the drive home, though it was unlikely she would have. She had only helped clear up his misunderstandings about how babies were made three years earlier. After their discussion, she constantly reminded him that sex was only for marriage, and anything else was a sin that had the potential to ruin this life and the afterlife.

Once home, she gave him some kind of pill for the pain that didn't knock him out like the anesthesia but gave him a glowing feeling that all was as perfect as it could be after having a couple of teeth yanked out of your head.

The television was in the family room in the walkout basement of a house that overlooked the vast Merrimac River Valley below. From anyone's standpoint, it would be the perfect setting to recover over the weekend from a dental procedure. Kevin's mother propped him up with pillows in a very comfortable overstuffed chair, pulled the ottoman up to just the right place to support his feet and legs, and then covered him with a blanket. After she went upstairs, he heard the blender whirring, and soon, she returned with the fresh banana milkshake that was his reward for what he had endured. It reminded him of the Bill Cosby record about getting the promised ice cream after having his tonsils taken out.

The usual problem with milkshakes is that they are so good you drink them too fast, and the sound of a straw sucking air makes you want more and wish that you had savored the milkshake just a bit longer. That was not the problem today. Kevin's mother warned him to drink his milkshake slowly or, with the pain medicine, it could freeze his gaping tooth holes or cause a problem for a stomach still troubled from anesthesia.

It was in the pure joy of painkillers and drinking a fresh banana milkshake slowly and pleasurably that the first news report about President Kennedy being shot in Dallas interrupted his bliss and blew a parallel hole in the fabric of his reality. It was almost as if he was being pulled back into the black again, where the dichotomy between the fresh banana milkshake in the warm comfort of the overstuffed chair and the news report about someone shooting the president made no more sense than getting a boner from an angel. Unfortunately, the announcement was not a dream; it was as real as his erection had been. Spreading like wildfire, the announcement became a continuing series of announcements, rumors, and speculation, unfolding minute by minute throughout the weekend to become a nightmare of group consciousness, consumed around the world by anyone that had access to a television or radio.

He called to his mother to come downstairs. As he watched her begin to comprehend what had happened, she looked ashen and frail, a look he had never seen surrounded his mother. Small tears began to run down her cheeks, but she didn't wipe them away because she still had her hands over her mouth, as if she was trying to keep something out—or keep something in. For what seemed like a very long time, she didn't even acknowledge that Kevin was in the room, lost in the matrix of her own overwhelming shock and sorrow. Then, without looking at him, she said that she was going to turn the channel to CBS to see what Cronkite would tell them.

Walter Cronkite would be the narrator of the unfolding horror show for Kevin's family and millions of other families in the United States. It wasn't as if he could really help anyone make sense of the twists and turns of the violent series of tragedies. Even Walter Cronkite seemed vulnerable and perplexed. But his steady and almost fatherly nature provided a gathering place of some comfort and a place to check in or stay tuned to try and make sense of it all. Mostly, the early news broadcasts were giving facts and figures that seemed to change dramatically every few minutes—and then the announcement came that President Kennedy was dead.

The events of the weekend continued to play out live on television, with Kevin's entire family watching together and not saying too much. Usually, the family gathered for the television series *Bonanza* on Sunday nights. They all consumed Jolly Time, white kernel popcorn, coated with wonderfully way too much butter, made by Kevin's father in vast amounts. The freshly popped corn was devoured by all of them in big handfuls, along with milkshakes made by his mother. His father made two giant batches of white popcorn that weekend, both with extra butter. One batch was being cooked while they were all watching TV at the time Lee Harvey Oswald was shot by Jack Ruby. The sound of Ruby's gun, firing just before it brought Oswald to a buckle, and the sound of kernels popping at the peak of their cooking frenzy were almost indistinguishable.

Kevin wasn't sure if it was the pills he was taking, but nothing that weekend made any sense within his perceptions of life before his oral surgery and before President Kennedy was assassinated. Why was Jackie still wearing the dress splattered with blood and brain matter? Who showed little John John how to salute or told him when his daddy was coming by in the casket? And then there was the drumbeat that continued in the same cadence for the full length of the procession as the caissons went rolling along. *Da-dump, da-dump, da-dump-dump-dump. Da-dump, da-dump, da-dump-dumpty-dump.* It was the drumbeat that he would remember all of his life, more than the popcorn or the milkshakes; the drumbeat he could pound out anytime without even needing to think about it. More prominent in his head than the drum roll on the song *Wipe Out*, it was a drumbeat that certainly didn't bring to mind images of bikinis on the beach.

If life can return to normal after a nation and a world witnessed a weekend of horror and sorrow together on TV, it did. But ahead of the expression, it was the "new normal," and the beginning of what no one could imagine was yet to occur over the next four years. For Kevin, it would never be the same again. Something beyond the fact that the president was assassinated was just not right, and even adults were talking about it. He was haunted by it, and while he hadn't taken much interest in current events before that weekend, now he consumed everything he could read about the assassination of President Kennedy. The more he read the various theories about who or why someone would kill the president, the more all that he had previously believed in, without any real consideration whatsoever, became shrouded in doubt. In that doubt that reminded him of all he didn't remember in the deepest stages of anesthesia, the presence of a "problem" called Vietnam began to slowly seep into his awareness.

Chapter 2

See the World

I n 1965, the choice for John David Berglund was just like it was for almost all young men graduating from high school. You could either go to college full-time or, in very short order, unless you were physically disabled, you were going to be drafted into the military for the war in Vietnam. What started with sending a few advisors to assist the South Vietnamese Army in 1963 had grown into a full-scale war by 1965 that required five hundred thousand American troops with what seemed to be no real plan and no end in sight.

John came of age in Ladue, Missouri, an affluent suburb of St. Louis, well-insulated from the social unrest percolating in other areas of the city. His father made enough money, so John didn't lack for much, though in Ladue, his family would not have been considered wealthy. While brilliant, John was not a diligent student. But with very little effort, he managed to get the B's and C's needed to graduate from high school, and with a grade average that guaranteed he would be accepted at one of Missouri's state colleges.

What John lacked in applied scholastic ability, his six-foot-three-inch height and powerful, magnetic personality made up for. He was an energetic presence in any situation he chose to occupy. John didn't try to be a leader or assert himself as a leader; he just was one. He was also a gifted and animated storyteller and had the ability to hold others captivated, as much by how he told a story as the story itself. For those who knew John, his storytelling only partially disarmed his tendency to surprise unsuspecting listeners with a slightly sarcastic quip or a verbal challenge to their point of view. His focused eyes would smile but burn in intensity, and his face seemed to mirror the rise in his voice when he thundered out of nowhere, "I don't know, Feldman!" or the last name of the person of his selected attention. After delighting in how uncomfortable his center of attention was, he would laugh and make everyone in the room feel at ease again and carry on with the story or the subject of the discussion. When you were with John, you knew you were going to be in the moment, slightly on guard, and sure to have a few good bouts of laughter.

Like many college freshmen, it wasn't easy for John to make the transition from high school to college that required a higher level of discipline to succeed within an environment that, for the most part, was undisciplined. In high school, they would call your house looking for you if you were even a half an hour late getting to school. In college, no one really cared if you came to class or if you didn't because you stayed out late three nights in a row drinking beer and smoking weed.

Unfortunately for John and many other young men at the time with the chance to defer going into the military by staying in college for four years or more, if you didn't carry a full load of sixteen credit hours per semester and get a passing grade average, you became immediately eligible to be drafted. In 1966, there was no draft lottery you could count on for a gambler's chance, so if you were eligible and had no deferment, it was almost certain you would be drafted into the Army or Marines. From the Army's perspective, about eight weeks later, you would be ready to defend your country's freedom and be on the way to Vietnam.

The U.S. government needed a constant supply of new young men to replace the dead and injured coming back to the USA. It also needed more men to replace the soldiers that reached the thirteen-month time limit for their tour of duty. In an attempt at shared responsibility, the law at that time stipulated that unless a soldier volunteered to return, all military personnel needed to be back on US soil within thirteen months from the day they arrived in Vietnam.

What was so conflicting for these young, college-age men was that, while they could see the images on the TV news about the raging war and the assembly line of caskets with dead soldiers being unloaded from the planes returning to the United States, it was hard to bridge the reality of the life they knew at home and a life they would live in the jungles of Vietnam if they were drafted. The images, news reports, and the stories from the soldiers returning home should have scared the shit out of them. That should have been enough to keep them focused on school and grades. But there was beer to drink, weed to smoke, and girls to conquer, with no one keeping score if they were going to class or not until at least the end of the semester. Day after day, they would seize the night, and as a result, the future painted its own story.

John embraced the social life and freedom of college more than he did going to class. Judging from his grade point average at the end of the first two semesters, it was clear to John and his family that it was just a matter of time before he would be drafted. The only alternative to being drafted into the U.S. Army that John or his family could see was for John to enlist in the U.S. Navy.

Being drafted into the Army or Marines required a two-year commitment. Enlisting in the Navy or Air Force required at least a three-year commitment, but it was more likely to keep you out of direct combat. There were no major sea battles being fought in Vietnam so, from the likelihood of dying or being injured standpoint, the U.S. Navy was a safer bet. For John, it also held the promise of what the U.S. Navy used as a slogan to promote enlistment; "See the World." The romantic idea of being on a ship at sea, going from port to port, was very exciting and, in reality, a better fit for John than going to college to learn a whole lot of nothing.

Compared to Army or Marine boot camp, Navy boot camp was a piece of cake, and John managed to make the experience even better by arranging his training in San Diego instead of Chicago. Within about ten weeks, John had learned all that the Navy thought he needed to know at the moment and received his first orders to report to Sasebo, Japan. For John, that meant he would meet his first ship at the Sasebo Naval Base and then head somewhere for an adventure at sea.

John had a last party with his friends and was truly excited about what lay ahead of him. Although his parents would have preferred that he stay in school, they believed his time in the Navy would be good for him and provide discipline and direction for going to school after his stint in the Navy. Most of all, they were very relieved that John was in the Navy and not the Army on his way to Vietnam.

There was a chill in the air on the day John departed St. Louis for his trip to Japan in November of 1966. Still adjusting to wearing a uniform and wanting to be correct, John wore the Navy's winter blue wool uniform. It seemed odd to him to be getting on a plane to California that would connect to a plane for Japan without knowing what ship he would be assigned to and what he would be doing in Japan. He was informed he would find all of that out when he arrived at the base in Sasebo. But in a way, not knowing was part of the excitement.

The flight from California to Japan was long but not uncomfortable. John tried to sleep for part of the flight and did doze off a couple of times but never for very long. His mind was an active swirl of questions and possibilities that uncertainty brings. He had never been outside of the United States before this trip, but he had gone to the library and checked out books about Japan so he would have some idea of what to expect.

The books had not prepared him for what he saw as the plane banked in a steep turn in its landing approach. Immediately, he knew by the topography of the land and the character of the buildings and cars he saw below that he was not in the "good old USA" anymore. He also wondered why the plane was landing inland from the ocean, with no ships in sight. The adventure had begun.

Chapter 3

Welcome to Japan

When the plane landed, John got off, collected his duffle bag and was ushered into the terminal. Once inside, John and the other Navy personnel were met by a petty officer that instructed them to join a long line in front of another officer with a clipboard and a stack of envelopes. When John reached the front of the line, he saluted the petty officer and stated his name and rank. With very little discussion, the petty officer handed John the envelope he had been waiting for that contained his ship assignment. John saluted again and went quickly to an out-of-the-way spot in the terminal to open the envelope. He was so nervous and excited that he was having a hard time opening the envelope without tearing it open. Finally, he just did.

He unfolded the papers. It was hard to focus because his mind wanted to race down the page and find the name of his ship before reading the boilerplate information in the orders. But at the same instant that his eyes found the name of the ship near the bottom of the first page, another word that he had passed over quickly in his scan from top to bottom came like a thunderbolt into his present moment—*Saigon*. Now the name of the ship was irrelevant. In a panic, his eyes went back to the top of the page to look for his name. Surely, there was a mistake, and these were not his orders but some other sailor's misfortune. Nevertheless, it was his name, and in a state of anxious disbelief, he had to read his own name twice to make sure. Then it was an out-of-mind, mental scramble to read each word of his orders as slowly as his racing mind would allow, trying to comprehend what the fuck the word *Vietnam* was doing on the page. A tsunami of nausea crashed onto the shoreline of his Japanese adventure. All that he had ever imagined his future to be was swept away in a matter of seconds, sucked out to meet the horror of the unknown in Vietnam.

Now sweating at the face, John read the rest of the orders that stated he was to board a plane for Vietnam in about six hours. Once in Saigon, he was to report to Captain Darren McCluskey III on the USS *Newton County*, a landing ship tank, or LST. An LST didn't mean anything to John other than he remembered from war movies that they were used in World War II, but that would soon change. Now, he was consumed by confusion and a sense of fear that was knocking at his temples, making him almost completely unaware of his surroundings. With adrenaline pumping, he no longer felt tired or hungry from the long flight to Japan. The only thing that occupied his mind was Vietnam and how this could have happened. John kept thinking about the promises made by the Navy recruiter about no possibility of going to Vietnam and saying, "Fucking asshole," over and over again while staring at the papers.

He wandered to another part of the terminal where all the military flights for Vietnam departed and reported to the Navy personnel in charge there. Many others were waiting for flights, though most of them were Army. They were either going to Vietnam for the first time, like he was, or headed back for another tour. It was very easy to see the difference. Not just because the soldiers returning to Vietnam were generally a little older or that they wore their uniforms a bit differently, giving the sense that their combat uniforms had been their skin for a while. What telegraphed the difference were their eyes. The new soldiers were still bright-eyed in spite of the fear and uncertainty that was now a part of their presence. The soldiers that were returning to Vietnam had dead eyes; eyes that had witnessed too many horrors and that could never perceive life again through their original lenses. They could not look at or experience anything anymore without the shadow dreams of all they had been through in Vietnam running like a separate film in the background.

John took a seat next to one of the returning soldiers without saying anything. It seemed to him, judging from the cold expression he saw on the soldier's face, that saying hello wasn't the best option. John didn't really feel like talking anyway. In fact, he felt uncomfortably disassociated and wasn't sure he could hold a conversation. At that very moment, he didn't really want to engage in conversation that might provide any insight into why the soldier's eyes looked like they did. In an effort to stop the hamster wheel of fear spinning unstoppably in his head, he tried to focus on the others waiting for the same plane.

Chapter 4

New Realities

It was an odd mix of characters that were waiting to board the military transport plane in Sasebo, Japan, bound for Saigon. Most of them were Army or Marines, and most were first-timers to Vietnam. John was one of a few Navy people on this plane, and in his winter blue uniform, he stood out like a tourist, wearing plaid shorts, black socks, Birkenstocks, and a plastic lei at a luau in Honolulu. The first-timers were mostly between the ages of nineteen and twenty-two. Only about eight to ten weeks ago, they were still living their limited high school or post-high school dreams and very likely didn't know how to find Vietnam on a map. Likely, they still didn't.

Similar to the way it was in high school, there were all the different personalities; the loud ones, the macho ones, the quieter ones, the loners. It was evident that the quieter ones, who were cocooned by the fear of knowing they were about to fly to a place where death was a daily event, didn't really know what it all meant or what to expect. The louder ones recounted the stories they said had been told to them by soldiers returning from the madness or that they heard from another person in high school who said that someone told them. They were already using derogatory words like gooks, hiding behind a hatred for an imagined enemy and a culture they had no knowledge of. They were pretending they weren't afraid and bragging that they were looking forward to shooting their first gook or lighting up a hooch with a flamethrower. The most conflicted of all were the new soldiers that had been philosophically or politically opposed to the war but then ran out of options and were now on their way to being part of what they had so objected to.

The soldiers returning to Vietnam for second or third tours of duty didn't really say much to anyone unless they were talking to another soldier that knew where they were going and the true realities of Vietnam. They were well aware of what the new guys were facing and how there was no possibility that these recent draftees could even imagine what it was like. To be in the jungle, in 110-degree weather, soaking wet with sweat and jungle-rotted feet, dealing with bugs and snakes, and living on maybe two hours of sleep a night, but every minute being worried about being fired on by the enemy. It was an enemy you rarely could see before they pulled the trigger, an almost faceless enemy that could just as easily be a woman with a child in a village as a man with a gun in the jungle.

The returnees, or "old boots," stopped thinking or caring about how the "cherries" would adapt or might die. It was certain, no matter what, that they would all become familiar with death and dying and living under its spell. It would be death a hundred or more different ways, with more combinations than anyone should ever need to ponder. There would be instant death with a bullet through the head, long agonizing death with organs hanging out, buried to death, death by booby trap, death by torture, death with the loss of one limb, death with the loss of multiple limbs, death by drowning, and the worst death of all, the death of their own souls and spirits. It didn't matter what religion you believed in or if you didn't believe at all, nothing could prepare you for the onslaught of death and dying in real-time with limited interruptions. The "here one minute, gone the next" part of death made death very personal very quickly, even if you barely knew the person that had been there and was now gone. And each death was also the death of another part of yourself; and that included the flip side of death, the death you might inflict, or the death you would participate in.

In the 1960s, most of the draftees would have gone to church or Sunday school at one time or another, and the Judeo-Christian concept of "Thou Shalt Not Kill" was well-known, even if the com-

mandment was not fully adhered to. But with war, that command-
ment was thrown right out the window. A soldier was trained to kill,
and the killing that had previously been something from the head-
lines of the nightly news, more of a concept of killing, was unlike
being in war that would wash them in death and squirrel its way into
every part of their being to become the complete focus of their new
reality. The mission they were on was to both cause death and escape
death, but each time they escaped death, they were keenly aware that
their number could be up next and how death could arrive in so
many ways.

As the draft law stipulated, thirteen months from the day a soldier arrived in Vietnam, they had to be back on U.S. soil. Inflict
death and escape death for three hundred and ninety-one days and
you could go back to the life you left in the *world*. Except that life,
viewed through previous lenses, before eating the first bite of the
apple of death, would no longer exist. Lying in the jungle, trying to
and trying not to sleep, straining to hear above the noise of the rain
any subtle sound of the enemy that would signal another firefight
or ambush, the death they had witnessed and inflicted would hold a
demonic party. Death grabbed the sound system and turned it up so
loud that nothing else in their mind had a chance to be heard. While
the devil spun the tunes, they found they could only dance to the
rhythm of "so what?"

Chapter 5

The Summer of Love

On February 7, 1964, less than fifteen months after President Kennedy's assassination in Dallas, the Beatles arrived in New York for their first appearance on *The Ed Sullivan Show*. Once again, millions of people were glued to their televisions in a collective moment of multiple emotions. The reactions ranged from frantic and hysterical teenage attraction to vocal parental disapproval and fear about why all these teenagers were out-of-their-mind attracted to four longhaired boys that weren't even American. Less than six months later, Kevin, who had been taking guitar lessons for a couple years, formed a band with three other junior high school friends and played every birthday party, talent show, or event they could get themselves invited to.

When Kevin entered high school in the fall of 1965, he loved the Beatles and the Beach Boys, everything Motown and, of course, girls. He wasn't bad on a steel-wheeled skateboard, longed to see California, read *Surfer* magazine from cover to cover every month, and considered himself a landlocked surfer. Kevin wore his hair on the edge of being too long for school policy, bought a fast car with financing from his parents, and kept looking for the fast girl. Other than not living in California, life was as good as Kevin could imagine it in Missouri.

In the summer of 1967, with the help of a family connection, Kevin was offered a job working in the kitchen of the Lazy "A" Guest Ranch in Encampment, Wyoming. Nothing in his too-cool, teenager-growing-up-in-the-suburbs-of-St Louis history had prepared Kevin for the discoveries and the events of that summer. The train trip from St. Louis to Laramie, Wyoming, gave him his first real look at how the farmland of the Midwest transitioned town to town, hill by rolling hill into the full-blown mountains and landscapes of the "out west."

When the train arrived in Laramie, a ranch hand from the Lazy "A" named Tom met Kevin at the platform. Tom was wearing cowboy boots, a cowboy hat, and had a buckle on his belt almost as big as Wyoming. He tossed Kevin's duffle bag into the back of a dusty pickup truck. With the duffle bag now sharing space with two border collies, they headed out for the ranch, with not much said between them. Kevin had not met a real cowboy before and assumed Tom had not met a landlocked surfer. It turned out they both smoked Marlboro cigarettes, and that seemed to break the ice and get them through the ride to the ranch.

Once he arrived at the Lazy "A," Kevin met Chef Jordy, his boss for the summer. Though Kevin eventually did become inspired by Chef Jordy, Chef Jordy immediately disliked Kevin. Kevin learned quickly that Chef didn't care too much for longhaired surfer-looking boys, landlocked or not. Chef managed the kitchen operations of the Lazy "A" Ranch in the summer and the Calistoga Inn in Scottsdale, Arizona, during the winter. He was a Swiss-trained old-school sarcastic taskmaster with very high standards for his food and dining experience and little tolerance for anything less, especially excuses. Preceding the television show by more than thirty years, Kevin was in Hell's Kitchen. But for the first time in his life, he had to really stretch beyond his comfort zone, and he began to glimpse what he was capable of, savoring the satisfaction of well-executed but difficult accomplishments.

The menu for the guests changed each day. Words, names, and terms, such as truffles, foie gras, mirepoix, roux, tartar, and hollandaise, became part of Kevin's everyday through the culinary dishes he was helping to prepare and to taste. He was also introduced to the wines that were components of the recipes they prepared and that complemented the food. Kevin took an immediate liking to

Chateauneuf-Du-Pape, Pouilly-Fuiseé and, of course, Champagne, and tasted the remnants of the partially consumed bottles that came back to the kitchen whenever he had the chance.

Fortunately, it wasn't all work and no play at the ranch. Kevin made friends with the head wrangler and had a horse to ride over the 70,000 acres of the ranch on his days off. A few times, Kevin and some of the others working at the ranch floated down the North Platt River in old inner tubes. Kevin enjoyed spending lazy afternoons gazing at the billowing white cloudscapes in a beyond-blue sky that moved in an endless parade over the mountain peaks that ringed the river. On these days, Kevin found himself captivated by the vastness of the West, new smells of sage, and Wyoming summer. He felt a growing energized contentment of being in the fully involved presence of such natural beauty.

There were also wonderful summer evenings drinking Coors beer and partying with new college-age friends. Kevin was introduced to music that he had never heard before that summer; The Grateful Dead, The Doors, and Quicksilver Messenger Service, along with an herb that they didn't have in the kitchen. The year 1967 was the Summer of Love in San Francisco, but for Kevin, at the Lazy A in Encampment, Wyoming, it was the summer of love in the hayloft, Sgt. Pepper, and Saint-Émilion.

Chapter 6

Sasebo to Saigon

The plane that John and the other soldiers going to Vietnam were boarding was an aging troop transport plane without airline-style seats and very little comfort. Beyond the seat belts bolted to the fuselage of the plane, one of the first things John noticed was that there was no bathroom on board. If that had been announced at some point, John didn't hear it. He felt a slight twinge of panic, since his stomach had been rumbling since learning he was going to Vietnam instead of staying in Japan.

After six hours of waiting in Sasebo and trying to make sense of why he was going to Vietnam in the first place, he was no further along in that understanding or in comprehending what he was going to do on an LST. The flight to Saigon would take almost eight hours. As the plane rattled down the runway straining to pick up speed, John was not really concerned about how long the flight would take, only where the plane was going, and he was in no real hurry to get there. That all began to change about halfway through the flight when the slight rumble in his stomach turned into a full-on angry churning and cramping. Trying not to bring any more attention to himself than his Navy uniform already did (surrounded by mostly Army personnel), John focused on pinching back the results of the churning to keep it from finding its way out of the only place it could. At one point, John was sweating profusely from the pain and desperation of trying to hold it all in and not become a consequence of blowing a seat-load of diarrhea into a very crowded transport plane with crude ventilation.

Eventually, Vietnam came into view, and the plane quickly circled the military airfield and made a hard landing. Desperate to get off the plane, John shouted he was about to puke, and the troops in front of him parted and let him through. As he rushed out the door of the plane and down the stairs, he was assaulted by the heat and humidity of Vietnam that was made significantly worse by the wool uniform he had chosen to wear in what now seemed like a lifetime ago in St. Louis. John was no longer just sweating. Every pore in his body had opened up, and he could feel a waterfall of sweat catching gravity and cascading toward his shoes.

As quickly as he could, given his condition of the moment, he headed toward the first person that seemed like they had some kind of authority. When he asked him where the bathroom was, the soldier pointed to a rectangular canvas enclosure without a roof and said, "The shitter's over there, squid," a derogatory term that John had already learned Army soldiers often called someone in the Navy. Quickly, John entered the enclosure through a break in the canvas that served as the doorway.

Once inside, he realized the enclosure was an elongated communal outhouse, and he was going to be shitting in a hole in the ground. At that point, John didn't have time to care about the nature of the latrine or who might be watching his drama. As quickly as he could, he unbuttoned and lowered his wool pants and got into a squat. The rumble, now truly in the jungle, became a river of nasty that exploded from his body with a cacophony of gas. Within only minutes of arriving in Vietnam, there he was, in 105-degree heat and humidity, wearing wool, squatting, and spewing diarrhea into a hole in the ground. He hoped this wasn't a sign of how much worse it could get.

Now sweating through his uniform but very relieved, John found his duffle bag and got on the bus that would take him to the USS *Newton County*. On the ride, John began to take it all in. He breathed deeply and scanned his new world for anything that might infuse him with a positive sense of adventure. The sights, the sounds, and the smells came at him almost too fast to process. It was all new and completely unfamiliar, but he immediately felt a strong sense of fear and concern rush through his body, commanding the hairs on his arms to stand at attention. Why he could feel and recognize war, destruction, and hopelessness in everything he laid his eyes on he wasn't sure, but he did.

Chapter 7

Spring Break 1968

After a summer at the Lazy "A" Ranch, Kevin came back home for his senior year in high school. By the end of the first semester and the start of 1968, Kevin knew that, unless he completely blew his final semester, he would be accepted at the University of Missouri that fall. The counterculture ideas, music, and marijuana he had been introduced to by college students working at the ranch were now taking hold and expanding across the country, though at a slower pace in Missouri and the rest of the South.

A year earlier, Kevin had never listened to FM radio, and for a good part of his life, he'd wondered what it was and why there were buttons or dials on some radios that indicated AM/FM. Now commercial-free, FM stations that played the music he was introduced to at the ranch and more were popping up in most U.S. cities, including KSHE in St. Louis. At first, it seemed like there were many coded messages about getting high in some of the music for the "experienced" to understand. At that time in Missouri, a teenager that was smoking weed on occasion had to be cautious who knew about his marijuana activities or another teenager might turn them in to the police for their own good. Over time, that would change, as one after another, the uninitiated were invited into the circle by their friends and turned on.

Kevin and his closest friends had always dreamed of going to Panama City, Florida, for spring break, and hatched a plan for 1968. Kevin's '65 Chevy SS convertible had bucket seats that would only hold two people in front and three in the back. The number of seatbelts was not a concern, since almost no one wore seatbelts then for any reason. A gallon of gas and a pack of cigarettes both cost about twenty-five cents each in 1968 and even less farther south. A twenty-four case of Busch Bavarian beer was less than four dollars, and they determined if they pooled their money, they could get by and stay buzzed.

Maybe the biggest challenge for the trip from Kevin's perspective was that the only other person going on the road trip that smoked grass was Billy Harris. They would both need to keep that fact a secret from the others. What should have been more concerning was that they were going to carry marijuana in the car while going through the Deep South. In 1968, if caught, that could mean a long prison sentence. But of course, teenage invincibility prevailed.

The drinking age in Missouri in 1968 was twenty-one, but everyone going on the road trip was experienced in rounding up beer and liquor. It was decided they would have an easier time buying beer in Missouri instead of trying to figure it out in Florida, so they bought enough to keep them fueled for a good part of the trip. On that day in April, when they left for Florida, there was more beer in the trunk, stuffed in duffle bags, than there were clothes. But if someone had a quick look in the trunk, all they would see were duffle bags with wrinkled clothes spilling out the top and a couple of suitcases. Without telling anyone else, Kevin hid his bag of grass in the steering wheel cap that he had figured out how to pop off and on with a little help from a screwdriver.

The spring breakers didn't get the early start they hoped for, so it was almost noon before they got on the road. The plan was to drive straight through all the way to Mobile, Alabama, only stopping for gas and food. Once in Mobile, they would stay a night with Kevin's Auntie Jo and three of his girl cousins that he was close to. He knew they would enjoy being invaded by the guys and that all of them would be well fed before heading to Panama City.

Sometime after 6:00 p.m., on the first day of the journey, they were driving through Memphis, listening to Koko Taylor singing "Wang Wang Doodle" on an R&B station, when the DJ interrupted the song for a news bulletin. Very emotional and somewhat stammer-

31

ing, the DJ read the bulletin that stated: "Reverend Martin Luther King Jr. has been shot at a motel in Memphis by an unknown assailant."

It was a shock for everyone in the car, but there was not really much said other than from Billy, the other "toker" on the journey, who kept saying over and over, "Fuckin' A, man, fuckin' unbelievable, they shot him." In less than an hour, they would learn MLK was dead. The car was quiet for a while, and somebody mentioned President Kennedy's assassination, but they found a radio station playing music and stayed the course for Mobile. They would have all thought it was even more fucking unbelievable if they knew at that moment that, within two months and one day, Robert Kennedy would be assassinated in Los Angeles.

When they got to Mobile, they were well received by Auntie Jo, who had prepared a huge table full of fried chicken, mashed potatoes, green beans, and a Mobile favorite, cold boiled crab, all of which the boys devoured. Showers were taken, pop-tops were popped on beers, and their cigarettes filled Auntie Jo's house with smoke. The cousins were definitely smitten by the boys, to the point that Kevin wondered if it might get interesting later in the evening.

Kevin settled in the kitchen and talked with Auntie Jo about MLK's assassination, but she couldn't seem to make any sense of it, other than she was deeply saddened and thought it must be racially motivated. As the night soldiered on, they eventually all found a chair or a couch or a place on the floor to sleep for a few hours. At some point in the night, Kevin thought he heard one or more of the cousins' bedroom doors squeaking, and he fell back asleep with a smile.

In the morning, Auntie Jo made them pancakes and sausage. After saying thank you and goodbye, and with what seemed like extra-long hugs for the boys by the cousins, Kevin dropped the top on the Chevy, and they headed for Florida.

Kevin first saw the Gulf of Mexico as they slowed down to drive through Destin, Florida, which, at the time, was not much more than a fishing pier and a few motels on the beach. Kevin had forgotten how much the multi-hued blue-and-green water set against the backdrop of white-sugar sand and dunes spoke to a place in him he didn't get to visit very often.

Just outside of Destin, where the road opened into a long, straight stretch, Kevin put the Chevy through a four-gear fast tango, quickly accelerating to over eighty miles per hour. The exhilaration of acceleration was quickly tamped down by an Okaloosa County Sheriff's red light flashing in Kevin's rearview mirror. As he pulled over for the deputy, the memory of beer in the back and dope in the steering wheel made his heart race and his face flush. Kevin sternly told the others to keep it in line as the officer approached the car looking like a poster boy for all the southern cops they had seen in movies. Through mirrored sunglasses, the deputy was asking him about how fast he was going, and Kevin was answering every question with "Yes, sir" or "No, sir," but all he could think about was the weed in the wheel.

The deputy instructed Kevin to step out of the car and open the trunk. When he did, the duffle bags in the trunk and clothes that had been randomly stuffed into the trunk when someone changed from long pants to cutoffs or discarded a coat or sock looked like the teen disarray they hoped would camouflage their beer. The deputy poked around a bit with his nightstick and then closed the trunk. He then asked Kevin how he intended to pay the seventy-five dollar fine. While Kevin was surprised he was being asked to pay the fine on the spot, he took out his wallet and handed four twenty-dollar bills to the deputy. The deputy peeled off a five from his wallet and gave it to Kevin and then walked back to his car without another word.

Everyone in the car was very experienced with dealing with the hometown cops, but they were genuinely relieved to be on their way again with all of their beer. Kevin and Billy were even more relieved.

Spring break in Panama City was everything they had all hoped for and more. They drank from morning to night, partied and danced with girls from everywhere, and according to each one of them, they all got laid a few times over the week. Almost out of money, out of beer, and unknown to three of them, out of reefer, they nursed their sunburns and headed the '65 Chevy north for home. Low on cash, they had to drive straight through, only stopping for gas and food. By this time, some of them had cash and some had none. Together, they had enough so everyone could eat, with promises of "You owe me."

About six hours from home, they came into Memphis around 7:00 p.m., only nine days after MLK had been assassinated. Over those past nine days, they had been so busy having fun that they didn't really think much about Dr. King or the shooting. They also never anticipated that there would still be so much unrest in Memphis or that more police and National Guard than they had ever seen in one place had the city in a lockdown. The main road north was partially blockaded, forcing traffic to slow to a crawl so that police or National Guard could have a look at each car as it stopped for a quick check.

As they approached their turn, Kevin rousted the guys sleeping in the back and told them to straighten up. When the policeman poked his flashlight into the car and scanned all the faces, he asked Billy Harris a question, to which Billy replied with a smart aleck answer, and once again, trouble became Kevin's companion. The officer told Billy to shut his goddamn Yankee mouth and for Kevin to step out of the car. The officer signaled for Kevin to open the trunk. After seeing only sand and dirty clothes, which were consistent with the spring break story Kevin gave, the police officer was completely in Kevin's face about how he wasn't going to take any smart-ass comments from a bunch of Yankee bastards. The "yes, sirs," "no, sirs," and "sorry, sirs" came out in rapid fire from Kevin's mouth with all the sincerity he could muster.

Finally, the officer told Kevin to get back in the car and get their sorry Yankee asses out of Memphis. The car was silent as they pulled away from the roadblock. After all the carefree fun in the sun in Florida, it would be the magnitude of Martin Luther King's assassination, not the sugar sand in the trunk, that would, over time, become the enduring memory of Kevin's spring break 1968.

When Kevin got home around 3:00 a.m. after dropping everyone off, he tried to be as quiet as possible and not wake his parents. When he turned on the lights in his room, he noticed two envelopes on his desk neatly placed there by his mother. One was a letter of acceptance from the University of Missouri for the fall semester of 1968. The other was a welcome letter from the Selective Service, along with his draft card.

Chapter 8

Brown Water Navy

By the time the bus arrived at the Newport LST piers in Saigon, John was the only passenger on the bus. The driver turned to John with a bit of a smirk and said, "This is your stop, squid. Your tub's over there." John grabbed his gear, exited the bus, and just stood in the heat trying to determine how to find the USS *Newton County*. He saw three LSTs, half out of the water on the amphibious tarmac with their sterns still in the river. John hoped that one of them might be his ship. With a crew of ten to thirteen officers and up to ninety enlisted men, and designed to carry a significant amount of cargo, LSTs were longer than a football field. They were much larger than John had imagined, though he had never given any real thought to an LST until he was stunned by his orders in Sasebo.

As John made his way to the three LSTs. he could see the name USS *Newton County* on one of them with a gangplank lowered to the tarmac for entry. John wasn't sure what the protocol was for coming aboard, but assumed from his training there must be some sort of formality, and he didn't want to make a mistake by just walking onto the ship. He stood at the bottom of the gangplank, still sweating in his wool uniform, waiting for someone to notice him and pipe him aboard or, at the very least, tell him to come aboard. After about five more minutes of waiting in the heat, John said, "Fuck it," and walked up the ramp.

Once on the ship, John still didn't see anyone. As he wandered toward the stern on the port side of the ship he got a strong waft of

35

pot smoke. Just up ahead, under a stairwell, were four men passing a joint. When they noticed John, the last one taking a toke exhaled quickly and cupped the joint in his hand. None of the men were wearing Navy uniforms, which puzzled John. All of them had jeans on but wore an assortment of different shirts. The guy wearing a denim shirt with a military-style patch on his sleeve that displayed Tonkin Gulf Yacht Club nonchalantly, but in a stoned sort of way, said to John, "What's happenin', sailor?"

John, exhausted, hungry, and still sweating, blurted out, "This is supposed to be my new ship. Are you guys smoking weed?"

After a brief denial in unison, the man holding the joint un-cupped it, offered it to John, and said, "Welcome aboard, man." Then, one by one, they introduced themselves to John as Stevie, Baxter, Beach Boy, and Gunner.

With the help of his new friends, John was introduced to the petty officer who showed John his bunk and told him where he could shower and get something to eat. Looking as disheveled and sweaty as he did, it wasn't apparent to the petty officer that John was stoned. But it was certainly apparent to John that he was more stoned than he expected to be after only two tokes. Once his head hit the pillow, he slept until reveille.

Now awake but severely jet-lagged, it seemed like he was still dreaming since he had no point of reference for his new reality. John got into uniform to formally report for duty, but as he headed to meet Chief Petty Officer Morrison, he noticed that from the mechanics to the cooks, no one was in full uniform and no one was saluting. Chief Morrison wasn't in full uniform either, but like many of the others, he wore a combination of regulation gear mixed with civilian clothes. He informed John he was going to be the gunner for one of the LST's four twenty-millimeter machine guns. In the meantime, Chief said John should work closely with Seaman Pahlmeyer, mostly referred to as "Gunner," who would show him what to do on the river.

The vast majority of the LSTs that served in Vietnam were commissioned during World War II. Though they had been refurbished, they were not much more than very leaky shallow-draft amphibious cargo ships designed to ferry soldiers and supplies to the beach or, in the Vietnam War, upriver. LSTs were not really fighting ships, and typically in Vietnam, had only one or two forty-millimeter anti-aircraft guns as well as four or more twenty-millimeter machine guns that could be mounted on various turrets around the boat. The USS *Newton County*'s main task, in what was called the Brown Water Navy, was to bring food, ammunition, spare parts, medical support, and fuel to the troop supply landings in the Mekong Delta. A typical run that started at the Newport LST piers in Saigon would go into the mouth of the Mekong River then upriver to the Bassac River as far as the LST ramp at Bien Thuy, or sometimes a bit further, and then back to Saigon to get another load.

Once on the river, with all of the crew performing their assigned tasks, it became even more apparent to John that there was little or no standard Navy protocol on board the USS *Newton County*. Certainly nothing that was similar to what he had been taught in basic training. Everyone did seem to know their responsibilities and to be functioning as a team, but without the formality and respect for rank that John had expected. According to Gunner, if you had to be in the Navy and you had to be in Vietnam, there was no better ship to be on than the USS *Newton County*. Although Gunner called the LST a "leaky piece of shit," he said what the LST lacked for in creature comforts, it made in the shade with not needing to salute and all. According to Gunner, "None of it really fuckin' matters once you realize that not one of those top brass motherfuckers really has a plan or knows why we are in Nam. That fuckin' dog just won't hunt, so all you can do is try to keep from gettin' kilt and make the most of it until you can get out of this shithole."

Thomas Lee Pahlmeyer, aka Gunner, was born and raised in Eminence, Missouri, an Ozark town close to where the Current River meets it largest tributary, the Jack Forks River. Up until he reported for boot camp at the Great Lakes Naval Station near Chicago, Gunner's life was the Ozarks and the river. He had never been further than St. Louis, and only one time, when his younger sister, Karen Sue, had to see a different kind of doctor than they had in Eminence. Fishing and hunting were not something you did for recreation; it was just a part of everyday life and keeping the family fed. Gunner had a rifle with him most of the time when he wasn't in school for about as long as he could remember. By the time he was twelve, he could shoot a water moccasin out of a tree with one shot while standing in a Current River johnboat going through the rapids. As Gunner would say, "The rivers in this hellhole are muddy fuckin' pieces of shit with floating dead gooks, but they are rivers just the same." He still had a gun or two with him every day. It was just a different kind of hunting, where what you were after could fire back at you.

John wasn't a complete stranger to guns, but he didn't know about guns and shooting in the sixth sense sort of way that Gunner did. Gunner took to John immediately, being another Missouri boy, though kind of a Yankee from an Ozark point of view. Gunner showed John how to adjust his aim with the machine gun to the speed of the boat when firing ahead of or behind the direction they were going on the river. They went through many rounds of ammunition on John's first few days on the LST, shooting at anything they saw in the river until Gunner was convinced that John had it down.

When John finally saw Captain McCluskey in the flesh and in action, it was acutely clear to him that the ship's unique culture flowed from the top down. Donald "Donny" Baxter, the sarcastic jokester from New Jersey, was the gunner of one of the Newton County's forty-millimeter anti-aircraft guns. He said he had a special relationship with "the 40" and called her "Jersey Girl" because she was hot and ready for action. He told John that "Captain McCluck," as he referred to him, was currently the youngest captain in the U.S. Navy and came from a very distinguished naval family. According to Baxter, with McCluck at the helm, his eccentricities were steering the ship and their fortunes. It was his eccentricities that also looked the other way regarding uniforms and formalities.

On his first voyage upriver, John witnessed Captain McCluskey sitting in a lawn chair on the top deck of the LST, firing a grenade out of a grenade launcher almost straight up in the air. If his timing was right, the grenade would explode behind the ship as it went into the water. Fortunately, it did, but it would not be the last time John would see that stunt by McCluck or a few others from his loose marble bag of tricks.

In addition to delivering the supplies the troops needed upriver, a main focus of the ship's crew was to keep the ship and themselves out of harm's way. The LST was the biggest boat on the river and was always within shooting distance from both banks. As a machine gunner, it was John's job to watch for the enemy—or suspected enemy— especially snipers and for any object in the river that might be a mine. As Gunner had stressed to John, it was the machine gunner's job to shoot at any unknown object floating in the river and explode it ahead of the ship in case it really was a mine. Even when docked at night, the men on watch kept lookout for Vietcong swimmers trying to attach explosives to the ship.

When the LST would receive random fire from somewhere on the bank of the river, all the machine guns, and sometimes the forty-millimeter anti-aircraft guns, would stream hellfire into the area where the shots were perceived to be coming from. During John's tour of duty in Vietnam, he never had a confirmed enemy kill, and he was glad he didn't. At the same time, he didn't like to think too much about the shower of bullets they fired into the jungle each time they took fire and who might have been shot or killed in the process.

"Just fucking gooks," Gunner and Baxter and so many of the crew would say, but John never saw it that way. The concept of dehumanizing the enemy was as foreign and repugnant to John's way of thinking as the Navy's policy of using the majority of the black soldiers on the ship as janitors and cooks. But when you allowed yourself, in spite of your fears, to consider the faceless enemy as human beings; that thought would become a haunting night-looping reminder of a sense of compassion the war could not allow. John didn't share these feelings with Gunner, Baxter, or anyone on the ship, and they certainly wouldn't have agreed with him. In spite of feeling so conflicted, he wanted to stay alive, and the entire crew of the ship needed to have each other's back to make that happen.

As the months went by, it was mostly trips up the river and back delivering supplies. It was always hot and sticky, and half the time, the areas of the ship that were supposed to be air-conditioned, weren't. It was bad enough for the crew working topside, but truly a living hell for so much of the crew that worked below decks. The ship was fired on each trip on the river and returned fire each trip, but since John had been there, no one of the crew had been seriously injured on the USS *Newton County*. But John learned quickly that the jungle was not your friend. The jungle was the marquee for the landscape of the Vietnam War and the unseen enemy that was waiting behind thick, dense foliage.

Stephen (Stevie) Anderson, who had been pursuing a degree in creative writing at the University of Michigan before his dreams of becoming a novelist were interrupted by the war, was always quick to remind John on many occasions that, "Jungle is as jungle does." John didn't need reminding. During his time in Vietnam, there had never been a day on the river that John wasn't aware that death's doorbell could ring at any time. He knew there were snipers on both banks of the river that would see their huge ship and the men on board as a shooting gallery. Each trip, he seemed to focus more intensely on the elusive enemy along the river that he knew waited patiently for them. He had become jumpy. Maybe it was from a lack of sleep. The boat was leaking more and more each trip, and no one he spoke to appeared to give a shit. The maintenance and engineering crew tried to keep the ship's pumps working, but it was almost never the case that all of them were working at one time. On the worst days, when the ship was taking in water from both the river and from the monsoon rains, the water in the lower part of the ship could become ankle-deep. Just to get to his bunk, John had to wade through the water in his bare feet so his boots would stay drier than they were from his constantly sweating and rotting feet. Once he got into bed and closed his eyes, it was difficult to sleep most nights because it was so hot and humid below deck.

Some nights, it was also impossible to shut out the question of why he and the United States military were engaged in a war in Vietnam. It was the question that had become the herd of elephants running through the rooms of his mind. It was a question with no answer, a riddle within a riddle. Over time, the riddle became its own moral dilemma, with a line that had already been crossed and a genie that wouldn't go back into the lamp. When the morning came or the ability to sleep had departed, it was another day on the brown river and another day to try and keep himself and the other crew members on the USS *Newton County* alive.

Stevie was technically a radioman on the ship, but in reality, he was fully involved in all aspects of the ship's communications, both officially and underground. If there was anything unofficial that a crewmember wanted to know, you could count on Stevie to know it. Stevie was the eyes and ears of the ship—and beyond the ship. He always knew what was going on stateside and was a source for that information for anyone that cared to listen. But most news from home seemed far away and disconnected from the world the USS *Newton County* sailors had populated.

One of Stevie's jobs was to communicate in code when the ship would be arriving at a supply landing so that everything was readied to bring the ship to shore. It was not a predictable or easy task to turn the 328-foot ship, with a 50-foot beam, crossways on a fast-flowing river for an amphibious landing at a specific place on the shore or against a pier sticking out in the river. There was a small powerboat on the LST that was stowed on davits and could be lowered into the water for short trips to shore when required. The coxswain's main job was running the small powerboat when needed which, on the river, was not too often. One task it was required for was assisting with landing the LST when the current was strong and the river higher than usual.

The coxswain for the USS *Newton County* was Trent David Wilson Jr., known by almost everyone on the ship as "Beach Boy." Some said they called him Beach Boy because he was a surfer from Seal Beach, California. Others onboard insisted Trent was Brian Wilson's second cousin, a factoid that Beach Boy never confirmed or denied. But without a doubt, Beach Boy was a first-class waterman. Born and raised in Southern California, Trent had been surfing since he was eight years old and came of age in Southern California at the time that was memorialized in Brian Wilson's songs, cousin or not. When he was younger, he attended Sunday school at St. Peter's By-The-Sea Presbyterian Church in Huntington Beach and still knew most of the cornerstone Bible stories at a comic book level. His real church, and his point of reference for everything, was the ocean. Without ever aspiring to be, Beach Boy was Pacific Ocean Zen.

Beach Boy was the only person John could talk to about what troubled him so deeply about the war in Vietnam. When they were stoned and alone, John would confide in Beach Boy that there had not been one day since he arrived in Vietnam that he felt good about life or about himself. John had no sense of accomplishment and felt he was stained by the war and covered in its stink. At times, he found himself incredibly angry at no one in particular but at his country and its appetite for making adjustments around the world through war and assassinations. "They" had created this horrific situation, with no honorable purpose he could comprehend, that required his and hundreds of thousands of other Americans' participation in a madness that he had grown to detest.

Beach Boy told John that he too was perplexed and saddened by the two-pronged dilemma. Why were all of them in Vietnam, on both sides, at this moment in time, having this shared experience, and what was the purpose in their lives of the death, destruction, and horror that they encountered each day? But he also more serenely stated to John that Mother Ocean, with her complexities and interconnected forces, was also beyond his understanding. To be in the ocean, to be allowed to ride and participate with its forces, to accept the ocean as unknowable on the ocean's terms and at its mercy, was the blessing. Sometimes Beach Boy's Zen tidbits would soothe John's raging frustration and anger for a while, but unfortunately, not for long.

Chapter 9

A Little Help from My Friends

I f there were any perks of being assigned to an LST, and especially to an LST captained by McCluck, it was that all of the crew was, essentially, sailing on a traveling store. Almost anything you could imagine, from bullets to booze, went upriver, not to mention cigarettes, fine china, silverware, and exotic foods that someone had determined they needed in the jungle to fight the enemy. The military has never been very effective or reliable with inventory control, and some of the crew of the USS *Newton County*, including the tight group of friends that John now called the "Weed Whackers," became like foxes guarding the henhouse. Most of what they helped themselves to were used to trade for what they wanted, and as a result, they didn't want for much, including crazy-good pot, a merry-go-round of girls in town, and state-of-the-art stereo systems. John traded contraband for a Sony reel-to-reel stereo system and the best pair of speakers he could negotiate to enhance his listening pleasure. That delight was further enhanced by the massive amount of weed he was now consuming, as close to out in the open as you could be without being completely stupid.

By June of 1967, John was promoted from a gunner to coxswain when Beach Boy was about to be transferred back to the States. He did get a little help from Beach Boy, who recommended John personally to McCluck. The Weed Whackers decided to throw a party for Beach Boy at their favorite hostess bar in Saigon, the "Hong Hanh," whose polite and acceptable translation meant "pink apricot

43

blossom." Stevie made all the arrangements with Mama-san, securing a special table and making sure the girls they enjoyed the most were reserved for the party. Baxter traded a rare bottle of tequila he had commandeered for two bottles of absinthe to take the night over the top. After the evening had reached its alcohol crescendo, two by two, the Weed Whackers and their girls of the night departed to rooms upstairs over the bar for their imagined delights.

For months now, when they came to town, John always spent time with Ha`ng. Ha`ng told John her name meant "angel in the full moon," but John mostly called her Hang 10 because of the way she gave him a back massage with her toes as she walked lightly across his back before they made love. He shared tender moments with Ha`ng, but they did not have a shared reality of any kind. He wondered what she thought about and what she felt, and if she really felt any different about him than the other men she slept with. He knew the cascading but fleeting emotions of their time together were all he could count on.

Now the coxswain, during the trips up and down the river, John mostly hung out and slept in the boat he was in charge of while smoking weed. From his perspective, and in reality, out of sight was out of mind in more ways than one. During a run on the river in January of 1968, John was lowered into the river with his boat in case the *Newton County* needed assistance docking at the last stop upriver, Bien Thuy. After the LST was secure, and while the cargo was being unloaded, John made small talk with some of the soldiers on shore. Recently, John had concluded that the further they went upriver, the more hardcore the soldiers seemed to be. Their faces showed the strains of war and fear beyond what John and the crew of the USS *Newton* had to endure with sniper fire on the river. These soldiers engaged the enemy and death during patrols in the jungle on a regular and sometimes daily basis. At least, after the crew of the *Newton County* unloaded in Bien Thuy, they would return to Saigon. The soldiers in Bien Thuy and other outposts were there until their time—or their number—was up.

On the way back downriver from Bien Thuy, the *Newton County* developed engine problems in both of its diesel engines and had to rely mostly on the current and a tugboat partway to get to Saigon. Once in port, the crew was informed that the ship would be in Saigon at least ten days for repair. The Weed Whackers were overjoyed, knowing they would have many glorious nights in Saigon and long days to recover.

Coincidentally, the USS *Enterprise* was also in Saigon and in sight of the USS *Newton County*. On the January afternoon when the USS *Enterprise* was conducting full dress inspection on its flight deck, John convinced the Weed Whackers that they should point his speakers directly at the *Enterprise* and play *Sgt. Pepper's Lonely Hearts Club Band* at very high volume. Being full-on whacked, that is exactly what they did. They all danced their own dance or played wild animated air guitar while singing the song as loud as they could shout it. As John pranced on the deck of the USS *Newton County*, he wondered if anyone standing at attention on the USS *Enterprise* had broken a smirk. At that moment, in John's weed- and war-addled mind, the USS *Enterprise* was the mighty symbol of the absurdity of the war and the perpetrator of an out-of-control plan—or non-plan—that had become their jailer for a sentence in hell.

Less than forty-eight hours later, the Naval Investigative Services (NIS) paid the USS *Newton County* a visit.

John had no idea the NIS was on the *Newton County* when he came back from seeing Ha`ng in town and boarded the ship. As he walked up the gangplank, one of the investigators was waiting to greet him. In a room alone, he was immediately asked point-blank if he had been smoking marijuana and taking other drugs while in Vietnam, to which John immediately answered no. At that point, the investigator told John he was underestimating how serious the charges were and produced photos showing John and all the other Weed Whackers partaking of the herb. There was not much John could say, so he didn't say anything. The NIS officer then informed John that using drugs during wartime that resulted in putting other military personnel in danger was a capital offense and could be punishable by death. With that bit of information, John almost shit his pants for the second time since coming to Vietnam.

Very quickly, John changed his attitude and demeanor and admitted he had been smoking marijuana while in Vietnam, on occasion. After that admission, he was ushered into a meeting room on the ship. When the door opened, Stevie, Baxter, Gunner, and the other remaining Weed Whacker were sitting around the table in the room looking, if not frightened, very concerned. The Weed Whackers were informed they were going to be held in custody while waiting for the results of a Captain's Mast that would determine their punishment and future in the Navy. Not really knowing what this meant, they were taken by MPs to the Annapolis Hotel in Saigon for house arrest.

A few days later, more than 70,000 North Vietnamese and Viet Cong forces launched the Tet Offensive in over one hundred cities and towns in South Vietnam. The chaos, confusion, and a small part of the fighting spilled over into Saigon. John and the others were issued weapons and stood guard at the windows of their rooms at the Annapolis Hotel in case the North Vietnamese and Viet Cong made it that far into the city. With his reputation, Gunner was given a few weapons to use as needed.

A month later, the North Vietnamese and Viet Cong forces pulled back, and things reverted to what had previously been called normal. Shortly after, John and the others were flown to a naval base near San Francisco, still with no clear idea of what awaited them.

Most of their days in California were spent painting ships while waiting to hear their fate. After sixty days of good behavior, John found it odd that they were able to get passes to go into San Francisco, but odd was good. Once in the city, they were introduced to the delights of Haight Ashbury, hippies, and LSD. Over the next two months, now painting ships in technicolor, one by one, the members of the Weed Whackers would be called away by the NIS. After they left, they didn't return to the base again. John and the remaining Weed Whackers didn't know if they went to trial and had been sentenced or if they had been discharged. No one in charge would let them know, so they could only speculate on their fate and their own future fate.

The first to go was Gunner, followed by Baxter. The remaining Weed Whackers had no idea what had happened to those that left so quickly. Were they sentenced to prison, and if so, for how long? After Stevie left, John knew his fate awaited him soon. When it was John's turn, he went with an officer from NIS and learned that he was going to receive a General Discharge with Honors, along with his back pay. He was then immediately driven to the main bus station in San Francisco.

At the bus station, John used a pay phone to call a young woman he had been spending time with whenever he came into the city. That night, they both dropped Owsley Orange Sunshine LSD and went to the Fillmore West to hear Quick Silver Messenger and Country Joe and the Fish. It is safe to say that most of the crowd at the Fillmore wanted to bring an end to the Vietnam War. For John, the war was over, and after dancing to Country Joe's anthem, "One, two, three, what are we fighting for…" he was glad he hadn't come home in a box. With all that had happened in eighteen months, he wanted and was waiting for a sense of elation. Just being alive and back in the United States should have been enough, but it wasn't. He courted the elation he so desired with a gift of Orange Sunshine, but within the undulations and chambers of his acid haze, he found he could not release all that he had seen and felt in Vietnam and had no idea what was next.

Chapter 10

Glory Days

Not long after Kevin came home from spring break, his parents informed him that they were going to put their home up for sale and build a newer home in a different area of Kirkwood. Only a few weeks later, the house sold for the asking price to a family that needed to move in within thirty days. Kevin's parents scrambled and found a home to rent while they built their new house. Unfortunately, with three bedrooms, it only provided comfortable room for Kevin's parents and his younger sister and brother. His parents assured Kevin he was welcome to share a bedroom with his brother but offered to pay for a room or apartment during the summer before he went to college if that was more to his liking. Kevin just happened to know someone looking for a roommate and gladly accepted the offer.

Joel Douglas was a year older than Kevin, but they had played together in a few bands since junior high. In many ways, Joel was one of the coolest people Kevin knew at that time. Way before it was acceptable in Missouri, Joel grew his hair out to shoulder-length and looked very much like the bass player for Jefferson Airplane. He made a decision to live and be who he wanted to be on his own terms, regardless of the social restrictions that decision might place on his life and even wellbeing. Currently, Joel attended Meramec Community College, played most weekends in a band, and lived on his own in a Kirkwood heritage home that had been converted into four apartments. Joel welcomed the idea of a rent-sharing roommate for the summer. Kevin welcomed the idea of a summer of smoke, music, and girls, out of sight of his parents.

The evening of the first day that Kevin moved into the apartment, Joel introduced Kevin to John, who was technically the landlord for the building and lived in one of the upstairs apartments. In reality, the apartment house was owned by John's father, who was desperate for John to find his way after returning from Vietnam. John living in one of the apartments also provided some welcome distance for John's family from what they considered his unusual behavior.

After some small talk, John suggested that Joel and Kevin come upstairs and listen to music on his reel-to-reel sound system. Joel's apartment wasn't modern or luxurious by any means, and Kevin didn't expect John's to be either. But he also wasn't prepared for what he saw when John unlocked the door and they entered his apartment. The floor was completely covered in wadded-up pieces of paper, shopping bags, pizza boxes, tin foil, bottles, cans, batteries, and an odd assortment of just plain litter. It was almost like John's entire apartment was one big recycling bin. To avoid stepping on anything that might be hiding beneath all of the trash, Kevin had to kick aside the paper to make a pathway to a chair that was piled with books and magazines. Added to that were ashtrays full of cigarette butts and the overwhelming smell of a cat box that obviously was heaping full and hadn't been changed in quite some time.

John didn't seem to have any problem navigating his apartment and went straight to a small wooden Chinese puzzle box that was unintentionally hidden by an opened St. Louis phone book. John quickly gained entry to the box and produced what at first appeared to be a chocolate bar with a gold-colored wrapper around the middle. With a giggle of delight, he showed it to Joel and Kevin and said, "Ever seen one of these before, boys?" Both Joel and Kevin shook their heads at first until they caught the scent of the bar and realized it was hashish. Besides the gold-colored seal, the bar of hash also had an embossed seal that John said certified that the bar came from Afghanistan.

According to John, this was Pak-Afghan Gold Hash that was rumored to contain goat's blood added to the hash by shamans for a more spiritual experience. With that, John reached back into the puzzle box and brought out a small hash pipe, and the night unfolded.

Surrounded by clutter but with good tunes coming through great speakers and a hash-infused mind, Kevin no longer found the unusual surroundings odd. He was fascinated with John's intellect and his animated storytelling. The subject of Vietnam came up once in the conversation, but it was evident that John didn't want to go there. Where he did go and dwell on were speculations and theories behind U.S. military expansion and the U.S. Military Industrial Complex, something Kevin had never heard discussed before. Somewhere during the conversation, John was able to locate an issue of *Rolling Stone* magazine that supported his theories about the topics they were discussing. He also told Kevin and Joel he had a few books they should read if they were interested in knowing the truth about "the shadow government" and what was really going on in the USA.

After a few more bowls of hash and some cheap plonk that John called "revolutionary wine" that inspired him to shout "Viva!" before each sip, it was time to call it a night. When Kevin settled into his bed, a mattress from home now on the floor in his designated spot in Joel's apartment, his mind swirled around so many questions that John had posed to him. For the first time in many years, he remembered the day President Kennedy was shot and the questions that still surrounded the event. He was supposed to be feeling amazing, stoned on good hash, with his new independence and the first night in Joel's apartment. Instead, he was very uncomfortable about the conceptual link that had now been established in his mind between his long-held feelings about the Kennedy assassination, more recent ponderings about MLK and Bobby Kennedy, and so many things John talked about that evening. Before he could stress too much more, the hash invited him to a sleep he didn't know how to refuse.

In the morning, his head was still in a fog, but the clouds of doubt and concern no longer enshrouded his heart. He was happy to be waking up in Joel's apartment, with a full summer of fun before college that would be theirs for the taking.

A frequent business lunch customer, Kevin's father had helped Kevin secure a job as a line cook at Al Baker's, one of the best Italian restaurants in St. Louis. Though Kevin didn't really have that much experience, his time with Chef more than prepared him for learning the menu and working the line at Al Baker's. Kevin mostly worked the day shift through lunch and preparation for the evening. Fortunately, that made most nights available for whatever might evolve. Unfortunately, he still had to get up in the morning.

With two less-than-twenty-year-old males living in an apartment, their residence became a merry-go-round of spontaneous nighttime activities and unexpected guests. The guest list included many young and beautiful girls that just wanted to hang out with them. It was a summer when many of their guests had never smoked marijuana when they came through the door but certainly did before they left. Weed then was, at best, Mexican field grown, and most imbibers could smoke big fat ones all night. The never-been but soon-to-be stoned experience by their guests was so frequent that Kevin and Joel began to anticipate an often-uttered statement, "I don't feel a thing." Soon to follow would be a hearty and sometimes out-of-control laugh about something as random as the idea of playing the game Pin The Tail On The Donkey, or pondering why Little Joe and the entire Cartwright family from *Bonanza* always wore the same clothes each episode.

Further down the cannabis trail, they would discover how hungry they were. After busting open a bag, they might wonder why they had taken the taste of Hydrox cookies for granted for so many years, or possibly, they would suggest a walk to 7-Eleven to get something salty. Usually by that time, they were beginning to admit they were stoned, and when they saw a world of food illuminated by fluorescent convenience store lights, they damn well knew they were. At that moment, the hard part was trying to not act stoned in the store when, an hour earlier, they had never been high.

Weed and women were better than Kevin had ever imagined. From junior high through most of high school, if you got any, it was because you spent many months cultivating a steady romantic relationship that led you, month by month, step by step, to the magic gates. Sometimes you got to knock on the gate or ring the bell, but it wasn't often you were invited inside. Not so with grass. Kevin wasn't sure if "the times were a changin'" or if dope was changing the times. Didn't really matter. For the first time in his short life, sex did not need to be pursued, it just seemed to find its way through the front door. And the sex itself was usually a passionate, fully engaged, unabashed, present-moment dance of delight.

There were nights that Kevin just hung out with John and they talked about politics, conspiracy theories, grander visions of the universe, and life after death. Recently, John had also begun to share the occasional story about Vietnam with Kevin. They were not told in any chronological order or in a way that gave Kevin a sense of John's Vietnam experience. They were just snippets of events that seemed so distant and difficult for Kevin to truly comprehend. The images these stories conjured up in Kevin's mind seemed to have darkened edges and morphed into emotions, expanding like smoke rings, to growling places in Kevin's stomach. They were images and feelings that Kevin wanted to put out of his mind but that also seemed intrinsically connected to new concerns that had effervesced into his consciousness from many discussions with John.

During more intense periods of their discussions, the expressions on Kevin's face and his body language were like a barometer for John that alerted him to change the subject. He was reminded not to follow his darkness down into holes he had revealed to Kevin that he had previously explored more thoroughly alone. A subject shift that seemed to provide energetic hope for both of them was the idea, though very far-fetched at first, of moving to another country. The Kirkwood Library was no more than a block from the apartment house, and John had checked out books on Papua New Guinea, the Netherlands, New Zealand, and Canada. What seemed to interest John the most were the political systems and social programs of each country, as well as its track record related to war or armed conflict. Kevin had never even pondered the idea of moving to another country before these discussions with John and really considered these verbal meanderings as flights of fantasy. John was back from Vietnam and Kevin had his draft deferment, so from Kevin's standpoint, all was just fine in Missouri.

At the end of August, Kevin stayed briefly with his parents before moving into the dorm at Mizzou in early September. Happily, Joel and Kevin were still friends after three months of being roommates, but the person Kevin was going to miss most after the summer of 1968 was John. John recently told Kevin that he had filled out immigration papers for New Zealand, and he expected to get an answer from the New Zealand consulate within six months. Kevin had a better understanding now of how much John felt the U.S. government had betrayed him and so many other young men by sending them to kill and possibly die in Vietnam. From John's point of view, with the war continuing, expanding, and supported by the majority of Americans, not to leave the United States, if you found an acceptable alternative, was an act of complacency. Kevin didn't hold that view, but it was one of many ideas or concepts Kevin had never really considered before meeting John.

The 1968 Democratic Convention was held at the International Amphitheater in Chicago from August 26 through August 29. The convention took place after riots, unrest, and violence occurred across the country during 1968, resulting from war protests but mainly from the assassinations of Dr. Martin Luther King Jr. and Robert Kennedy, the front-running Democratic presidential candidate. In anticipation of 100,000 antiwar protestors coming to the convention, 23,000 police and National Guardsmen were mobilized throughout the city. Over three days, with the world watching, Dan Rather was roughed up on the convention floor by security live on television during a remote with Walter Cronkite, and the Chicago police led an unprovoked violent riot against 10,000 protestors in the city's Grant Park when one protestor lowered a U.S. flag.

Once again, Kevin and his family watched very disturbing events unfold on television. However, this time, while in the same room, they were miles apart on their opinions of who was to blame and why this was happening. As Kevin tried to contain his horror and anger at what he was witnessing, he couldn't help thinking about John and all they had talked about over the summer. Maybe John was right; that it would never be right again in the United States. Maybe John was right that the United States was not the best country in the world anymore, and there were other countries founded on democratic principles that now had higher moral principles than the United States. Maybe John would find the peace he was looking for in New Zealand. Maybe there was no peace to be found.

Chapter 11

1969

After the great summer of 1968, Kevin was determined to make the most of his freshman year at the University of Missouri, and he did. Just as his parents and his teachers had reminded him on so many occasions, going to university was quite different than attending high school. Kevin fully enjoyed the greater academic and social freedoms of university, and fortunately, quickly cultivated a self-discipline that allowed him to indulge in his social life while also maintaining a 3.5 grade average.

The political events that unfolded during his first year echoed the discussions he'd had with John the previous summer. The Vietnam War, along with social change and unrest, remained front and center in the news and on campus. Politics and opinion were now well entrenched on most college campuses, though the University of Missouri did not have the political intensity of Berkley, Columbia, Madison, or the University of Michigan. The election of Richard Nixon for president, along with his vocal vice president, Spiro Agnew, threw gas on the flames of the opposition to the Vietnam War. It also flared the divisions between peaceful protests and more radical, sometimes violent, opposition to the war gaining strength through the activities of the Students for A Democratic Society (SDS), Weatherman, Black Panthers, and other groups.

By the end of Kevin's second semester, Harvard University's administration building had been seized by three hundred members of SDS and resulted in more than forty injuries and nearly two hundred arrests. Kevin's parents were certainly pleased with his grade average but were more in alignment with Spiro Agnew's Silent Majority and hoped Kevin would not become part of the "nattering nabobs of negativity" that Agnew spoke about.

Kevin got his summer job again at Al Baker's restaurant in St. Louis and was welcomed back to the apartment at North Taylor Road by Joel and John since his relationship with his parents was a bit strained. Joel's band was now steady with work, and Kevin and John went to the gigs with Joel whenever they had a chance.

John's application for immigration to New Zealand was declined, and he had turned his immigration focus to Canada. John gave Kevin information on Canadian immigration, and they spoke often about Canada's policy of sanctuary for draft evaders and U.S. military deserters. According to John, there was an underground of young Americans living in Canada that supported others that needed protection and helped them through the process. Canada was certainly more familiar to Kevin, and closer to the United States than New Zealand or Papua New Guinea, but Kevin struggled with the idea that those who fled to Canada to avoid the Vietnam War might never be allowed back into the United States. Fortunately for Kevin, he had his college deferment and the draft, for him personally, was not really an issue at the moment.

The summer of 1969, for the most part, was working during the day and evenings full of weed, women, music, and parties. But unlike the previous summer, it was also a high-speed rollercoaster ride of current events that included Woodstock, the first man on the moon, Charles Manson's new level of evil, and a brighter spotlight on the endless procession of body bags arriving back in the United States from Vietnam shown nightly on the television news.

With prompting from John, Kevin and Joel were initiated to LSD that induced an altered state of reality far beyond what Kevin and Joel had ever experienced with marijuana. For Kevin, LSD brought him more confusion and darkness than the insights he read about and had hoped to achieve.

Summer was fading, and it was time for Kevin to head back to school. For the first time in his life, Kevin had been experiencing bouts of depression and paranoia that seemed to be walking hand in hand with his concerns about world events. He hoped the new semester at school and renewed focus on his studies would wash all of that away.

Chapter 12

Woodstock Nation

B ack at school, university life began to provide the renewed sense of spirit and joy that Kevin had hoped for. It was immediately evident to Kevin that there was a dramatically different mood and energy on campus than there had been the previous year. Maybe it was because of Woodstock just a couple of months before, but instead of hippies being a small and isolated subculture, now longhairs, bearded radicals, and free-flowing all-natural hippie chicks appeared to be the predominant campus demographic. Even the Greeks were becoming freaks and were having a difficult time recruiting without severely relaxing their rules and dress codes.

New stores featuring bellbottom jeans, boots, peasant blouses, and hippie-style clothing were established and ready to help students make their fashion transition. There were also head shops that sold rolling papers, pipes, beads, stash bags, and black lights. Another new campus favorite was the Goodwill store that provided an almost endless supply of old clothing to customize your look. In addition to these legal counterculture enterprises, weed and other drugs were widely available from enterprising underground entrepreneurs.

The start of the fall semester in 1969 was like attending a festival, and the unity on campus was magnified by a sense of a tribal belonging to the growing Woodstock Nation. Almost everyone Kevin met was trying on a new level of kindness and love. For many, any form of irritation, anger, or aggression was seen and openly judged as socially incorrect. During this group-mind flirtation with Age of

Aquarius values, even hitchhiking was as easy as flashing the peace sign to a car with like-minded brothers and sisters who were only too eager to assist a tribal stranger. More than likely, once you got a ride, there would be at least an offer to pass the new rolled-up form of peace pipe while motoring to your destination with newfound kindred spirits.

Within that afterglow of love and peace in the fall of 1969, dystopian events were certainly not taking a holiday. In September, U.S. Army Lieutenant William Calley was charged with war crimes related to the My Lai Massacre in Vietnam. September was also the beginning of the five-month-long spectacle trial of the Chicago Seven, who were charged with conspiracy, inciting a riot, and other crimes related to anti-war protests at the 1968 Democratic Convention.

October 1969 brought on the Days of Rage, Vietnam War protests, and anarchy organized by the Weatherman faction of the SDS. From October 8 through 11, the Weatherman and their supporters battled in the streets of Chicago with over 2,000 police, setting cars on fire and vandalizing businesses and homes. On October 15, a more peaceful Moratorium to End the War in Vietnam became a massive collective of protests and teach-ins, with millions of people participating across the United States and around the world. A month later, the Moratorium March on Washington was a magnet for half a million demonstrators to come to Washington DC and peacefully, but vocally, express their opposition to the Vietnam War.

If there was any saving grace or diversion for the chaotic and highly divisive events of the fall of 1969, it was the United States release of the Beatles new album *Abbey Road*. For Kevin and many others, the album cover with Paul walking barefoot and the alleged hidden messages in some of the album's songs substantiated the rumors that began with the Beatles *Sgt. Pepper's Lonely Hearts Club Band* album cover in 1967—that Paul McCartney was dead.

Kevin still kept up with the anti-war movement and unfolding political events, but under the influence of a growing assortment of drugs that he was now taking, he became consumed with understanding and unraveling the "Paul is dead" conspiracy. He listened to the record at slower speeds and played songs on the album backward to find hidden clues. Kevin even tried, like many others, to determine a secret phone number that it was said could be revealed by listening to the rolling and syncopated drumbeats on the song *Come Together* that mimicked the sound of a rotary phone returning to its starting position after each digit was singularly dialed. Determining this phone number and calling it was supposed to lead to deeper answers.

Kevin enthusiastically shared his new findings in great and sometimes exhausting detail with anyone who would listen, including his parents over Thanksgiving. He even tried to convince them, to their great dismay, that there were links between "Paul is dead," the Kennedy assassination, and the dark and secret plans for global domination by the hidden puppeteers of the United States government. But the biggest disagreement around the Thanksgiving table in 1969 was the upcoming U.S. military draft lottery. This attempt to randomize the selection of manpower needed to fight the Vietnam War was put into effect by President Richard Nixon's Executive Order the day before Thanksgiving on Wednesday, November 26, 1969.

The first draft lottery drawing since 1942 was held on December 1, 1969. It was broadcast live, nationwide, on radio and television, even preempting the regularly scheduled Mayberry RFD on CBS. This first of two Vietnam-era draft lotteries was for men who were U.S. citizens or immigrants born between 1944 and 1950. Because of February 29 occurring in leap years, 366 blue capsules, each one with a different calendar day of the year inside of them, were put into a large glass container that tumbled the capsules. One by one, the capsules were drawn by hand to determine the order that draftees would be called up for service. The group of draftees born on the calendar day inside of the first blue capsule drawn would be the first to be drafted, followed in sequential order by the men corresponding to the calendar day in each subsequent blue capsule picked.

The night of the lottery at most universities, including Mizzou, was more chaotic than the actual drawing of the capsules and definitely louder and more emotional than the somber event itself. What could be seen on television were blue capsules being drawn, one by one, with the paper inside unfolded to reveal the date on the paper.

In a staid and very matter-of-fact manner, the calendar date inside the capsule was announced before the paper with the date was pinned onto a board with 366 squares. At draft lottery gatherings across the country, many of the affected viewers were fueled by alcohol, drugs, and anxiety or a combination of some or all of that. With each capsule drawn, there were clear winners and losers. It was an odd game of chance that forced participation, and one where you did not want your number to be picked.

Kevin watched the drawing with many others at a draft lottery party he had been invited to. Kevin smoked some hash just before walking into the party and continued to smoke any joints that came his way as well as sip on the wine from jugs that were being passed around. But once they started to handpick the blue capsules, all of his attention was focused on the lottery. The hoped-for outcome was that your number would not be picked before 195 capsules had been drawn. The Selective Service estimated that it would not need more men each year than those provided by the first 122 capsule picks, and beyond 195 picks, it was very likely you would never be drafted.

For forty-one picks, Kevin cheered with those who had escaped selection for the moment and watched the troubled reaction of those who were not so lucky. But when the forty-second capsule was picked and they read his birthday, July 13, there was no need to watch the television any longer. Kevin knew that number forty-two almost assured he would be going to Vietnam as soon as he finished school or lost his school deferment, unless the war ended before then.

For the first time ever, he felt an uneasy, and now very personal, connection to the war in Vietnam. He was no longer looking at or pondering the war from a philosophical distance that allowed him long periods of time he could choose not to think about the war at all. In an instant, he was now mired in and on the losing end of the government's mechanism for providing the manpower required to fight its seemingly never-ending war. Kevin's new and frightening revelation was playing out amongst the cheers and jeers of each new capsule pick without an awareness of being present in the room. Overwhelmed and feeling slightly nauseous, he decided to go back to his dorm room, but as he headed for the door, he saw Lorraine for the very first time.

Kevin was attracted to many girls and always had his radar up and running, but when he first noticed Lorraine, his whole body rushed with an unfamiliar focused intensity. What he was feeling was every bit as strong as a spontaneous adrenaline rush generated by a fight-or-flight situation. In this instance, Kevin had no desire to flee but an urging to know more. Kevin's shimmering perception of Lorraine was deeper than how beautiful she appeared to him in every physical way. He perceived a sense of her inner beauty that radiated outward and surrounded her, showcased by her calm and poised elegance. All of these emotions were quickly tempered when he remembered why he was leaving the party in the first place and further realized that beauty he had just encountered was unapproachable for him.

Back in his room, with lights out and eyes closed, Kevin tried to sleep in a mental loop of worry about how the results of the draft lottery would affect his future. But his last thoughts before he drifted off were images of Lorraine.

Over the next few days, Kevin saw Lorraine on campus a few times, but not in any circumstance that would allow him to engage with her. He did ask friends who were at the lottery party about her, and learned she was from Southern California, and that this was her first semester at Mizzou.

On Friday night, December 5, Kevin went to a concert and dance at Mother Earth, a big barn that had been turned into a party venue about five miles from campus. The evening was a true peace-and-love freaks gathering, with everyone in their hippie garb, stoned, or on their way to being stoned, and ready to dance. Not only were they celebrating the gathering of the tribe at Mizzou, many felt a connection to the free concert being put on by the Rolling Stones in the San Francisco Bay area the following day that was being heralded as Woodstock West.

Kevin was supposed to meet friends inside Mother Earth, but when he got inside the barn, it was darker and more crowded than he expected. He wandered through the crowd looking for someone he knew. Before he ever saw Lorraine, she was standing directly in front of him with a no-holding-back high-voltage smile. The band had just started playing, and it was already hard to hear, but the first words Lorraine ever spoke to Kevin were, "I think you must be Kevin, and I hear you want to meet me."

Kevin was truly tongue-tied but managed to mutter, "Yeah, that's right."

To which Lorraine responded, "Well, good to meet you, Kevin. Let's dance." Lorraine took Kevin's hand and led him into the crowd that was already dancing near the stage. All of this was happening so fast and unexpectedly that all Kevin could do was break into a smile and dance.

Just like the first time he saw her, Kevin was captivated by Lorraine. Everyone on the dance floor was attired in their hippie best, though most were looking very earthy in a back-to-the-land sort of way. While Lorraine's outfit was definitely counterculture couture, everything about the way she looked accentuated her elegant, quiet, joyful confidence and poise. Lorraine's long and beautiful brown hair showcased her almond eyes that were a grand mystery of their own. It flowed down her back, spilling over the shoulders of her autumn-colored paisley blouse that was loose-fitted but definitely styled. The bottom of her blouse stopped right above her hips where her low-cut and perfectly fitting jeans became the marquee for everything that the jeans were clothing. They belled out below the knees to break perfectly on tan leather boots that could have only come from California.

Watching her dance, Kevin noticed that Lorraine didn't look stoned or lost in the music. Instead, her eyes were clear and bright, radiating her joy for that moment. While dancing, Lorraine reached out and touched Kevin's shoulder and trailed her hand down his arm, briefly allowing her fingertips to linger on his palm before her hand moved on with the rhythm of the music.

When the band played its first slower tempo song, Kevin and Lorraine moved easily into slow dance together with no sense of awkwardness and with both of them electrified by their unspoken attraction for each other. Toward the end of the song, Lorraine spoke into Kevin's ear and asked him if he wanted to get a beer. When the song was finished, Kevin got two beers, and they went to a table at the back of the barn where they finally got to just talk. Within less than an hour, in a fixated conversation that tuned out everything else around, it became clear to Kevin that Lorraine, in every way, was like no girl he had ever met before. When Lorraine's hand would touch him, even briefly, he felt assured that she was feeling the same way. When he woke up late the next morning lying beside her in her bed, he had no doubts.

Saturday, December 6, was a lazy and romantic winter's day for Kevin and Lorraine, cocooned by their new love. The following day, Kevin and Lorraine learned that, on that very same day they were celebrating the birth of their new relationship, brothers and sisters attending Woodstock West at Altamont Speedway were beaten, raped, and murdered by the Hells Angels. The horrific violence all happened in front of the stage and in sight of the Rolling Stones playing the third song of their set, *Sympathy For The Devil*. As more details came to be known about the dark events of the free concert at Altamont Speedway, December 6, 1969 would be remembered as the day Woodstock Nation died, less than four months after it began.

Chapter 13

Four Dead in Ohio

L orraine's parents had decided to spend the Christmas of 1969 in Germany with friends who lived near Heidelberg and wanted Lorraine to come home and spend Christmas with her sister, Kate, who was still going to high school. Lorraine went home for Christmas break, but unknown to her parents, with Kevin in tow. For ten days, Kevin came to know Southern California through Lorraine's eyes and was enchanted by all that charmed so many. But the laid-back sunny magic of California came with an undercurrent of overcrowded and congested franticness. Even then, the freeways were crowded and gridlocked much of each day, and unless the Santa Anas were blowing, smog was a constant companion.

For Kevin, California was both the best and the worst. He could imagine how incredible it would be to live a life in the sun, close to the beach, and be able to surf every day. He could understand why California became a post-World War II magnet for so many GIs who had discovered all that California had to offer on their way to and from the war in the Pacific in the late 1940s. But whatever California was in the 1940s and '50s, as the 1970s were about to begin, California was already overpopulated, with people still wanting a piece of the dream but now rushing to relax and waiting for a time to delay.

As the plane carrying Kevin and Lorraine lifted from the runway at LAX for the flight to St. Louis, the view from the 707's window of all the houses and cars, surrounded by brown hills below a layer of smog, for some reason, brought to mind John and so many things they had discussed.

Back at school, both Kevin and Lorraine settled into their new semester schedules but spent as much time together as possible. Some weeknights and almost all weekends, Kevin stayed at Lorraine's. Her balanced approach to life was a good influence for Kevin in many ways. Since meeting her, he hadn't taken any hallucinogens and only smoked weed and drank wine on the weekends. Lorraine also made Kevin much more aware of what he was eating. There were days when he ate more fruit and vegetables than meat, and even the odd day when he ate no meat at all. He tried a few times to stop smoking cigarettes or cut back, but that wasn't working out very well.

Kevin continued to do well in his classes, and outside of school, Lorraine had most of his attention. But the war in Vietnam was always present in some way on the campus and in the news—and never very far from Kevin's mind.

Kevin and Lorraine talked almost daily about the war and war resistance. They were both troubled by the growing acceptance of the idea that violent resistance to the war in Vietnam could be justified by the brutal domestic and international policies of the Nixon administration. Walking through campus on an early spring-like day in March, they met young Quakers with a table full of information that reinforced peaceful resistance to all war. The book Kevin left with and read more than once from cover to cover was the *Manual for Draft-Age Immigrants to Canada*, written by Mark Satin, a U.S. citizen and conscientious objector living in Toronto. The manual explained, in great detail, all that was required to immigrate to Canada, including the special planning and documentation required if the primary purpose of going to Canada was to avoid the Vietnam War. It also clearly portrayed the differences between life in the United States and Canada, including highlighting Canada's history, politics, culture, and weather. Within all of the how-to information provided, the manual emphasized that anyone making the decision to move to Canada as a draft evader or deserter needed to fully come to terms with the fact that they would likely never be able to go back to the United States again without risking arrest and imprisonment.

Given Kevin's comfort with the familiar and his deep feelings for Lorraine, this was a very troubling element. Lorraine was quick to remind Kevin that, for as long as he remained in school, this was an option he did not need to consider or be troubled about. Though he never brought it up with Lorraine, he doubted John would agree with her reasoning.

On April 29, more than fifty thousand U.S. and South Vietnamese troops crossed the border into Cambodia in an assault designed to disrupt the Viet Cong forces taking refuge in Cambodia and to destroy their Cambodian sanctuaries. The following day, President Nixon's televised address to the nation announced the invasion of Cambodia, justifying the action as necessary "to win the just peace that we desire." The Cambodian invasion became the catalyst for nationwide demonstrations on college campuses that resulted just four days later, on May 4, in the shooting deaths of students at Kent State University by the Ohio National Guard. Another four days later, on May 8, antiwar demonstrators on New York City's Wall Street were violently attacked by construction workers in an anti-protestor backlash that became known as the Hard Hat Riots.

Many campuses, including the University of Missouri, imposed curfews and strict limits on the number of students allowed to assemble in one place. In spite of what Kevin and so many others believed at that time, the real goal of these restrictions was not to limit expression, but just to bring some order to the chaos on campuses, allowing the students to complete the term and head home.

Kevin and Lorraine passionately participated in all of the non-violent protests at Mizzou before curfew and limits of assembly were enforced, but the deaths of the four students at Kent State and the violence perpetrated by the construction workers in New York devastated them both. Even though their relationship remained dynamic, they now shared an overwhelming despair that trumped their other emotions and seemed impossible to set aside.

The last day of exams should have been a time of relief and some joy. Instead, on a phone call home and through her mother's tears, Lorraine learned that her father lost his job with the advertising agency he worked for in San Diego and that she would now need to attend college the following fall in California.

Two days later, Kevin and Lorraine drove to St. Louis and stayed at a motel near Lambert Field. After a long night of no sleep and not much more one could say, Kevin found himself looking into Lorraine's now sad almond eyes as he said goodbye and told her once more how much he loved her. With a tear running down her cheek that betrayed her attempt at a smile, Lorraine told Kevin that she loved him more than anyone she had ever loved, and if that love is meant to be, it will be. With a hug and a last kiss, she turned and walked directly to the gate and down the loading ramp, pivoting to wave briefly before stepping inside the plane. Kevin stayed and watched Lorraine's plane take off from the observation deck and then drove home to his parents' house in a fog of sadness and confusion.

Once again, Kevin was offered a job at Al Bakers in St. Louis filling in for different cooks on summer vacation. Joel was no longer living in the same apartment, so Kevin reluctantly moved in with his parents for the summer. The commute from their house to the restaurant took at least thirty minutes each way, providing too much time for Kevin to spin the confusion and despondency that still persisted from his last term at school and his goodbye from Lorraine.

The days passed quickly, and the nights did introduce new friends. Kevin sent a few letters to Lorraine and she wrote back each time. He talked to her by phone when he needed to hear her voice, but the cost of a long-distance phone call to LA didn't allow them to talk very long or really discuss anything. Possibly it was the brevity of the calls, but though Lorraine seemed happy to hear from him, she also seemed a bit detached now, almost a world away, living her days in a life that Kevin was a stranger to. The time between calls to Lorraine became longer as the summer progressed, and Kevin found a friend with benefits that helped fill the void left by Lorraine. He wondered if Lorraine found someone too or was back together with her former high school surfer boyfriend. Kevin didn't really want to know and never asked her.

By the end of summer, he was still haunted by his feelings for Lorraine, but then, it didn't seem to really matter if he and Lorraine loved each other or not. She was in California, and he was going back to school in Columbia, Missouri. Neither Kevin nor Lorraine had any money for cross-country travel, so there was really no way to see each other. They could only afford to call on the phone for a very short time, once in a while. The likelihood of them being together was, as they still said at the time, about as good as a Chinaman's chance in hell.

Chapter 14

Where the Hell Is Vancouver?

Kevin was fully enveloped by a bottle of red wine he was sharing with his non-significant other. It was a plonk the California wine industry was allowed to call Burgundy at the time, but the buzz it provided at that moment was just about perfect, and it took the edge off the Thai stick he had smoked earlier in the afternoon. In what is often referred to as "out of the blue," Kevin got a call from John. He told Kevin he was in Toronto taking a deeper look at Canada but would be returning to St. Louis and intended to leave for British Columbia in a couple of weeks. Confusing British Columbia with British Honduras, as many others would do in the days to follow, Kevin thought John was headed south. Though British Columbia had been a province in Canada for many, many years, knowing then as much about Canada as most Americans don't, that was a news flash for Kevin.

Once he figured out John was talking about Canada, it made a bit more sense... sort of. Kevin had gone on fishing trips to Red Lake, Ontario, with his father a few times. Other than the information he got from the Quakers at school, the trips with his father were his singular point of reference for Canada. As John's excited voice streamed through the phone, the only images Kevin could conjure up were pine trees, cold water, walleye, moose, and bear—not much that appealed to Kevin at that moment. In spite of being in university, he had never stopped to consider that Canada might be something other than Red Lake, Ontario.

What he had read about Canadian winters didn't help either. Kevin's most recent fantasies of travel had him cooking his way through Europe, drinking wine with every meal, and making frequent weekend visits to Amsterdam. Not once had he dreamed about Red Lake, Ontario, or policeman with red coats.

As Kevin hung up the phone, still in a bit of a Thai stick/ red wine haze, he was puzzled and even oddly amused by the fact that in his entire life, he had never heard of Vancouver and British whatever it was called. He knew there must be lots of snow and ice, that's for sure.

Chapter 15

The Best They Could Imagine

It was Labor Day weekend when John arrived at Kevin's parents' house in his VW Beetle loaded with camping gear, most of his remaining possessions, and laden with maps. Kevin was energized by John's enthusiasm for the adventure and genuinely excited by all of the facts and details he learned from John about the Pacific Northwest. But over dinner with Kevin's family, John broke the news that it was his intention not just to explore British Columbia but to seek permanent residence by formally immigrating to Canada. Kevin's parents were stunned by the idea that a veteran from the U.S. Navy, who had fought for his country's freedom, would now want to leave the USA for Canada. Possibly even more shocking to them was the idea that Kevin was now considering riding along with John to have a look at Vancouver himself.

He'd arrived at that decision earlier in the day, after devouring John's maps and his excitement. Of course, that was the first time in his life that he really knew where Vancouver was. The aspect that intrigued him the most was the fact that British Columbia (he could remember the name now) was on the Pacific Ocean. John spit out some fact about a warm Japanese current and an "almost" subtropical Vancouver Island that even had a palm tree or two. In Kevin's mind, he was already in his wetsuit paddling out to catch the perfect Canadian wave. Maybe British Columbia wasn't California, but neither was Missouri.

Later, in a private conversation with his parents, Kevin tried to soften their concerns by letting them know this was mostly a two-week vacation and a chance to be with John on the traveling leg of his adventure. He reinforced his story by reminding them he was still registered to go back to school and could go back as late as mid-September. From the look in their eyes, he was sure they were not convinced. Considering the difficulty Kevin had sleeping for the next couple of nights, churning and turning in the tumble of excitement, fear, and rationalizations, he realized he wasn't convinced either.

The night before Kevin and John left for Vancouver they liberated a bottle of true French Burgundy from Kevin's father, who had received the bottle as a gift from one of his European clients. Since his father had left town on a business trip, and Kevin knew his father preferred California Burgundy to Burgundy from France, he easily escaped his fleeting feeling of guilt about consuming the wine. For the first time in a while. he was drinking wine that had the smells and tastes of some of the wines he'd experienced working in restaurants. It was dramatically different than the California jug wine he had been drinking since he got back home or the wines that were often consumed with fat joints at school. With the stamina that youth grants, Kevin and John finished off the Burgundy and moved on to another bottle of wine they found lurking for their pleasure in Kevin's father's stash. Drinking and laughing long into the night, pulsating with the excitement of the journey ahead, and speculating about what Canadian girls would be like, Kevin and John truly didn't have a care in the world at that moment.

Chapter 16

We Left Missouri in Kind of a Hurry and Headed Up Canada Way

Kevin's mother believed in kindness, courtesy, and the triumph of love over all. As long as Kevin could remember, she'd lived her life and her beliefs in an unspoken expectation of how it might be if everyone lived and was guided by virtue. Kevin had certainly tested her beliefs on too many occasions, but she continued to hold out hope that it was just a matter of time until the virtues she believed in would become his own. But on the morning Kevin and John were leaving for Vancouver, the shadows of her doubts seemed to block the light of her hopes. She struggled to her goodbye, finding a way to a hug and a smile that seemed challenged by her concerns. And for a moment, Kevin wanted to stay and wave to John from the porch with her… but only for a moment.

Kevin filled what little space there was left in the VW with his duffle bag and guitar. John's hand produced a key from his pocket and he inserted it into its German-designed place in the dashboard. A turn of the key to the right and the recently tuned, air-cooled engine popped to life with the sound of tappets and fan belts that only a VW makes. John's foot and the clutch pedal rose from the floor in unison, and in a low gear giddy-up, the four wheels of the VW began their first rotation of the journey. Two right turns and three gears later, they were rolling at seventy miles per hour, with Kevin's home, his family, and his life as he had always known it, quickly vanishing in a VW-sized side mirror.

Bringing himself back to the journey ahead, Kevin felt the intense surge of excitement that comes in the first moments on the road, when the where you are and the where you are going seem to briefly reside in one spot. It is the same place where the never-been-there shares space with the imagined, and $400 in your pocket buys the unconcerned confidence required to fully embrace the future and welcome the unknown. The romance and excitement of travel were not new to Kevin, but his journeys to previous destinations had always been round-trip. This time, though he hadn't ruled out returning to school in a few weeks, Kevin felt his first slight twinge of the one-way.

Chapter 17

I Never Shut the Back Door and You Never Looked the Other Way

There was a huge sporting goods and outfitter store somewhere in Minnesota that John had put on the itinerary before leaving so they could both buy new sleeping bags and camping gear. They made it there by midafternoon of the first day and then had their first night's sleep in the new bags at a campground still south of the Canadian border.

Morning arrived shouting Indian summer, and with a new level of excitement for crossing into Canada that day. Kevin and John made the Manitoba border by early afternoon. There were only two or three cars in the line-up for the border crossing. They quickly put their long hair up into their hats, put their smiles on, and greeted the border guard with careful enthusiasm when it was their turn at the border. After a few standard questions such as "where are you going?" and "what is your purpose?" as well as questions about alcohol and firearms, the border guard said with a smile, "Welcome to Canada, gentlemen." John had already mentioned to the border guard that they were going to head west on Highway 1 and now asked him if he had any recommendations for camping. The border guard named a couple of provincial parks that were up the road but then smiled and said to them, "This is Canada, gents; camp where you like, but clean up when you leave." After a couple of very happy thank yous, once again John's foot and the clutch pedal rose from the floor, and the VW Bug that contained all their worldly possessions and most of their dreams of the moment rolled north into Canada.

The sign simply said, "Welcome to Manitoba," but both Kevin and John were surging with the got-what-they-wished-for. Their excitement for being in Canada predated the high five and any bumping of body parts, but they did manage to get off a good *yahoo* as they pumped a peace sign into the sky through the sunroof.

They stopped at the first town to get gas, change some money, and buy a few supplies for the road. It didn't take long to learn that Manitoba was truly in another country and not just a state called a province north of a line agreed to by politicians many years ago. The imaginary line separated very similar yet sometimes vastly different ways of looking at the world. They would come to know that these differences were underscored by the Vietnam War and accentuated in the opposing worldviews of Richard Nixon and Pierre Trudeau. While President Nixon was adding to his growing enemies list that included philosophers, writers, artists, and musicians, Prime Minister Trudeau was adding to his list of new friends that included philosophers, writers, artists, and musicians. Many people, including John Lennon, were on both lists.

But on that day in September of 1970, Kevin and John's first brush with a new cultural reality included colored money, Cadbury's instead of Hershey's chocolate, GM cars and trucks with the body styles that they were used to but with different names, a queen and her mother (or the Queen Mum, as they called her), cigarette brands that James Bond would smoke, and Canadian beer. They quickly grew to listen for and love the Canadian accent. In the days, weeks, and years to come, they would learn and embrace that there is not just one Canadian accent any more than there is one U.S. accent. They would discover that the real Canadian accent is not only the "owt and abowt" or the "bean and a-gain," but a Queen's English and countrified French overlaid by a rhythmic variation in pronunciation that is punctuated by the multicultural influences of Canadian policies and first-generation immigrants.

They pulled out of town and headed west toward the Rocky Mountains that were less than eight inches away on their map, but in reality, were a prairie's ways away. They took a new interest in Canadian radio stations, trying to understand the news and the politics through the filter of all things Canadian that, at the moment, they didn't have a clue about. That night, Kevin and John camped at a small park that seemed to appear as a treed oasis in the shadows of the late day. They drank a cheap Canadian wine called Baby Duck and fell asleep by a small fire as their eyes became heavy in the awe of a star-intense night sky.

The next morning, they started out early, hoping to get as close to the mountains as possible by the end of the day. The sky was cloudless and brilliant blue, and the angle of the September sun brought a shadowed glow to the autumn colors of prairie grass. Hours and miles passed, and while there were many subtle changes in the landscape and in the chatter of their dreams, Kevin was becoming uncomfortable in the loneliness that echoed from the unfamiliar expanse of the land and the never-ending ribbon of road that sliced through it.

By late afternoon, they knew they wouldn't see the mountains, or even a hill, that day. They did find the blue sky changing to grey marshmallow clouds from the remnants of a storm that found its way from the Pacific Ocean over the Rockies.

Having learned that prairie gas stations were few and far between, they stopped in a less-than-twenty-building Saskatchewan town whose principal reason for being was the railroad of the past. Kevin asked where the restroom was and was politely informed that the washroom was "around back." The restroom he expected to find turned out to be an outhouse. The spring-loaded door closed behind him with a creak. Looking at the grey light between the cracks in the boards, Kevin felt a distance from all that he was comfortable with as vast as the landscape he had been traveling through. It was a loneliness he couldn't share with John, since John was committed to a new life in Canada. The begged-for solution was the companionship of the familiar. Right there and then, returning to school, family, and friends seemed the most desirable and likely outcome. Even more desirable, since somewhere along the Trans-Canada Highway, in the revolving door queue for his mental attention, Lorraine, whom he had been trying to forget about, moved to the front of the line. And in the whispers from the absurd that wait to be listened to in times of pain, Kevin discovered a brief moment of delight in a new understanding of how the cheese stands alone.

Chapter 18

Banff

Kevin and John decided they needed a break from camping, along with showers, and found an inexpensive motel for the night in Saskatoon. They were now only about seven hours away from Banff, and excited by what they anticipated they would see along the way tomorrow. By 7:30 a.m., they were on their way. By 1:00 p.m., the city of Calgary began to emerge in a shimmering distance, shadowed by the foothills of the Canadian Rocky Mountains that camel-humped out of brown prairie flatness. As they got closer to Calgary, it appeared as a metropolis in the middle of nowhere and like no other city Kevin had seen or imagined. The distant perspective, coupled with expectations, brought to mind Dorothy and her traveling companions, and Kevin decided Calgary might just be Canada's Oz.

They stopped in Calgary for lunch and were both intrigued by its blend of urban sophistication and rugged cowboy spirit. But the Rockies were waiting, and they wanted to be settled in a campsite well before dark.

Shortly after leaving Calgary, the Trans-Canada Highway says goodbye to the flat terrain it has shared for more than a thousand miles and hello to an uphill, repetitive undulation that grows steeper and deeper as the mountaintops along the path grow higher. On that cloudless, sunny September day, the mountains presented themselves brilliantly against the sky. They were accented by a deep bright blueness that brought distinction to each sharp edge, geometric peak, and crevice. These majestic gray giants, which seemed to be so distant at first, became the point of entry to a stunning natural wonderland that informed you that you were a stranger as it closed the doors on everything but the compelling present. The highway was now lined by an endless parade of trees, fading summer grass, and struggling wildflowers with the cars, passengers, and the road itself being the only intruders. At certain points along the highway, a murky turquoise-colored Bow River played peek-a-view between the trees, adding to the color palette of the vast surrounding.

The overwhelming beauty and sense of new experience became a desire in Kevin to belong to and become familiar with all that he saw and all that he was feeling. Less than twenty-four hours ago, at an outhouse in Manitoba, he had been ready to abandon adventure for the comfort of the familiar. Now he was held captive, in unison, by what he had just seen, what he was now seeing, and what might be around the next bend just up the road. Within the swirl of that presence and emotion, he pivoted to his longing for Lorraine, imagining what it would be like to share all that he was discovering with her.

It hadn't occurred to either Kevin or John that they had barely spoken for the past thirty minutes and John was feeling, every bit as much as Kevin, in awe with all he could never have imagined but was now immersed in. But in John's mind, there was no question if he would come to belong to this magnificence. He'd shut the back door to his life in the USA when they crossed into Canada two days before. Having decided to immigrate to Canada while touring Ontario with his aunt, what he was experiencing now in the Canadian Rockies exceeded all of his expectations about the magnificence of Canada, and they hadn't even reached British Columbia yet.

The town of Banff projects a sense of place in its destiny to share space with a wilderness region so vast and beautiful that it dwarfs any and all of civilization's discoveries, innovations, trinkets, and trash. Banff and its architecture are perfectly suited to welcome guests from around the world and humbly showcase all that surrounds them.

John and Kevin strolled through the main streets of Banff, looking at the shops and restaurants, breathing in the clean mountain air while still craning their necks to look at the wilderness icons surrounding the town. Kevin spotted a pub and suggested to John that they should take time for a Canadian beer. The drinking age in Alberta was nineteen, so for the first time in his life, Kevin would be able to have a drink in a bar legally.

As they approached the pub, they noticed two entrances. The sign over one entrance indicated "Men Only," while the sign over the other entrance said, "Ladies and Escorts." Once inside, they saw a simply decorated and poorly lighted rectangular hall full of small round tables, all with fitted, terrycloth tablecloths. Male waiters, with round trays full of draft beers, were dispensing the glasses of brew to their customers, generally leaving more than one per customer. Tables with four or more customers were typically being filled with as much beer as the little round table could hold.

When the waiter stopped by John and Kevin's table, he just asked, "How many, gents?" Kevin held up two fingers, meaning two for the table, but the waiter put two beers in front of each of them and grumbled, "Eighty cents for the lot, big spenders." Kevin gave him a dollar and told him to keep the change.

The waiter came by again just before they finished their second beer and asked them how many they wanted this time. John said they were done but asked the waiter about the men only sign at the entrance. The waiter said, "Not to worry, Yanks. That's how it was a few years ago, but they haven't gotten round to changing the signs. Women can come and go as they please now, with or without a man." John then asked about the line around the top of all the beer glasses. The waiter told them that was the pour line mandated by the Alberta government to make sure all guests got a full pour.

"Why do most of the tables take so many beers at one time?" Kevin asked.

"Just habit," said the waiter. "When it gets busy in here, you want to make sure you don't run out of beers. Thanks for stopping by. See ya."

Kevin and John walked back through town, bought some food for the evening and then drove to the provincial campsite. Not too long after dark, it got much colder than either Kevin or John had expected. After shivering on the ground in their sleeping bags for a couple of hours, they both ended up back in the car, running the heater every time they got too cold.

As soon as it got light, they headed back to Banff and found a restaurant. During breakfast, they shared the local paper, and Kevin noticed a help wanted ad for the Banff Springs Hotel. Despite the cold and mostly sleepless night, both John and Kevin were still captivated by Banff and the Rocky Mountains. They both agreed it was worth looking into the job opportunities at the hotel that was just a short drive from the restaurant.

When they got there, they parked the car and walked to the hotel entrance specified in the ad. What they found posted at the entrance was a sign showing a drawing of two distinctly different couples. The first was a young man and young woman with well-coiffed hair and conservative clothing. The second couple looked hairy, dirty, and disheveled, had guitars, and looked like they might have just come back from Woodstock. Beneath the conservative-looking couple, the poster indicated: If you look like this, please come in. Under the hippie-looking couple the message was: If you look like this, you need not apply. With that bit of information, John and Kevin walked back to the car, left Banff, and continued west on the Trans-Canada Highway to Vancouver.

Chapter 19

The Banana Belt of Canada

T he roadmap of British Colombia indicated two main routes to Vancouver. The most direct route continued on the Trans-Canada Highway along the Fraser River Canyon and then through the Fraser Valley all the way to Vancouver. The alternative route headed south on Highway 97 at the town of Sicamous, following the Okanagan Lake system down to the Hope Princeton Highway that begins in Kaleden, British Columbia. It was a bit of a toss-up, since John and Kevin were anxious to get to Vancouver, but with the map showing towns named Summerland and Peachland along the southern route, that became the deciding factor.

The scenery between Banff and Revelstoke was spectacular and rivaled any mountain drive that John or Kevin had ever made previously. What neither of them expected was how different the topography would be on the west side of the pass at Revelstoke. The drive from Revelstoke to Sicamous is only 45 miles, but in that relatively short distance, the elevation of the highway drops from 5,600 feet to 1,100 feet.

The change in temperature that September day was just as dramatic. By the time they reached Sicamous, the temperature had risen from forty-nine degrees at the pass to seventy degrees. The front windows and sunroof of the VW were open, and their sweatshirts and jackets had been tossed into the backseat by the time the town of Sicamous came into view.

In their lack of understanding about British Colombia, they had expected it to all look much like Banff. Instead, the town of Sicamous was situated on a channel between Mara Lake and Shuswap Lake, with a vast natural water system stretching southwest surrounded by forested wilderness.

From the junction at Sicamous, Highway 97A goes almost directly south for forty-six miles to the town of Vernon. Again, the topography changes dramatically over that short distance from the green forested mountains bordering the lakes at Sicamous to the dry brown desert landscapes of the Okanagan Valley. The Okanagan stretches southward all the way into Washington State from Vernon along a vast system of lakes fed by the Okanagan River and the intersecting mountain streams along the way. Vernon is at the head of both Lake Okanagan on the west and Kalamalka Lake on the east side of town.

When Kevin first saw Kalamalka Lake's sparkling hues of blue, green, and turquoise, it reminded him of the colors of the Gulf of Mexico. For some reason, the brown, dry landscape that ran down to the lake brought to mind impressions of Israel that he remembered from biblical movies. Realizing that both of these stray thoughts were at complete odds to what he was experiencing, he settled into his first awareness that British Columbia was quickly becoming the Canada he had never expected.

After Vernon, Highway 97 follows Kalamalka Lake and Wood Lake south past orchards, vineyards, cattle ranches, and fruit stands until it meets and crosses Lake Okanagan in the city of Kelowna. Beyond the floating bridge in Kelowna, Highway 97 follows the west side of Lake Okanagan to the end of the Lake in Penticton. Sixteen miles from Kelowna, directly on Lake Okanagan, is the municipality of Peachland, where John and Kevin hoped to camp for the night.

It was now 4:30 p.m., and they found a very basic campground with beachfront access to the lake that only charged them off-season rates for the night. After pitching their tent, they walked along the lakeshore back to the pub in Peachland. A few beers later, they walked a half a block up the street to the local café and both had fish and chips for dinner. After dinner, they walked back along the beach to the campsite and watched a colorful sunset dim to twilight, outlining the mountains in sharp shadows just as the first stars began to appear.

Sitting around a campfire on a night that was cool but not near as cold as the night before, they talked about how much their adventure had changed in the twenty-four hours since they'd arrived in Banff. The Okanagan Valley was a unique and unexpected surprise. Just like with Banff, they were both tempted to seek opportunities in Kelowna, but at the end of circular conversation, they decided they needed to see Vancouver first and then decide where to put a stake in the ground.

In the morning, they took hot showers at the campsite and drove south for breakfast to the city of Penticton, which sits between Lake Okanagan and Skaha Lake. Penticton was smaller than Kelowna, and much more of a town that seemed dependent on tourism and agriculture. With summer over and fall progressing, the town had a feeling of closing down until next season. The exception to that were the busy fruit stands that offered a cornucopia of locally grown fruits and vegetables for eating, storing, and canning, to customers coming from as far away as Calgary and Vancouver. After breakfast, John and Kevin stopped at a fruit stand outside of town and purchased apples, pears, and Concord grapes for the six-hour drive to Vancouver.

A couple miles south of the fruit stand, they turned west on Hope Princeton Highway for the last leg of the trip to Vancouver. Forty-five minutes later, just outside of Hedley, British Columbia, which is for the most part in the middle of nowhere, John discovered that the uneven bumping of the road was, in reality, a flat tire. They changed the flat to the spare tire which, unfortunately, turned out to be very low on air. Slowly, they drove into Hedley to discover that Hedley was a one-gas-station, former gold-mining ghost of a town with a population of less than one hundred people. The mountains surrounding Hedley were made of rock and stone, decorated by scrub pines struggling to grow between the rocks. The decaying remnants of the gold mine and its entrance were perched on the stone face above the town.

As they slowly drove into the gas station, both of them had a sense that their trip was going to take an odd twist—and maybe not a good one. But instead of being greeted with the hostility that long-haired men often encountered at the time in rural areas of the United States, they were greeted with a smile by a twenty-four-year-old bear of a young man in mechanic's overalls named Colin. Colin noticed the Missouri license plate, and as John and Kevin were getting out of the VW, he called out, "Looks like you Yanks can use a bit of help!" John smiled and agreed while Kevin wondered, once again, why anyone would call someone from Missouri a Yank.

"Just pull that bug into the bay and I'll take care of it," said Colin. John did just that, and Colin lifted the rear wheels of the car just enough so he could take off the tire and then dunked both the original flat tire and the nearly flat spare tire into a water tub to find the leak. During these procedures, Colin was very chatty and seemed delighted to answer the stream of questions John and Kevin posed about Hedley, the Okanagan, and the road ahead to Vancouver. Even after both tires had been fixed and put back where they belonged on the car, John and Kevin were still peppering Colin with questions that he continued to answer with joyful enthusiasm.

After paying Colin what seemed like way too little for all the time they had spent with him, both John and Kevin thanked Colin and thrust out their hands for soul-style handshakes. As palm smacked palm, Colin said, "If you're not in a big hurry, you can come up to the house and meet my gram, who has some cool stories about her days in Vancouver. Hell, you guys could have dinner with us and stay overnight, I know Gram would love it."

John made quick eye contact with Kevin, who had a big smile on his face, and said, "Right on, Colin. That would be great."

With that agreed to, Colin closed up the gas station, and they all headed off up the hill to Gram's house along a rickety boardwalk. On the way, Colin looked back and said, "Watch your step, boys, the rattlesnakes like to hide in the shade under the walkway at this time of day. Won't bother you unless they poke their head out and you happen to be there," followed by a hearty laugh. It was eyes to the ground for John and Kevin for the rest of the way to Gram's. They didn't see any snakes, but they did hear a couple buzzing underneath the boards.

Colin's grandmother's house was Victorian in style with a large porch in obvious need of repair and reflected what must have passed for grandeur in Hedley at some point back in time. They entered through the screen door to old wood floors, high ceilings, wallpaper, and an eclectic hodgepodge of furniture, all smelling of old house but overlaid with the welcoming scents of roasting food coming from the kitchen.

Colin called out, "Gram, I'm home, and I brought you a surprise!" Gram came out of the kitchen with a smile of expectation that grew wider when she saw John and Kevin. She was small in stature, but her presence was strong and confident, adding a glow of beauty to the one that once was. "Gram, this is John and Kevin from Missouri, in the States. They're moving to Canada and stopped at the shop with a flat. They have so many questions about British Columbia I invited them for dinner and to stay the night. Hope that's okay, Gram."

"Why of course, Colin," said Gram. "That would be just wonderful. Good to meet you, John and Kevin. Let me get some beers, and I want to hear all about your plans."

When Gram mentioned plans, it occurred to John that he didn't really have any, and it reminded Kevin that his previous plan to return to school was long gone. Beers with Gram and Colin were followed by the roast beef dinner they smelled, accompanied by Yorkshire pudding. Dinner flowed into numerous Canadian ryes and stories from Gram about her days in Vancouver that included nights hanging around the opium dens of the time. As eyelids got heavy, Gram showed John and Kevin to the room they would sleep in. They were at complete ease, hugging Gram and giving her a kiss on the cheek. When Kevin went to give Gram a peck, she quickly turned her head and kissed him on the lips. He knew he had just kissed old Gram, but he also had an electric sense of the young, vibrant, and adventurous woman that had frequented opium dens. It was the first time Kevin had ever really experienced or recognized the true nature and spirit of an older person, now with youth no longer evident behind the mask of age.

Kevin and John woke the next morning to the smell of bacon cooking in Gram's kitchen, and their temples throbbing from the too many ryes of the night before. When they got downstairs to the kitchen, they found Gram in all her spirited presence, seeming no worse for wear from their evening together, and Colin in overalls, ready to head down to the gas station. "Got to open up the shop," said Colin. "I'll see you before you head out."

Gram's coffee, along with eggs, bacon, and real hashed browned potatoes, helped them to "smarten up," as Gram called it. After breakfast, they thanked Gram profusely, and both John and Kevin gave her a hug. Kevin welcomed Gram's kiss on the lips this time and gave her an extra hug when he said goodbye. The last thing Kevin told Gram before he walked out the door was he had never really met a woman like her before. With those words and emotions hanging in the air, John and Kevin headed down to the gas station on the boardwalk, keeping a keen eye out for snakes.

There were slapping palms and bear hugs with Colin, with promises to come back again to Hedley as soon as they could. Giving a last wave to Colin as they drove out of the gas station driveway, it would have been hard to believe that they would never see Colin or Gram again.

Chapter 20

Lotus Land

The drive from Hedley to Vancouver takes about four hours, going over Alison Pass in Manning Park down to Hope, where Highway 3 intersects with Highway 1, the Trans-Canada Highway. From Hope, Highway 1 is a straight shot to Vancouver through the Fraser Valley, passing the towns of Chilliwack and Abbotsford. As they crossed the Port Mann Bridge from Coquitlam to Surrey, it was already evident that Vancouver and the surrounding Lower Mainland had a population of well over a million people. Since John and Kevin were used to the suburbs of St. Louis, which were sheltered from the traffic and hubbub of the city, they were slightly overwhelmed by the congestion they encountered so far from the city center of Vancouver.

Kevin joked, "We're not in Hedley anymore," while experiencing an anxious sense of not belonging to, or even understanding anything about, the metropolis they were entering. His confidence about the decision to stay in Canada and not to return to school was quickly waning. John said nothing and just seemed to be trying to cope with traffic and follow the signs to downtown. On the final stretch of their journey to Vancouver, they had no actual destination in mind, and no one they even knew within more than one thousand miles.

The Trans-Canada Highway turned into city streets, and John told Kevin he was the navigator to get them to a park near the water where they could stop and figure out a plan. With a well-worn map crumpled on his lap, Kevin told John to make a series of turns that only left them more confused about where they were and how to get to any park. Adding to their stress was their hunger, since they hadn't eaten since breakfast at Gram's. At the corner of Fir and Broadway in a very busy area of Vancouver, they saw a Smitty's Pancake House, and John made a spontaneous decision to get out of the traffic and get something to eat.

The hostess seated them at a booth and gave them menus. A couple of minutes later, a server named Dale presented her smile at their table. John asked Dale what was good this time of day, and she suggested the battered cod. John smiled and ordered the cod with steamed vegetables. Kevin ordered a cheeseburger with fries and asked Dale if they had a newspaper they could look at. Dale said she thought there was one at the staff table.

A short time later, when she brought the morning's Vancouver Sun to them, she asked them, "You guys are Yanks, aren't you?"

"How did you know?" asked John.

"Oh, I could tell by your accents," replied Dale.

"That's so bizarre," Kevin chimed in. "I grew up in Missouri and always thought of myself as a rebel, never a Yank. But you're the third person to call me Yank since we left Missouri for Vancouver."

"Why did you come here?" asked Dale.

"We're immigrating to Canada," John stated.

"Far out!" exclaimed Dale. "You are going to love it here. It's really a mellow and very together city and, guess what—no Vietnam War."

"That's for sure," said John.

John and Kevin looked closely at the classified section of the newspaper during lunch, looking for rooms or apartments to rent and for jobs. They saw a couple of what seemed like reasonable places to rent but really had no idea what part of the city they were in and how long it would take to get there. One of them was an advertisement for a furnished basement suite on 4th Avenue.

When they were paying the check, John asked Dale if 4th Avenue was a good part of town and how far it was. Dale chuckled and told them, "There really are no bad parts of town, just different

91

parts of town. Fourth Avenue is cool, with a health food store and natural food restaurants. Real close to here, as well. Lots of heads live there and rent is pretty cheap."

"Cool," said Kevin. "Now if we only had jobs."

Dale told them they needed a couple of dishwashers at Smitty's, but the job didn't pay very much. "No problem," said Kevin. "Isn't that what being an immigrant is all about?"

"Don't know," responded Dale, "but guess you're right. You've got to start somewhere. I suggest you talk to Brian, our manager, on the way out. He's over there at the staff table and likely he can help you out."

John and Kevin thanked Dale and told her, with luck, they would see her again. They went over to the staff table and said they were looking for Brian. "That's me," Brian said in a friendly way.

"Heard you were looking for dishwashers," Kevin asked in a statement. From there, it just got better. Brian did need dishwashers and told them if they were up for the task, they could start right away. When they told him they didn't have their immigration papers just yet, Brian said he could work something out for a bit until they got Social Insurance Numbers. "Today's Thursday," said Brian. "Take a day to get settled, but I need you both here on Saturday. One of you can start at 7:00 a.m. and the other one needs to come in on Saturday at 3:00 p.m. and stay until closing. Whoever is coming in for the late shift, come in at two thirty and we can sort it all out while you're both here."

Kevin and John thanked Brian over and over and said they would cover both shifts on Saturday. They found Dale before they left and told her they both got jobs. "Far out, guys, and see you again soon!" said Dale. "Hope the place on 4th works out for you too."

They called from a pay phone outside of Smitty's and inquired about the basement suite on 4th Avenue. A woman with an accent who answered the phone in Portuguese invited them, cautiously, to view the suite. John told her they would be there within thirty minutes, but it only took about fifteen to drive there, park, and knock on the upstairs door. Mrs. Francisco Silva answered the door, glanced at John and Kevin from top to bottom, and told them to come have a look. They went back down the outside stairs from the front door to a street-level door that was the separate entrance to the suite.

The suite had linoleum floors and a minimal amount of old and unmatched furniture. There was a sitting area with a small kitchenette right inside the front door. Behind the sitting room were two small bedrooms that were separated by a sheetrock wall that was no more than three-quarters of an inch thick. Instead of doors, each bedroom had a curtain that could be closed, with no beds but mattresses on the floor. In what little space remained, there was a very small "washroom" with a toilet, prison-sized sink, and a standup shower that was barely big enough to turn around in.

John confirmed the price with Mrs. Silva, glanced at Kevin for his approval, and said, "We'll take it." They paid Mrs. Silva cash for the first month's rent, found out where they could park, and moved all of their possessions from the VW into the suite, which took all of about ten minutes. Still nursing a bit of a hangover from the night at Gram's, Kevin suggested they walk to a pub and have a few beers. They were happy to learn that beer was still twenty cents a glass in Vancouver. A couple of hours and two dollars later, they started walking back to the suite, stopping along the way at the green grocer for snacks and some of the essentials they needed.

Once at the suite, with no television, they both settled in for the rest of the evening with a book. After the beers, Kevin had a difficult time staying awake and reading and just turned off the light and looked at the ceiling until he fell asleep. Thinking about the day, as well as the moment and where he was, Kevin was reminded again that, other than John, there was no one he really knew within thousands of miles. Maybe even more troubling was the idea that he could spend all of tomorrow wandering around Vancouver and never run into anyone he knew or even recognized, unless of course he happened to run into Dale or Brian from Smitty's. Fat chance of that.

Kevin wondered if his grandfather that immigrated to the United States from Germany ever felt the same way when he first arrived. What about Mrs. Silva? Kevin never really thought about being an immigrant, only the concept of immigrating. But now, he was an immigrant, with a job as a dishwasher, and sharing a dark basement flat with a fellow immigrant. *It can only get better from here*, he told himself just before he drifted off to sleep.

Chapter 21

Draft Dodgers, Deserters, and Immigrants

T he majority of the staff at Smitty's Pancake House was close in age to Kevin and John. While being dishwashers was certainly tedious and somewhat humbling, their jobs at Smitty's provided an opportunity to interact with young Canadians, helping them begin to grasp the social differences and nuances of Canadian culture. John and Kevin's different work schedules limited the free time they had together, and both of them were soon socializing outside of work with other Smitty's employees. At the same time, they both knew that, until they formally immigrated to Canada, there was no guarantee they could stay in Canada or continue to work at Smitty's, a fact that Brian reminded them of frequently.

Both John and Kevin had read or referred to the *Manual for Draft Age Immigrants to Canada* so many times it had become quite tattered. The manual indicated that there was a loosely knit group of organizations in the major Canadian cities that were staffed with trained counselors to provide advice and assistance to young Americans trying to avoid the draft or who were deserters from the U.S. military. Most of these counselors were immigrants themselves and were very familiar with all the prospective immigrants were going through. To make sure they fully understood the process, Kevin and John met with a counselor at the Committee to Aid American War Objectors in Vancouver. At their first meeting, they were given a series of pamphlets published by the committee that covered a wide range of topics related to immigrating and living in Canada. They were also given a checklist of the personal documents they would need to secure for the immigration interview, which included a certified birth certificate, social security card, high school and college transcripts, job history, letters of recommendation, and if possible, a U.S. passport and offer of employment in Canada. All of these needed to be gathered before the counselors could conduct mock immigration interviews with them, and prior to making an appointment for an immigration interview.

Leaving the offices of the committee, they had a clear understanding of their first steps to becoming Canadians, along with a sense of shared purpose and experience with all the people they met there.

Because of their familiarity with the manual, both John and Kevin had most of the documents they required but, unfortunately, not all of them. Well before affordable courier service, fax machines, internet, or e-mail, it took a series of expensive long-distance phone calls and six weeks to receive the remaining documents they needed by mail.

With all their documents in hand, including offers of employment from Smitty's, John and Kevin arrived at their appointments with the committee for final guidance and mock immigration interviews. Before the mock interviews, they met with a counselor who looked to be in his mid-twenties and introduced himself only as Danny. According to Danny, many Canadian immigration officers had been in the Canadian forces during World War II. Given their service in combat, some of the officers did not look favorably on U.S. draft dodgers or deserters.

Danny also told them that, in spite of that, there was a federal Canadian law that prohibited Canadian immigration officers from inquiring about an applicant's military service or draft status during the interview, unless the subject was brought up or shared by the applicant. The committee counselor stressed that nothing about draft status or military service should be volunteered during their actual interviews, even if the Canadian immigration officer guided their interview close to those boundaries. "For example," Danny said, "they might unexpectedly ask you something like, 'At your age, what motivated you to move to Canada, so far away from your family and friends?' You've got to be prepared to respond to that, very confidently and without hesitation, and not get nervous and blurt out the wrong thing. That's what the mock interviews are all about. Don't worry about making a mistake in the mock interview; we will stay with you until you have it right and help you frame your answers correctly. Just as importantly, have your documents organized and in good order. Only give them the documents they request when they ask for them. Never volunteer any document unless it is requested. We know this because we've all been through these interviews ourselves and from the information we have learned from hundreds of other Americans that have gone through the process. Have a seat over there, guys. Someone will come and get you for your interviews in a few minutes."

The mock interviews went well, though John was much less stressed in his interview than Kevin. For the most part, military service had no relevance to the conversation he was having in the mock interview nor would it be in the actual one. John had served in the Navy, had a general discharge, and his desire to immigrate to Canada was based on his principles and the strong belief that Canada was a better democratic experiment than the USA, providing a different lifestyle and more opportunity. His passion to move to Canada, as well as his optimism and desire to succeed, were real. This passion and determination were all he would need to convey, along with the documents required for the interview.

It was not the same for Kevin. Though he had not been drafted yet, he knew he would be, since he had not returned to school in September. Kevin's desire to live in Canada was as strong as John's, but he faced a different set of circumstances if he was not allowed to stay. At the same time, Kevin's personality allowed him to express his passions and determination with ease and sincerity. During the mock interview, he was coached to keep the fear of not being allowed to stay in Canada out of his mind, while keeping his passion to come to Canada and succeed front and center.

The counselors conducting the interview knew the circumstances of both John and Kevin. John's interview was very straightforward, mostly focused on the questions that would be asked and the way documents would need to be presented one by one during the interview process. The counselor conducting Kevin's mock interview probed for why Kevin, at just twenty years old, would quit university and pack up and leave for Canada, asking the same question a number of times and in a variety of ways during the interview.

The two months that Kevin had spent in Vancouver reinforced his decision to move permanently to British Columbia, Canada, and provided the confidence he needed to display his desires and enthusiasm for what he was now committed to. When Kevin first crossed the border into Canada in September of 1970, he was very conflicted about if or why he would want to stay in Canada. But after living in Vancouver for just over sixty days, he was completely captivated by all he had learned about Canada, as well as the beauty, lifestyle, and multicultural nature of British Columbia. He wanted to join the club, and according to his counselor, that seemed to be coming through in his mock interview. Kevin's only challenge during the mock interview was keeping his documents organized and presenting them easily when requested. Kevin ended the mock interview counseling knowing that presenting the documents was just the mechanics of a process he now had a better sense of.

After the mock interviews, John and Kevin had a last meeting with Danny, who told them that as far as the committee was concerned, they should confidently make the appointment with Canadian Immigration for the real immigration interviews. Danny advised them to make the appointment to immigrate at the Huntingdon border crossing between Abbotsford, British Columbia, and Sumas, Washington, because it was much smaller and more laid-back than the primary point of entry between Surrey, British Columbia, and Blaine, Washington. He also strongly suggested that they cut their hair, wear suits and ties, and that each of them should have at least five hundred dollars in cash to show they could support themselves until their first paycheck in Canada.

Later that same day, John and Kevin called the Canadian immigration office at Huntingdon, British Columbia, and made their appointments for immigration interviews the following week. Danny from the committee told them they could make the appointment from Canada, but John was very concerned that the immigration officials at Huntingdon might be able to tell if the call originated in British Colombia. The alternative was to drive to the United States to make the call and then hope they could come back into Canada without a problem, which had more real risk than the risk of the phone call in Canada that John was concerned about.

The appointment for their immigration interviews was scheduled for 10:00 a.m. on Friday, November 20, 1970. Late afternoon on November 19th, John and Kevin crossed into the USA at the main border crossing between Surrey, British Columbia, and Blaine, Washington. It was the first time they had gone back to the United States since they'd entered Canada in Manitoba in early September.

The crossing back into the United States was a bit more intimidating than they had anticipated. Both of them were asked to show ID as well as their draft cards. The border guard asked them very probing questions about why they had been in Canada and for how long. John said they were up in Canada as tourists and had only been in the country for a few weeks. The border guard peered into the driver-side window and seemed to be focused on the backseat that only contained two duffle bags and a guitar. He walked around the car, came back to the driver's side, and stared directly into John's eyes for what seemed like way too long, then Kevin's eyes and finally, without any display of emotion, told them they could proceed. John drove ahead, and they entered into Washington without speaking until they were far enough from the border to be sure nobody could be listening to them. When they finally did speak, they both agreed that the emotions of fear and paranoia that they used to experience living in the United States and that they had been able to put aside in Canada had now come home to roost.

About two miles past the border crossing, they turned east and followed the U.S./Canadian border a little over sixteen miles to Lynden, Washington. Before they left Vancouver, Kevin made a reservation for them to stay the night at the Windmill Inn at Lynden, a town large enough to have a motel about twelve miles south of the Huntingdon, British Colombia border crossing. By the time they arrived in Lynden, the sun was setting in the west and their paranoia had vanished, but their concerns that either one or both of them would be turned down by Canadian Immigration were settling in.

After checking into the Windmill, they ate dinner at a café down the street and then passed some time before they went back to the inn for the night. When Kevin turned on the television in their room, they both realized this was the first U.S. television station they had watched in almost three months. It was all very familiar but an odd contrast to Vancouver, which was so close in miles but now seemed so far away.

By the time they turned off the television at 11:00 p.m., they had watched *Pat Paulsen's Half a Comedy Hour* on ABC, *Ironside*, and *Dragnet* on NBC, and most of the *CBS Thursday Night Movie*. Kevin put a few quarters in the Magic Fingers Vibrating Bed during the last half-hour of the movie, but when they finally turned off the TV and the lights, his mind was racing ahead to tomorrow's interview.

Kevin continued to toss and turn most of the night, and while John never said anything, Kevin noticed he was turning over in his bed quite often. Kevin finally found some sleep around 3:00 a.m., but his eyes popped open at 6:30 a.m., worried that they had slept through the alarm. At that point, he called it a night and went quietly to the bathroom to shave and shower for the day ahead. *It will be what it will*, he said to himself, just before he heard John say, "What the fuck in hell are you doing up so early, Kevin?"

Chapter 22

Give Me Shelter

That November morning in Lynden, Washington, was Pacific Northwest postcard perfect, with bright sunshine and clear, blue skies dotted with puffy, white clouds moving very slowly from west to east. When Kevin walked out of their room at the Windmill Inn and engaged the beauty of the morning, he remembered that Thanksgiving in the United States was only six days away. He wondered what the weather was like back in Missouri. He wondered what the mood would be like around the Thanksgiving table at home with his parents, so disappointed in his decision not to return to school and instead stay in Canada. He knew it would not be something his parents would want to talk about with people outside of the family. He also knew it was a subject that would not—or maybe even could not—be avoided during Thanksgiving dinner.

Kevin's decision to immigrate to Canada echoed the political divisions within the United States about the war in Vietnam and the direction the country was taking. Those same differences of opinion were now well entrenched within his family and had been hotly debated for the past few years each time they were all gathered together. He longed for the taste and smells of Thanksgiving, the football games, and the feelings of warmth and security he remembered from his childhood but not for the unrest around the table that overshadowed all they wanted to be thankful for. Thanksgiving in Canada had been more than a month earlier, in October. Kevin and John spent their first Canadian Thanksgiving rinsing Smitty's version of Thanksgiving dinner off of plates before they put them in the dishwasher, completely detached from any sense of family or tradition.

With the interviews scheduled for 10:00 a.m., there was plenty of time for coffee and breakfast at the same café in Lynden where they ate dinner the night before. Just before leaving Canada, John and Kevin got haircuts for the interviews, as Danny had suggested, and both of them wore grey suits that they found at The Salvation Army in Vancouver. John was full of confidence and exuberance and ate a hearty breakfast of eggs and bacon with hash browns and biscuits. Kevin only had toast and coffee, while trying to keep his nervousness in check. A few times during breakfast, Kevin went through all of his documents with the hope that he would be able to present them smoothly when requested.

By 8:45 a.m. they were done eating and all coffee'd up. It was only twenty minutes to the border, so Kevin and John took a walk around Lynden to kill some time. By 9:15 a.m., they were back at the car and drove out of Lyndon heading north to the border.

As they approached the border crossing, with all of their anxieties for the interviews ahead, what captured Kevin's conflicted attention were the U.S. and Canadian flags flying so predominantly on each side of the border. The Stars and Stripes waved in the wind with the aura of its military power and might as they crossed the U.S. border into Canada, welcomed by a radio station in Vancouver playing the Rolling Stones' song "Give Me Shelter" and an understated fluttering maple leaf flag "just a kiss away."

John told the border guard they were both coming to Huntingdon for immigration interviews at 10:00 a.m. The guard welcomed them to Canada and showed them where to park. Once inside the border office, John and Kevin presented themselves to Canadian immigration. They were told to take a seat and that the immigration officer would come to get them soon.

Within ten minutes, an immigration officer who appeared to be in his early or mid-fifties walked over to where they were sitting and introduced himself as Blair Richardson. He explained that he was going to interview John first and then conduct the interview with Kevin.

John followed Officer Richardson into a hallway that went to the interview offices. About thirty minutes later, Blair Richardson came back for Kevin. Kevin didn't see John but was reluctant to ask where he was as he followed Officer Richardson to the interview office. Officer Richardson sat at the metal desk in the office and motioned for Kevin to take a seat in one of the two chairs that faced the desk. Once Kevin was seated, Officer Richardson said to him, "I understand you would like to immigrate to Canada, young man."

"Yes, sir," indicated Kevin as confidently as possible.

"Okay, let's get started then," said Officer Richardson. "We need to see a few documents. Can I please have your birth certificate, social security card, and U.S. passport, if you have one?"

With a bit of fumbling, Kevin reached into his right-side suit pocket for his passport, his left-side suit pocket for his birth certificate, and into his wallet for his social security card, giving them all to Officer Richardson without saying anything. In complete silence, Officer Richardson looked at each of the documents and jotted down information on the immigration form he was filling out. Once he was finished with each one, he put them in a pile on the right-hand side of the desk.

"Do you have your school records?" Officer Richardson asked.

"Yes, sir," replied Kevin, reaching again into his left side pocket, pulling out his folded high school and college transcripts and giving them to Officer Richardson. Again in silence, Officer Richardson reviewed the transcripts, spending more time on them than he did with the first documents he'd requested. Finally, he broke his silence. "Kevin, it looks like you only have two years of university. Do you plan on finishing and getting your degree?"

"I'm not really sure yet," said Kevin. "I need to get established in Canada first and make enough money to support myself while I am going to school."

"How did you support yourself for the past two years?" asked Officer Richardson.

"By working summer jobs cooking in restaurants; but I also had help from my parents," answered Kevin.

"Why would you give that all up to come to Canada?" asked Officer Richardson.

"I read a great deal about Canada," said Kevin. "After visiting British Colombia and seeing how beautiful it is here, I am convinced there are opportunities here for me in Canada that will allow me to live a more adventurous life. Once I was offered a job, I knew I had to give it a try."

"Did you bring that job offer with you, Kevin?" asked Officer Richardson.

"Yes, sir," Kevin replied, once again reaching into his left coat pocket and struggling a bit to get the folded letter out to present to Officer Richardson.

Officer Richardson seemed to spend even more time looking at the letter from Smitty's than he did on any of the previous documents he'd requested. It looked to Kevin like he was reading the letter from top to bottom more than once. His face was stern but otherwise expressionless, and Kevin could now feel sweat beginning under his armpits but fortunately disguised inside his suit coat. After what seemed like way too much time looking at the letter, Officer Richardson looked up from the letter and looked Kevin in the eyes and said, "How did you obtain this offer of employment?"

Kevin's armpits inside the suit jacket were no longer just moist, but definitely wet, as he responded, "I have a friend I met while visiting Vancouver that works at Smitty's, and she got me a job interview. I showed them my work history and they were impressed by the caliber of training and experience I have. After getting the offer, I made sure it would provide me enough to get an apartment and cover my living expenses, and it does. I still have $600 of the money I saved up from working last summer to live on until my first check from Smitty's. My goal is to start at Smitty's, but eventually, I intend to find other employment at a more upscale restaurant, similar to the ones I have worked for in the United States." Kevin then opened his wallet to show Officer Richards the six $100 bills he had.

There was a long period of silence as Officer Richardson read the offer of employment letter once more and then made a series of notations on the immigration form. Finally, he looked up again from the paperwork and directly into Kevin's eyes. His face now seemed to have softened slightly, but his eyes displayed seriousness in their focus.

"Kevin, truthfully, at your young age, I'm not sure you know the full impact of immigrating to Canada and all that it might involve for you. While Canada is similar to the United States, it is quite different in many respects, and it will definitely be an adjustment. It could be a lifetime commitment you are making, young man. Do you understand that?"

"Yes, sir," said Kevin. "I think I know what you are saying, but I have given the decision lots of consideration, and I know that this is what I want to do. I want to live in Canada and become a Canadian."

"Well, young man," responded Officer Richardson, "I'm not convinced that you know all the hurdles that may be in front of you, but it sounds like your friend John clearly has you in his plans." With that, Officer Richardson stood up, extended his hand across the table to Kevin and said, "Welcome to Canada."

"Thank you, sir, thank you, thank you, thank you!" said Kevin, continuing to shake Officer Richardson's hand. After that, it was a bit of a blur. Kevin followed Officer Richardson into another room to complete final paperwork. John was already there and waiting with a big smile on his face.

"Looks like you're in too!" John said with a grin.

"Yes!" Kevin all but shouted. "This is a day to remember!" With that, John gave Kevin a bear hug, and they laughed with joy while the immigration officer that needed to complete Kevin's paperwork waited patiently. Once completed, Kevin and John were given temporary Landed Immigrant cards stamped with the date and Huntingdon, British Columbia, and a form that they needed to take to a doctor for physicals. They were also informed that, unless there was something unexpected with the results of their physical, they could apply for British Columbia's single payer medical program within sixty days. One more bear hug later, they said thank you to everyone in the room, strolled out to the car, and started up the road to Vancouver. About one hundred yards from the border crossing was a big blue-and-white sign that said, "Welcome to British Colombia." John pulled the car over in front of the sign, and they both took pictures of each other smiling and pointing at the sign.

The juice was pumping as they drove to Vancouver and back to their apartment. They were now Canadian immigrants, but it all seemed like a bit of a dream. So much had happened since their first discussions about leaving the United States in John's Kirkwood apartment. For John, this was it. He was done with the United States, and he shut the door behind him. Kevin knew this was just the beginning. He was joyous about obtaining Landed Immigrant status in Canada, but he also knew he could not just shut the door on the United States. There was more to come, and he would likely get a draft notice from Selective Service very soon.

And then there was family. And then there was Lorraine. Once these thoughts gained access, the words of Officer Richardson reverberated in his mind. "It could be a lifetime commitment you are making, young man. Do you understand that?" Kevin wasn't sure he did, but he was sure he didn't want to think about it now.

After a couple of tokes on a needle joint, rolled so perfectly by John, they headed to the Marble Arch pub for a few of those twenty-cent beers, each one poured to the line.

Chapter 23

Christmas 1970

K evin was still happy and grateful that he had been allowed to stay in Canada, but as November progressed into December, the days continued to get shorter, and with mostly rain and clouds, they seemed to blend one into the other. The only bright spot was the peek-a-boo of the sun that too often appeared, if it did at all, in the very late afternoon just before it set behind the mountains.

Brian promoted Kevin from dishwasher to cook, and because of Kevin's skill level, that was working out well for both Brian and Kevin. John was promoted to cook's helper and, with Kevin's help, was progressing to becoming a cook very quickly. Their separate schedules still allowed John and Kevin to spend some time together when they weren't working, but John was now spending more and more of his free time with Kathrin, whom he'd met at the Canada Employment Centre while exploring other job opportunities. Kathrin was only eighteen, five years younger than John, but her independent air of indifference and anti-establishment outlook on life was very appealing to John. It didn't hurt either that she was young, petite, and enjoyed frequent sexual activity as much as John did. Just before Christmas, John informed Kevin that he was going to move in with Kathrin at the beginning of the New Year.

John's decision to move in with Kathrin was just one more reason that the first Christmas in Canada was so dreary and depressing for Kevin. The lights and decorations of Christmas in Vancouver only reminded Kevin of all he missed, not being with friends and family during the Christmas season for the first time in his life. Kevin spoke briefly with Lorraine by pay phone in October, letting her know he had successfully immigrated to Canada. She was friendly and truly seemed happy for him, but minutes went quickly as the operator continued to request that Kevin put more coins in the phone. All too soon, Kevin put in his last quarters, and with only a couple of minutes left, he told Lorraine he missed her and still loved her. There was a moment of silence before Lorraine, in a choked-up whisper, said, "I love you too, Kevin, very much. Guess we better say goodbye now."

"Goodbye, Lorraine," Kevin told her just before the phone clicked to silence.

He had tried to call Lorraine a number of times during the week before the holidays to wish her a Merry Christmas. Each time, he let the phone ring at least twenty times but there was no answer. Kevin wondered if it was just bad timing and maybe Lorraine was working long hours over Christmas to make money for school. Feeling desperate to hear her voice one night, he tried to call her just after midnight, but still, there was no answer. As he hung up the phone, a panicked and fearful surge, curated by insecurity and jealousy, sent a warm flush to his face and then up through the top of his head. He was cocooned by the phone booth as the rain beat out its wet syncopation on the roof, echoing his sadness at not being able to reach Lorraine.

John spent Christmas Eve and Christmas Day with Kathrin. Kevin spent Christmas Eve alone in the apartment, without a television, once again listening to the cold Vancouver rain that hadn't stopped in days. His parents sent him a Christmas card and a brand of jeans he liked and couldn't find in Canada. He knew the rest of the family would gather around a Christmas tree on Christmas Eve that would be surrounded by a vast amount of colorful and perfectly wrapped presents. The presents would be presented to their intended recipients, one at a time, by his father, who would delight in his role as the MC for the family tradition. A well-laid fire would be crackling in the fireplace, and those of age, or close enough to it, would be drinking bourbon and eggnog or a glass of wine.

The only other present Kevin received that Christmas was from Laurie, a girl with a motherly nature who was the main hostess at Smitty's. He wanted to wait until Christmas morning to open it. Though it was wrapped, Kevin was sure it was a book. In the end, he decided to open it Christmas Eve, hoping the book would provide a diversion from his loneliness. He fell asleep reading *Never Cry Wolf* by Farley Mowat, a renowned Canadian author he had never heard of.

Kevin was still lying in bed on Christmas morning at 11:00 a.m. reading his new book, when he heard a knock on his door. He opened it to find his new Canadian friend, Michael Murray, with a cigarette in hand and a big smile on his face.

"Merry Christmas!" boomed Michael. "Get your ass ready, Kevin my boy. Mum says you need to come be with us for Christmas."

"Wow, sounds great," said Kevin. "Got to get cleaned up, but if you don't mind waiting, it won't take long."

"No problem, my friend," assured Michael. "It's Christmas Day, and all we have to do is eat a whole bloody bunch of good food and pound a few drinks. Ready when you are."

On the way to the Murray family Christmas, Michael sparked a joint, and within a couple of tokes, Christmas wasn't looking so bad. The weed also set the stage for the food that was waiting. Kevin stopped at two tokes, knowing he had to meet the Murrays. By the time they arrived at the Murray's stately home that looked out over Howe Sound in West Vancouver, the Murray clan was well past the first round of Bloody Caesars and had no inkling that Michael and Kevin were lit up from a different power source.

All the Murrays welcomed Kevin and immediately insisted that he have a Bloody Caesar. Kevin said he had never had one before, to which Mr. Murray roared, "Well then, it's bloody time you start, Kevin! They say it's the perfect way to start the morning when all you have to do that day is screw the pooch. And they don't go too bad with Christmas Day or New Year's Day, either!" Mr. Murray slapped Kevin on the back while the laughter in the room grew louder. "Come on, lad. I'll show a Yank how to make a Bloody Caesar, though basically you're just substituting clamato juice for tomato juice. Very Canadian, you know."

Christmas dinner with all the trimmings was served late afternoon. The Murrays had both turkey and ham and a spread of extras that included mashed potatoes and gravy, peas and carrots, cranberry sauce, homemade rolls, pumpkin pie, and plum pudding. There were also some amazing French wines that Mr. Murray brought up from his wine cellar and decanted. The only real difference for Kevin were the colorful poppers in front of each place setting. They looked like a toilet paper roll that had been wrapped and tied at each end. Just after the prayer and before the toast, everyone picked up their popper, found the small slip of cardboard inside the wrapping at each end of the popper, and pulled the cardboard slips in opposite directions. The poppers went off like the sound of a cap gun and then they were unwrapped. Inside were little toys like you would find in a box of Cracker Jacks and a folded-up crepe paper crown that each person put on their head for dinner.

In Canada, like the United Kingdom, the day after Christmas is Boxing Day, which is also a holiday. Smitty's was open on Boxing Day, and Kevin had volunteered to work, since he didn't expect to be doing anything over the Christmas Holidays. Mr. Murray called a taxi to take Kevin home. There were numerous thank yous from Kevin and hugs all around for him from the Murrays before he got into the cab. On the drive home, the Christmas lights on Lion's Gate Bridge and throughout downtown Vancouver brought Kevin more than one smile. The Murrays had completely turned around his view of his first Canadian Christmas. The warmth and welcome they showed him had helped him to realize that, in time, Canada could truly become his home.

For the first time in a very long time, he said a prayer of thanks for all that he had at that moment before he rolled over and surrendered to what dreams might come. Falling asleep in a contentment he hadn't experienced in many weeks, he had no idea that only six days later, on December 31, 1970, the U.S. Selective Service would issue an Order to Report for the Armed Forces Physical Examination scheduled for 6:30 a.m. on January 22, 1971, at the Joint Examining & Induction Station in St. Louis, Missouri. Happy New Year!

Chapter 24

Bend Over and Drop Them

On January 20, 1971, Kevin flew from Vancouver to St. Louis to comply with the Selective Service order for his Armed Forces physical on January 22. By this time, he had already moved to a smaller apartment on 4th Avenue in Vancouver that he could afford on his own, without John. More importantly to Kevin, he had finally connected again with Lorraine by phone, and she explained to him that he couldn't reach her because she spent most of her Christmas holidays at her girlfriend's home in Palm Springs. While unloading a pocket full of quarters into the pay phone, they hatched a plan for Kevin to visit Lorraine in San Diego after his physical on his way back to Vancouver. The thought of being with Lorraine again within less than a week expelled the worries and concerns he had about his physical. He was also looking forward to seeing family and friends again in St. Louis but really wasn't sure what his time with his parents would be like, given the uncertainty of the circumstances.

When Kevin arrived at Lambert Field in St. Louis, his mother and his younger brother, Russell, were waiting with smiles, big hugs, and a kiss from his mother. Arriving home, Kevin was warmly greeted by his father and the family's Australian shepherd named Pookie. Pookie knew it was Kevin before the door was even opened and engaged Kevin with a body-bumping wag dance while simultaneously loudly vocalizing a full range of verbal expressions that only Australian shepherds seem to be capable of.

The evening he arrived, Kevin was cautiously relieved that there was no mention of the upcoming physical or his decision to emigrate to Canada. It was late, and his parents went to bed shortly after he arrived, once his mother was sure Kevin had something to eat. Kevin stayed up for another hour talking with Russell who, though five years younger than Kevin, was very interested in Kevin's adventures in Vancouver. When he settled into his room and finally turned off the light, he felt the warmth of family and familiarity that he had not sensed since he'd left for Canada four months ago. He fell into sleep in that glow and the thought of seeing Lorraine within days.

By the time Kevin woke up the next morning, his father had already left for work and Russell was just heading out the door for school. His mother was home and anxious to cook Kevin something special for breakfast that turned out to be her amazing French toast. Over breakfast, he noticed his mother unconsciously gently drumming her fingers on the table. Kevin knew that was a sign she was troubled and had something she wanted to say. Kevin opened the door to that discussion by telling his mother about how incredible Vancouver was and how much he liked his new life there. He also gushed about how he was going to see Lorraine on the way back to Vancouver.

"That's great, Kevin, I'm very happy for you," said his mother with sincerity. "But what are you going to do if you get drafted? As happy as I am that you are enjoying your adventure in Canada, your father and I are very concerned about the draft and the possibility that you intend to stay in Canada if you do get drafted."

Kevin tried to reassure his mother by telling her that he would cross that bridge when and if he got to it. He reminded her that, for now, he was here complying with the order to take the physical, and he had strong hopes that, because he had pronated ankles and wore corrective shoes for many years, he would flunk the physical. He reinforced his confidence by sharing with his mother that he had a letter from Doctor Harnel, who had treated him for many years, stating his condition.

"But what if that doesn't work out, Kevin? What will you do?" his mother asked with nervous concern.

"Let's not go there, Mom," said Kevin. "You know that discussion will only lead to an argument. I know clearly how you and Dad feel about the possibility of me being a draft dodger. But you need to open your eyes and understand that what is happening with the Vietnam War has no relationship to World War II and why the United States was fighting that war. If the situation now was the same as then, or even close to it, I would fight for the defense of this country. But it's not, and after lots of thought and confliction, I have made up my mind that I will not be a part of killing people on the other side of the world that are no threat to America. When I went to Canada and realized there was an entire country of people, just across the border from the United States, that have no concern about Vietnam except for the concerns about what the United States is doing, I realized, for sure, that all I had been feeling about this horrible war was right. These same people have welcomed me into their beautiful country, knowingly providing a refuge that allows me to make my decision based on my moral and spiritual principles, and not because of some kind of trumped-up patriotic obligation or fear of imprisonment that the U.S. government holds over the children of its own citizens that fought in World War II."

"But, Kevin!" cried his mother. "People will think you're a coward and a traitor and if you stay in Canada to avoid the draft. That decision will haunt you for the rest of your life. Your father is so upset he won't even talk about it. It's killing him that, after fighting in the Pacific for more than four years, having no idea if or when he would return home, his own son is a coward with no sense of duty to his country."

"Mom," said Kevin, louder now, "that's exactly why I didn't want to have this discussion. I love you both, and while I don't agree with your opinion, I respect it because of what you both went through during World War II, when you were basically my same age. But I need to do what is right for me right now. This is not World War II, and in my opinion, this is not the country you defended anymore. There is a growing secret government that is meddling in people's lives all over the world having nothing to do with the interests of U.S. citizens. It's all there to read and understand, but for some rea-

son, you and so many others of your generation don't even want to
look at it. You just blindly go along with whatever the government is
telling you, with your hand over your heart because this is the great-
est country in the world. Well, it's not anymore, it's far from that.
The church you attend, and all of the churches down the street—and
most of them around the country—that profess to follow the teaching of Christ are saying nothing! Why? How is that possible when
there is nothing Christian about the whole fucking thing? I'm sorry
for using that language but I am not going to be a part in this plan
that involves killing millions of innocent people for the benefit of
the military industrial complex and those that benefit greatly by war.
Maybe this decision will affect me for the rest of my life, but maybe it
will shape me too. I'm only here for a couple of days. I'm not going to
change your mind, and you're not going to change mine. I love you,
Mom, so let's please not spend our time arguing."

Kevin's mother started crying uncontrollably and sobbing into
her hands. Kevin pushed back from the table and quickly went over
and put his arms around his mother to comfort her, but tears were
now flowing from his eyes. The crying, stuttering, shudders of their
chests bumped out of unison enveloping them in the deep interconnectedness of a mother's love for her son. They were still holding
onto each other when their breathing became more regular and signaled it was time to break from their embrace.

"I love you, Kevin, and always will, no matter what," his mother
said in a soft but deeply sincere voice. "Let's just put this aside for
now and hope for the best with your physical. Please don't bring this
all up to your father, and I will try to make sure he doesn't bring it up
either. I want to enjoy the little time we have together."

"I will, Mom," said Kevin. "I love you, and sorry I said a word
like that in front of you. Let's wipe off our tears and make this a really
great day," Kevin said with a smile to his mother, who smiled back at
him, looking deeply into his blue eyes.

Kevin's mother took Kevin shopping at the store that carried
the jeans Kevin liked so much, and she told him to pick out a couple of shirts and a jacket that would keep him dry and warm in
Vancouver. They were home by mid-afternoon, and by six o'clock,

Kevin could catch the first aroma hint of the leg of lamb his mother had promised to make him for dinner. At six thirty, his father arrived home.

In a workday ritual, his mother opened the freezer door of the refrigerator and handed him a perfectly made Beefeaters martini on the rocks with a twist of lemon peel that accompanied him to the bedroom to change out of his suit and tie. Since the children were young, Kevin's mother told them it is best not to bother their father with questions until he emerges from the bedroom. As they got older, they knew this was really code for don't bother your father until he has had his first martini.

Just before seven fifteen, his father came into the kitchen smiling, gave Kevin's mother a kiss on the cheek, and said, "How was your day, dear?"

"Wonderful, Paul," said Kevin's mother. "Will you please open a bottle of Lancers rose to go with the lamb?"

Dinner that night was Kevin's favorite: leg of lamb, medium rare, with mashed potatoes and gravy, peas and carrots, and home-made German red cabbage made from a recipe passed down by his grandmother. Kevin would have chosen a different wine, but Lancers rose had always been part of the family tradition for this meal. Kevin's father said the standard family prayer, but as he often did, he ended with the words special prayer and then segued into whatever thoughts of hope or thanks were on his mind. "Heavenly Father, please be with Kevin tomorrow at his physical. Help him to be guided to make right decisions in the coming weeks and months. Thank you for blessing this family and this country. In Jesus's name, amen." For the rest of the evening there was no further mention of the upcoming physical or the war in Vietnam.

Kevin's father had gone to Ontario, Canada, on a number of trips for lake trout and muskie and wanted Kevin to tell him all about fishing in British Columbia. Kevin pointed out that he hadn't been fishing since he'd arrived in Canada and that British Columbia was quite different than Ontario, with salmon and trout the fish of choice in that neck of the woods. If the elephant was in the room that evening, he remained well hidden and broke no china.

Kevin was still on West Coast time and couldn't find sleep, even though he needed to report for the physical in downtown St. Louis by 6:30 a.m. the next day. His mother offered to drive him there, and they set the alarm for 4:30 a.m. so they had time for Kevin to shower and have coffee. At 6:15 a.m., Kevin's mother dropped him off at the Examining and Induction Station in the Mart Building at 12th and Spruce Streets in downtown St. Louis. Well over one hundred young men, both black and white, were already there, and many more seemed to be arriving each minute as the clock ticked down to 6:30 a.m.

As Kevin stepped out of the car, he heard men in military uniforms shouting orders of where to line up in single file. The crowd moved slowly as it narrowed to single file at the entrance doors. Once inside, there were other people shouting about other lines based on the spelling of your last name, and Kevin found the next line that showed F-J and flowed into a room with small desks, where another man in military uniform handed out questionnaires that they were ordered to fill out. The very last question required that the potential inductee swear that they had never been a member or involved with any groups listed on the Attorney General's list of subversive organizations. That was not a problem for Kevin but certainly was a reality check.

Once the questionnaire was completed and picked up, they were given a multiple-choice intelligence test. It was hard for Kevin to imagine that anyone could fail the test, though stories circulated on campus and in underground newspapers that some men tried to fail the test to avoid military service. The conclusion was, if your test score was at odds with your school records, you would pass anyway, and some stories suggested that the attempt could get you drafted into the Marines instead of the Army.

Kevin had heard other stories about people coming to the exam stoned on one drug or another or claiming to be homosexual to avoid the draft. A story that was more of an urban legend and that mirrored the racial bias of the '60s and '70s suggested that, during the chaos of the examination, a white male could ask a black male to fill up his urine sample with an offer of five or ten dollars. The hope was, according to the story, that the black man was more likely to have a venereal disease that would then exclude the white man from military service. Also, according to the legend, if that were the case, it would still be all good for the black man since, as a black man, he was capable of producing enough urine for both of them almost on demand. Kevin never considered any of these options as a real strategy because he doubted that they would work, and he knew his best bet was with the letter from Dr. Harnel about his feet.

After the multiple-choice test was completed and picked up, the men were told to strip down to their underwear and stow their clothes in one of the bin lockers outside of the room. Once stripped down to their gonch, the draftees were taken to a series of rooms to test their hearing, eyesight, and to collect blood and urine samples. For the urine sample, they were allowed to use the large lavatory with a very long urinal trough that allowed many men to crowd together and relieve themselves into small bottles. In the midst of this madness, Kevin smiled when he circled the roundabout of his mind back to the urban legend and realized that, hypothetically, it was possible for one man to fill up another man's urine sample bottle without detection.

After the series of tests were completed and noted on their chart, the men went back to their original room with the desks where they had filled out the questionnaires. Once inside, they were told to line up on opposite sides of the room facing each other and stand at attention. Then a man in a military uniform, who looked like a square-jawed poster boy for a drill sergeant, ordered them to drop their shorts to their ankles. With slight murmuring, but with no real hesitation, all the men dropped their underwear and displayed their genitals for a walk-by inspection. Kevin wasn't sure what they were looking for but didn't really ponder that very long.

About a minute later, they were told to face the wall, bend over, and hold their ankles. Another walk-by now inspected their anuses and the other side of their testicles. No one failed the test, and Kevin never really knew what they were looking for. He was greatly relieved that there was no finger insertion of any kind, which had also been rumored sometimes happens in certain states.

With Kevin appearing to have passed every test so far, he was sent in his underwear to another room to present the letter from Dr. Harnel to the U.S. Army Medical Corps doctor, Captain Alan Walker. As he entered the room, Capt. Walker asked Kevin for the letter from Dr. Harnel and then told him to take a seat. Watching Capt. Walker review the letter, Kevin realized that this was the first time he had really been nervous all day and felt sweat beading up in his armpits. To Kevin, it seemed like Capt. Walker was taking a long time to review the letter and he didn't know if that was good or bad. Finally Captain Walker asked Kevin to stand up straight with his knees as close together as they could go. Kevin knew that because of the pronated ankles he was knock-kneed, and that this should become very apparent to Capt. Walker. He also allowed his ankles to roll over as far as they could go so that the severity of his problem could be easily observed.

Capt. Walker then asked Kevin to stand on one leg and then the other, all the time observing Kevin's feet and ankles without saying a word. Finally, Capt. Walker told Kevin to sit down again. After a few minutes of making notes, Capt. Walker told Kevin that he certainly did have pronated ankles, but that he wasn't sure the Army environment would really cause him any more problem or pain than everyday life as a civilian. At the end of his pronouncement, he told Kevin that, for now, he was qualified for induction into the Armed Services and that his physical was complete and he was free to go. He did add that he was willing to review any additional related information Kevin might provide prior to or on the day that he was to be inducted.

With that bit of news, Kevin's positive attitude and outlook collided instantaneously with a new reality that he would likely be drafted within weeks. Kevin found his way back to his clothes, got dressed, and called his mother for a ride home from a pay phone in the lobby of the Mart Building.

Chapter 25

A Second Opinion

When Kevin's mother pulled up to the curb in front of the Armed Forces Induction Center, she could tell by the expression on Kevin's face that there was a problem. Kevin opened the car door and slid into the seat without saying a word. As his mother pulled out into traffic, she asked Kevin what was wrong. "Only that the Army doctor decided after less than ten minutes that my feet are no problem and I am fit for induction," said Kevin in evident frustration.

"Now what do you do?" asked his mother.

Kevin explained that the Army doctor did say he would accept and review additional information on his feet and ankles if it was provided. Almost at the same time, they both knew that they needed to go straight to Dr. Harnel's office and speak to him, since Kevin was leaving for San Diego the following day.

At the Doctor's office, they were told that he would see them, but they would need to wait for quite some time. After more than two hours, they finally got to meet with Dr. Harnel.

Kevin explained to Dr. Harnel the results of his examination by Capt. Walker and the opportunity to provide additional information, including a medical opinion letter from Dr. Harnel. After listening to Kevin and a long period of silence, Dr. Harnel told Kevin and his mother that he was not prepared to write an opinion letter that stated Kevin was not fit for military service. However, he was willing to provide additional information, including x-rays and another letter that would detail the history of Kevin's treatment since childhood and his concerns of a related slight curvature in Kevin's spine. Both Kevin and his mother thanked Dr. Harnel, who then told them that he would have the letter and information sent to the local draft board within a week.

Once outside of Dr. Harnel's office, Kevin's mother gave him a long hug and said, "Let's look at this as good news, Kevin. I think this will all work out." Kevin wasn't so sure, but he smiled at his mother and said that he agreed it would.

At dinner that night, Kevin's father asked how the physical went. Kevin provided the short version of the day, indicating that Dr. Harnel was going to provide additional information that would be taken into account before the final decision was made. To Kevin's surprise, his father suggested he send a letter to both U.S. senators for Missouri, letting them know that more information was going to be presented to the draft board and requesting a delay in issuing an induction notice until the information was thoroughly reviewed. Kevin agreed that was a good idea, and then there was no further discussion about Kevin's draft status that evening.

In the morning, Kevin's mother drove him to Lambert Field for his 11:00 a.m. flight to LA. She offered to walk him to the gate, but Kevin insisted he would be fine. When they pulled up to the curb at the departure area, Kevin's mother put the station wagon in park, and Kevin could tell she was holding back tears. "Take care of yourself, Kevin," said his mother in a slightly cracking voice. "We're all going to miss you very much. Please don't forget how much I love you."

"I won't, Mom," said Kevin as he reached over and hugged his mother still behind the wheel. "I love you too, Mom, so much. And like you said yesterday, it's all going to work out. You and Dad should plan a trip to British Columbia. As much as Dad likes Ontario, I think he'd be amazed by British Columbia, and you will be too. Bye, Mom." With that, Kevin got out of the car, collected his suitcase, and headed inside the terminal without watching his mother drive away. Only then did he feel the rush in his fingertips when he remembered he would see Lorraine in hours.

When Kevin exited the plane at LAX, Lorraine was waiting at the gate, looking every bit as radiant and beautiful as Kevin remembered. She was up on her tiptoes straining to see him in the crowd of passengers getting off the plane. When she finally saw Kevin, she smiled and giggled almost to the point of tears while bouncing up and down slightly, like a delighted child. They went straight to a hug that slid into kisses, with the unspoken concerns about their love evaporating into meaninglessness.

LAX and the freeway drive to San Diego reminded Kevin of all that he didn't like about California, though the weather was California perfect for a winter's day. At Oceanside, they got off the I-5 to take the Pacific Coast Highway to Encinitas, where Lorraine had made reservations for them to stay at a small motel overlooking the Pacific Ocean near Moonlight Beach. The drive down the PCH to Encinitas showcased everything Kevin loved about Southern California. With the windows rolled down and wind in his hair, most of Kevin's attention was on the ocean and the surfers in the lineup at each break they passed. When he turned his attention back to Lorraine, who was driving them along the ocean wearing her sunglasses, radiating all of her California-ness, he had a moment of déjà vu. It wasn't just the recognition of fleeting familiarity with the past or something yet to come. The multi-dimensional moment was more like a quantum entanglement of two souls, where information and perspective not bound by time or space was flowing between them faster than the speed of light. In that instantaneous timelessness, all that was Lorraine, all that was Kevin, and all that was the two of them together intertwined with the universe and was experienced without words, attachment, or judgment.

Before they checked into the motel in Encinitas, Lorraine took Kevin to a Mexican restaurant where they each had two fresh-squeezed margaritas, along with homemade tortilla chips and salsa. An hour later, with a buzz on that further amplified their passions, they opened the door to their motel room, quickly found their way to deep kisses, and then tumbled into bed to become reacquainted with the magic of their attraction.

The beautiful weather continued during the remaining three days of Kevin's visit, and time went by way too fast for both of them. Kevin didn't have a wetsuit, and the winter swell was too big for his surfing skill level, but he loved being at the beach with Lorraine and watching surfers in their effortless ballet with the waves. On his last day in California, he bought a long-sleeve t-shirt from Mitch's Surf Shop in Solana Beach to remind him of his time with Lorraine once he got back to Vancouver. The night before Kevin left, they didn't get much sleep, but in the quiet of their embrace, no words were needed for both of them to know this was the beginning of all they would become together.

Kevin's flight to Vancouver didn't leave until 3:00 p.m., so they had time to drive back up the PCH to Oceanside and stop for lunch along the way. At LAX, Lorraine walked Kevin to the gate and lingered next to him until it was the last call for boarding. After a final kiss, and with tears in their eyes, Kevin went through the gate, turned and waved, and was gone. Lorraine stayed in the terminal until the plane moved out of the gate. She waved out the window to the plane a couple of times, hoping Kevin might see her, but knew he likely couldn't. She wasn't sure what was next in her life, but she knew, for the first time, without any doubt, that it included Kevin. "Let the adventure begin," she said to herself with a smile.

When the plane landed on a wet, cold, and grey end of January day in Vancouver, it was the first time Kevin had ever gone through Canadian immigration and customs since his immigration interview at the Huntingdon border crossing. Canadian flags were predominant throughout the walkway from the plane to the immigration area, and Kevin was surprised how comfortable he felt coming back to his new home. He had filled out the Canadian Customs and Immigration form on the plane and checked the box for "Landed Immigrant." When it was his turn to see the Canadian immigration officer, he handed him the form he'd filled out along with his passport and Landed Immigrant card and waited for questions. The officer smiled at Kevin, stamped his passport, and said, "Welcome home."

Chapter 26

Okanagan Dreaming

Kevin picked up his luggage, breezed quickly through customs and out the door into the sea of people awaiting the arrival of friends and family. He scanned the crowd and saw Michael Murray waving his hand back and forth and jumping up and down. Michael slapped palms with Kevin and said, "Welcome home, you fucking newbie Canuck." Michael then told Kevin that they were going straight to the Murrays for drinks and dinner.

"The old man's looking forward to seeing you again, Kev, and he's got some ideas for you to think about," Michael said with a twinkle in his eye.

"What kind of ideas," asked Kevin?

"Not to worry, man," assured Michael. "I'll let the old man tell you all about it; don't want to be a downer for his excitement. He really likes you, Kev, and is fascinated that you aren't like any Yank he's ever met. You know, kind of like not liking hippies until you meet a good one."

With that, Michael pulled out a small joint and lit up. "Just a couple of tokes to tune up for dinner, Kev."

Kevin waved a no-no with his hand and said, "Not today, Michael. I was up most of the night with Lorraine, if you know what I mean, and I don't think I can make it through dinner if I get stoned."

"Whatever suits you, my friend," said Michael. "I'll fly solo for now."

As soon as he walked through the Murrays' front door, Kevin was greeted warmly by Mrs. Murray, and by the smell of roast lamb coming from the kitchen. Mr. Murray marched quickly down the stairs and greeted Kevin with a booming, "Kevin, my boy, so good to see you again! What do you want to drink? We've got lots to discuss."

"Just a beer for me, Mr. Murray," said Kevin.

"Great lad," said Mr. Murray. "You and Michael have a seat by the fireplace and I'll get the drinks."

Back with the drinks, it didn't take long for Mr. Murray to get to the point. "Kevin, my boy, when I met you at Christmas dinner, I was quite taken by the culinary background you have that seems to include an interest and understanding of good wine beyond your years. After you left, I couldn't stop wondering why you were wasting your time flipping pancakes at Smitty's. Even in the best restaurants, Kevin, cooking can become a bit of a dead end. How would you like to get closer to wine, lad?"

"Sorry, Mr. Murray, I'm not really sure what you mean," said Kevin with a puzzled look on his face.

"Of course you don't, lad!" boomed Mr. Murray. "But you will when I'm finished laying it out for you."

Over the next forty-five minutes around the fire, with the smell of the roast lamb dinner becoming more and more seductive, Mr. Murray presented his vision for Kevin's future. He explained that the Murrays were longtime friends of Peter and Anna Van der Meer, who owned and managed a large orchard and vineyard operation in the Okanagan Valley. According to Mr. Murray, there was an expanding interest in growing wine grapes in the Okanagan because of the number of European families that were moving there for just that purpose. Compared to Germany, Switzerland, France, and Italy, farmland in the Okanagan Valley suitable for growing European wine grape varietals was cheap, and most of it came with an amazing lake view. The Van der Meers had been in Okanagan Centre for over twenty years and led the tree fruit industry in its understanding of dwarf apples and high-density tree fruit plantings. Now they were shifting their focus to vineyards and the possibility of a winery, if they could someday get the British Columbia government to consider farm gate wine sales. According to Mr. Murray, the biggest problem the Van der Meers had was finding a hardworking and reliable farm manager to assist them in growing their operations.

"That's you, lad!" said Mr. Murray with great excitement.

"Me?" said Kevin. "I don't know anything about farming. I barely remember how to cut grass."

"That's not the point, lad," said Mr. Murray. "You already have the determination and most of the skills they need. The rest they will teach you."

"Wow," said Kevin, "I'm really not sure I understand what skills I have that relate to vineyards."

Mr. Murray explained to Kevin that there were a lot more similarities between running a restaurant kitchen and managing a vineyard than Kevin had likely considered. Both a restaurant kitchen and a vineyard worked with perishable commodities, had low entry labor positions with a high turnover rate, and required long hours at an often frantic pace to accomplish tasks with quality. "Besides, lad," said Mr. Murray, "the Van der Meers will teach you everything you need to learn, one bite at a time."

"How do you know they will like me?" asked Kevin.

"Don't worry so much, Kevin. They'll love you. Just let me take care of that," said Mr. Murray with confidence and assurance.

With that, Mrs. Murray came into the room and announced that dinner was ready. Mr. Murray was excited to show Kevin the Chateauneuf-du-Pape he had selected for dinner.

"They're not making wine in the Okanagan even close to this now, but it's just a matter of time, Kevin. And you have the opportunity to be part of that," enthused Mr. Murray.

Over dinner, Kevin became very excited about the vision Mr. Murray was selling him, though part of him was quietly concerned about the challenge of something so potentially overwhelming that he knew nothing about. The plan became more interesting when Mr. Murray told Kevin that he would make arrangements with his pilot friend, Jack McDonald, to fly Kevin, Michael, and himself up to the Okanagan so that Kevin could meet with the Van der Meers. Less than a week later, Jack McDonald's Cessna 185 Skywagon float plane lifted off from Vancouver's downtown harbor with four people bound for Okanagan Centre.

Kevin had been in an airplane many times, but he was not prepared for the ever-changing, but always majestic, landscape of British Columbia that he was now flying over on a clear and cold February day. The mountains and the terrain below seemed to change constantly, and Kevin was wide-eyed and astounded by the number of small lakes he noticed that could only be accessed by foot, horse, or possibly four-wheel drive. Flying over the Coast Mountains, the peaks seemed almost close enough to reach out and touch with the bright February sunshine highlighting each crag and crevasse filled with sparkling, new, white snow.

Past the Coast Mountains' lush green Pacific side, with its forested abundance, the topography transitioned to a less treed and sparser landscape. Still captivated by what was immediately below him, Kevin was surprised by his first view of Lake Okanagan, a body of water so vast that he could not see the beginning or end of the lake.

"There she is, lads," echoed a slightly distorted voice of Mr. Murray as it came through the headset. "Isn't she a sight?"

Ten minutes later, they were making their descent just north of Westbank, British Columbia, then continued almost due north, flying low up the middle of Lake Okanagan. By this time, Kevin could see the orchards and vineyards covered in snow on the east side of the lake, running all the way down to the shoreline where the slope of the land would allow. By contrast, the west side of Lake Okanagan in this area was mostly undeveloped, though a few summer cabins dotted the shoreline.

Jack eased the Skywagon lower and lower, providing an even better view of the orchards, vineyards, and houses along the hillside and lakeshore. Fortunately, with the warmer winter, there was not a speck of ice on the lake and it continued to be a bright, sunny, and beautiful winter day with an almost blinding, cloudless, blue sky. Jack slipped the Skywagon smoothly into the glassy morning water parallel and right in front of the small village of Okanagan Centre and then taxied in and tied up at the old dock by the summer swimming area.

The Van der Meers saw the Skywagon landing on the lake from their home that was built on one of the highest points of the hill, at the top of Goldie Road, and drove down in their GMC Suburban to the dock to collect their guests. Anna Van der Meer greeted everyone with a beaming smile, gave big hugs to Mr. Murray and Michael, and gave another smile and a welcoming handshake to Jack McDonald. With no hesitation, she smiled directly at Kevin and said, "And this must be Kevin. Welcome to Spion Kop Ranch." Peter Van der Meer was puffing on a pipe and was a bit more reserved than Anna but also welcomed his guests with handshakes and a sincere smile.

Everyone piled into the Suburban for the three-minute drive to the Van der Meers' home. At the top of Goldie Road, the Suburban turned onto a winding, snow-covered driveway with Peter driving much faster up the driveway than Kevin would have expected. As he got out of the car, Kevin looked back at Lake Okanagan to take in a view from the Van der Meers' that was just as stunning as the view of the lake from the plane.

Once inside the house, they sat in the living room by the fireplace near a picture window that took full advantage of the lake view. The Van der Meers' home did not have the grandeur of the Murray home but was charming and warm in its elegant simplicity and eclectic European furnishings, most of which the Van der Meers brought with them from Holland. Anna organized coffee for the men and tea for herself, which was served with scones and the offer of butter and homemade raspberry jam.

Anna's outgoing friendliness was welcoming for Kevin and put him at ease immediately. After small talk with Mr. Murray, Peter turned his attention to Kevin and began to tell him about their orchard and vineyard operations and vision for the future. While Anna never interrupted Peter or corrected him in any way, at certain points of a pause, she would expand on what Peter was explaining to Kevin, providing somewhat more interesting and compelling detail. Peter, along with Anna's help, outlined the roles of the farm manager they were looking for.

During that part of the discussion, Mr. Murray pointed out, on a few occasions, just how perfect Kevin was for the job. Kevin was very intrigued with the opportunity that came along with being able to live in such beautiful surroundings. In the back of Kevin's mind, throughout the conversation, were the questions of his capability for meeting the expectations of the Van der Meers, as well as Mr. Murray. He also wondered if the vineyard lifestyle would be of any interest to Lorraine who, at this point, had no idea what Kevin was considering.

After about an hour, Peter politely indicated to the group that he and Kevin had a few things to discuss in private. As Kevin stood up to follow Peter to his office, he saw Mr. Murray give him a wink and a smile. Peter sat across his desk from Kevin, packed and lit his pipe, and then asked Kevin what he thought about becoming a key part of the operations of Spion Kop Ranch. Without hesitation, Kevin indicated that he welcomed the opportunity and the challenge and that he was confident he was capable of exceeding the Van der Meers' expectations. That confidence transitioned into the more awkward question about compensation.

Peter initiated that part of their discussion by telling Kevin that he would be starting at the bottom rung of a ladder that provided an opportunity to climb and define his expanding role in the operation. Kevin knew that was the lead-in for what was going to follow about the actual starting salary. While the salary Peter offered was low, it did come with a small rent-free house and a pickup truck, along with a bonus program that could grow into profit sharing if everything worked out between them. Peter also indicated they would review Kevin's salary at the end of the first season, and then each season thereafter.

"When would you need me to start?" asked Kevin.

In his dry humor Peter responded, "Today would be perfect but... by April 1 will work."

Part of Kevin wanted to say to Peter that he needed a bit of time to think about it, especially because to answer yes now was to commit to a path forward that he had not discussed with Lorraine. While that thought was treading water in his subconscious, time seemed to be standing still in the present as he watched smoke rings from Peter's cherry tobacco rise slowly from his pipe to the ceiling. In those suspended moments, he thought about all Mr. Murray had organized to get him this chance. Almost a surprise to himself, Kevin stood up, extended a hand to Peter and said, "I appreciate this opportunity and look forward to being a part of Spion Kop Ranch." Peter shook Kevin's hand energetically and gave him a relaxed and welcoming smile Kevin had not seen from Peter up to this point.

"Guess we better tell that Scotsman that thinks so much of you we got a deal," chuckled Peter.

"Yes, I think he will definitely be happy about this," said Kevin.

Kevin followed Peter back to the living room. Peter looked over at Anna first and said, "Kevin is going to join us, Anna."

Anna beamed and gave Kevin a hug as Mr. Murray shot out of his seat, shook Peter's hand very vigorously, and exclaimed, "Thank you, Peter! You won't regret your decision. This is one fine lad. And he knows if he lets you down he has me to reckon with!" All of his words were punctuated with a hearty laugh.

"Jack can't have a drink, but the rest of us would love a glass of the wine you make before we fly out of here," Mr. Murray said loudly.

Anna got out the glasses. Peter poured a glass of Spion Kop Ranch Merlot for all of them, even a small glass for Jack McDonald. Peter made a toast to Kevin and the future of Spion Kop Ranch, glasses clinked, and Kevin tasted his first Okanagan wine. While it wasn't the same quality as the wines poured around the Murray's table, Kevin thought it was definitely a "yum".

Very soon after, Jack reminded them they needed to be in the air within thirty minutes so they didn't run out of light before getting to Vancouver. Anna quickly made some small sandwiches for the plane and then they all got back in the Suburban for the short ride to the dock. Hugs and handshakes were exchanged before Mr. Murray, Michael, and Kevin climbed into the Skywagon. Jack did his visual safety check of the outside of the plane before getting into the pilot's seat and firing up the engine. Peter untied the plane and pushed the pontoon away from the dock with his foot. Shortly after, Jack taxied the plane out to the middle of a much choppier lake than the one they were welcomed by earlier in the day. Facing almost due south into the wind, Jack pushed the throttle to the max. A mechanical, high-throated power growl roared from the engine, and in spite of the chop on the lake, the Skywagon soon lifted off the water with ease. Just before sight of the dock disappeared, Kevin saw the Van der Meers still waving from the dock. Once airborne and with the engine much quieter than at takeoff, Kevin heard Mr. Murray's voice in the headset.

"Congratulations, Kevin! This is going to be the start of something good for you."

"Thank you, Mr. Murray, I owe it all to you," said Kevin. "I promise I won't let you down."

But in reality, Kevin was not really sure what he had committed to, and hoped that his quick decision would be the beginning of something for him and Lorraine and not the end. Mr. Murray's voice came through the headset again. "Are you going to call your little lassie about all this, Kevin?"

"If I can round up enough quarters to explain it all to her at a pay phone," said Kevin.

"Fuck the quarters," laughed Mr. Murray. "You can call your California girl from my office and take all the time you need."

When they got back to the Murrays', Mr. Murray poured Kevin a glass of wine and showed him to the office. Leaving the room and closing the door behind him, he wished Kevin good luck. Not that he really needed it. After trying to explain how excited he was about his day in the floatplane to Spion Kop Ranch and the opportunity they offered him, he was rambling his way to try and tell Lorraine that he'd made a decision without talking with her. Before he got there, Lorraine noticed a sigh in Kevin's voice and a pause that provided the moment to just say straight out, "Are we going to do this adventure, Kevin?"

"I think we should," said Kevin.

"It's the start of something amazing, Kevin. I love you, and will be up to join you as soon as I can," said Lorraine with no hesitation.

"I love you too," said Kevin, "so much. But I'd better go, since I'm on Mr. Murray's nickel. Real soon, sweetheart."

"Real soon, Kevin," said Lorraine just before they hung up the phone.

Chapter 27

Good News, Bad News

I t seemed to Kevin that good news followed by bad news was becoming a pattern. Ten days after he accepted the job at Spion Kop Ranch, he received an order from his draft board in St. Louis to report for induction into the U.S. military on Friday, March 26, 1971. While Kevin had prepared himself for this day, he was not prepared for the multitude of emotions and fear that descended on him so quickly. In spite of Kevin's need to seek consolation from someone he was close to, a call home or to Lorraine was only possible by pay phone. Even if he could just pick up the phone and call his mother or Lorraine, he wondered if he would find the emotional support he needed or if he would be the one doing the consoling.

Kevin knew John was working the afternoon shift at Smitty's and went there just before John's shift was over to talk to John about his induction notice. Unfortunately for Kevin, when he arrived at Smitty's, he saw Kathrin at the staff table also waiting for John. For whatever reason, it had become clear to Kevin that Kathrin didn't like him at all. Kevin wasn't sure why, since he had never said anything derogatory about Kathrin or had an argument with her. But there was no question about her disdain as she greeted Kevin with a cold stare and finally said only, "Hello, Kevin." She then got up and left the staff table, walked outside, and had a cigarette by herself.

John walked out of the kitchen, tossed his apron into the laundry bin and came over to see Kevin. "What's up, Kevin?" said John. "You look like the dog you don't have just died."

Kevin told John he needed to speak to him in private, and asked John if he had time to have a beer. "Not tonight, Kevin, Kathrin and I are going to a movie," stated John. "Hey, if it's that bad, we can go for a quick walk. I'm sure Kathrin won't mind waiting a few minutes."

On their walk up Broadway, Kevin told John he had been drafted. "So what's the big fucking deal about that? You must have known it was coming!" John said with heated emotion. "You're in Canada, those bastards can't fucking touch you. And I hope to hell you aren't even thinking about reporting."

"Not a chance," said Kevin. "I just didn't think I would feel so conflicted about my decision to stay."

"Jesus, Kevin, you're living in paradise here. You know what's going on with the war and the U.S. government. You've done the hard part and got your ass up here where they can't touch you and force you to be part of their killing machine madness. I saw things you never want to see or imagine, Kevin. Don't be such a pussy. Fuck the U.S. government. Live your life based on your values, not some that are tarred and feathered in patriotic bullshit lies. Sorry, Kevin, I don't have any sympathy for you. If you think manning up is making a decision to stay in Vancouver, you just don't fucking understand the reality of the other alternative. Canada is not a consolation prize, Kevin, it's the grand prize, and you get to live here and be part of maybe the best democratic experiment happening in the world today. Sorry you didn't flunk your physical, but if that's the only reason you are here, I feel sorry for you. Got to head back and go to the movie with Kathrin."

John didn't say another word but immediately picked up the pace of his stride and left Kevin to walk back alone behind him. Kevin didn't like anything John said to him and was deeply hurt that John, who had never spoken to him like that before, seemed to have turned on him. But in spite of his shock about what John said and the way he said it, Kevin also knew that what John was saying was true.

In the fog of sorting out what just happened, Kevin remembered the offer from Spion Kop Ranch and all that Mr. Murray had done to make that happen. For the first time, it was clear to Kevin that none of what he was experiencing or concerned about had any real meaning or point of reference for most Canadians. They were living their lives and pursuing their dreams without any influence or threat from the nightmare of the Vietnam War. Beyond all that, their prime minister, Pierre Trudeau, was so opposed to what the U.S. government had been doing in Vietnam for a decade and its global impact that he offered sanctuary from the madness for U.S. draft resisters and deserters.

"This is the moment of truth; this is where the shit hits the fan," Kevin muttered to himself just before he got back to Smitty's. John and Kathrin were just coming out the door, and Kevin walked up to John and stuck out his hand. "Thanks, John, guess I needed that reality check," said Kevin, looking deeply into John's eyes. John shook Kevin's hand briefly and then put his arms around Kevin and gave him a hug. Pulling back from his hug with Kevin, John put his arm around Kathrin as he said to Kevin, "Go learn to farm in the Okanagan, have fun, and forget about those crazy motherfuckers south of the border, Kevin. You're free, just go create the life you want and one you can believe in without regret. Love you, brother, let's grab a beer tomorrow night."

"Thanks, man," said Kevin. "Love you too, and beer at the Marble Arch tomorrow it is."

Walking home alone from Smitty's, Kevin felt a lightness and sense of contentment that he had not been visited by for many months. John's words had awakened his strength of purpose and the sense of adventure that the possible offers. For the moment, he was able to push aside his fears of what he could not control and what those he cared for might think about his decision.

Three weeks later, Kevin received a letter of response from Missouri Senator Stuart Symington, who was a member of the Senate Armed Services Committee, indicating he had requested Kevin's draft board to postpone his induction until the new medical information provided by Dr. Harnel could be evaluated. Kevin was definitely pleased by the letter and the postponement of his induction order, but he also remembered what John had told him recently. "In the big-picture scheme of things, whether you get drafted or not doesn't mean shit."

Chapter 28

The Dry Side

The route that Kevin took from Vancouver to the Okanagan Valley headed east from Vancouver, up through the Fraser Valley on Route 7, and the Trans-Canada Highway to the town of Hope. From Hope he would take Highway 3, the Hope Princeton Highway, to the juncture at Kaleden. At Kaleden, Kevin intended to head north on Highway 97 all the way to the Spion Kop Ranch in Okanagan Centre.

Vancouver was then, and still remains, a visually stunning city that comfortably shares space with mountains and the Pacific Ocean. But unlike the present, in the spring of 1971, Vancouver transitioned very quickly into the countryside and the houseless mountain gateways to British Columbia's wilderness. In less than ninety minutes, Kevin was in Mission, where the farms seemed like the natural outcome of the lay of the land between the mountains and the Fraser River.

The Fraser River and the railroad gave birth to the towns along both sides of its banks by providing fertile farmland and transportation options for the food, fish, and logs that were so bountiful. While Canada seems endlessly vast, its prime agricultural land lays out across the country in a land strip only about a hundred miles wide, south to north, with the southern edge of the strip defined by the U.S. border. Within that limited agricultural possibility, one of the most fertile and climatically forgiving regions is the Fraser Valley in Southern British Columbia. Soils are rich and deep and do not require irrigation, and for the most part, winters are defined by rain rather than snow. Dairy, berry, and vegetable farms spread across the main valley and up into the smaller valleys that are tucked between the timber-laden mountains that supply lumber, cedar shakes and shingles, and the high Coast Mountains to the east that capture the rain clouds flowing in off the Pacific Ocean.

If you drove through the Fraser Valley on the Trans-Canada Highway or on the other side of the Fraser River along Route 7 any time after 1990, there would be nothing evident to suggest this area had once been an international cradle of the back-to-the-land movement in the 1970s. Instead, farm land battles for position and survival with ongoing residential development and strip malls that all seem to have adopted a commercially imposed architecture blending earth-toned stucco and colored metal roofs with faux clock towers. The roads, highways, and new-age strip malls are chock-a-block full of chain restaurants, mom-and-pop Asian eateries and Starbucks-inspired coffee shops. When Kevin first saw the Fraser Valley, it had none of the above. He was emotionally energized by its combination of grandeur and quiet beauty that invited an independent lifestyle and reinforced his decision to learn how to farm.

Darkness in British Columbia still comes early in late March, and Kevin didn't want to miss seeing any part of his road trip or risk an encounter between his pickup and a deer. He found a small motel in the town of Hope close to the river and near a small café. Kevin arrived in Hope just in time to watch the valley clouds and descending darkness merge into a night blanket that settled above the river and then slowly spread itself over the town.

In the moments just before darkness took full possession of the day, Kevin felt a sense of loneliness and uncertainty, a feeling that hadn't revisited him since his outhouse experience in Manitoba. And just like in Manitoba, it was a loneliness that was briefly stilled with memories of the familiar, which quickly surrendered again to the emptiness fear manifests with ease. But then he thought about Lorraine and how boldly she had embraced an adventure that she had almost no information about to measure its risk. The only certainty she had was her love for and trust in Kevin. Remembering the depth of her love and the commitment to the unknown she made shifted Kevin out of fear and provided renewed confidence for a shared adventure with Lorraine.

Morning arrived early in the Fraser Valley, bright and brilliant, with shimmering blue skies. It would turn out to be the warmest day of the year so far, and Kevin was anxious to get on his way and cross the mountain pass to his new home. After a quick breakfast at the café, Kevin left Hope and headed east on the Hope Princeton Highway toward the Okanagan Valley.

British Columbia's Lower Mainland is green and lush, with moderate temperatures throughout most of the year as a result of a succession of storms that come ashore after long journeys across the Pacific Ocean. As these low-pressure systems flow east, they eventually butt up against the coastal mountain ranges, forcing the saturated clouds to surrender most of their moisture in vast amounts of rain and snow as they climb over the steep peaks. Having given up most of the moisture on the windward side of the mountains, the air descends and warms on the leeward side. The warmed air makes condensation and rain even less likely, creating the rain shadow weather in the Eastern British Columbia valleys. Where parts of British Columbia's Lower Mainland receive more than sixty inches of precipitation per year, the Okanagan Valley only receives, on average, between eight and ten inches of annual precipitation. Kevin would come to acknowledge and respect the subtle microclimates within the Okanagan Valley that greatly limit or enhance the selection of what can be farmed successfully year to year.

As Kevin continued along the Hope Princeton Highway, he could see and smell the influence of the rain shadow effect as the landscape transitioned from tall firs, waterfalls, and ferns to a dry high desert climate with ponderosa pine, scrub cactus, and sage. After descending into the town of Princeton, Highway 3 continued east following the Similkameen River flowing between the valley, with cattle ranches and alfalfa farms touching its banks on both sides.

Just before the small town of Keremeos, the agricultural cornucopia of the region became evident. In a visual shout out, a long and seemingly endless procession of cobbled-together-style fruit stands line the highway. They were all vying for the travelers' attention, selling everything from last season's apples and pears to elephant garlic, winter onions, and homemade perogies. But even at this time of year, Kevin could easily determine what bounty summer held, since many of the previous season's signs that were not put away or that were permanently nailed to a post or a building proclaimed fresh-picked asparagus, tree-ripened Bing cherries, super-sweet corn, Roma tomatoes, freestone peaches, Blenheim apricots, strawberry and rhubarb pie, mega blueberries, and "world famous" Zucca melons.

Kevin stopped at one of the larger fruit stands and purchased a couple of apples and a glass of cherry cider. It was mid-morning and continued to be a sunny day with cloudless skies. If you stood in the sun, out of the wind, the warmth of spring felt luxurious as its soft heat penetrated the skin. But the wind still carried the chill of the snow and ice that remained on the mountains as it blew its way across the valley floor. Sometimes it would gust, blowing pieces of paper and leaves across the parking lots of the fruit stands or swirl the dry, dusty soil into miniature twisters that dissipated almost as quickly as they took shape. Many First Nations and other aboriginal cultures have different legends or interpretations of "dust devils." The one Kevin remembered was, if the dust devil turned clockwise, it was a good spirit, but if it turned counterclockwise, it was a bad omen. The whirlwinds Kevin observed were definitely turning clockwise, and he accepted this as a positive welcome to this side of the mountains.

Back in the car, Kevin continued east on the highway, slowing briefly through town, catching a glimpse of men and women in layers of work clothes, drinking coffee and talking story at the local café. As he was leaving town, he noticed that the highway, was framed by orchards. The parcels of land seemed to be defined one from the other by a house with an outbuilding or two, along with its own tractor and implements that were waiting to be called into action. By this time of year, a large percentage of the fruit trees had already been pruned, with the ground covered in the fruitwood that had been so carefully removed. The pruned tress reminded Kevin of stark and stubby works of art, their leafless limbs stretched to the limit of the allotted space, beckoning the sun to bask on their dormant fruit buds.

The un-pruned trees were shaggy by comparison. The areas of the orchards with trees that still needed to be pruned had one or more people with various pruning tools systematically shaping them, somehow knowing just what branches to cut or save. Kevin marveled at the amount of wood that needed to be trimmed for the un-pruned trees to become the bonsai-like agricultural art forms they are for a brief time each season.

It was clear that this procedure must be mandatory in the growing cycle, allowing the trees to bear the fruit that would be sold at the fruit stands or to the packing houses later in the year. It was also clear to Kevin that he had no understanding about how to prune nor any idea of what else must be accomplished in the orchard after the pruning was finished. In one respect, that thought was daunting. In the foodservice world, he had some knowledge and experience to guide his decisions. Now he was entering a completely new world that involved working with and managing living trees and vines within the context of other environmental factors he knew nothing about and that he didn't know how to measure or even consider. Kevin decided to allow the unknowingness to be part of the excitement of his adventure. He committed to himself that he would stay in awe of what he didn't know and take delight each day in what he would learn and discover. It also came to mind that, unlike the sausage in the restaurant cooler that wasn't destined in its essence to be part of a pasta, pizza, or breakfast, the trees and vines were anchored in the earth, "being" only what they must be, yet dancing with the seasons in a rhythm that everything implies.

At Kaleden, the Hope Princeton Highway ends at the juncture of Highway 97 and goes both north to the principal Okanagan towns of Penticton, Kelowna, and Vernon or south to Okanagan Falls, Oliver, Osoyoos, and the U.S. border. Almost immediately after turning north on Highway 97, the full magnificence of the Okanagan Valley is apparent as the road descends into the town of Penticton, which is beautifully sandwiched between the north shore of Skaha Lake and the south shore of Okanagan Lake. Forest, orchards, vineyards, and homes tier their way down the mountains on both sides of the lakes as fruit stands and campgrounds welcome visitors to the area.

Sometimes called the "banana belt of Canada," the Okanagan Valley, with its warm and dry spring, summer, and fall, is one of Canada's favorite retirement areas and holiday playgrounds. While farmers work in the orchards, vineyards, and vegetable farms, those on holiday soak up the sun on the Okanagan's beautiful beaches; swim, boat, canoe, sailboard, and water ski in the warm waters of its lakes; or hike, bike, and camp throughout the valley. More recently, the wineries in the Okanagan Valley have taken center stage as a year-round attraction. But it was the tree fruit industry that shaped the character of the valley, attracting immigrants from all over the world wanting to build a life growing fruit in Canada's "Garden of Eden." The name Kaleden materialized in someone's imagination by joining part of the Greek word Kalos (beautiful) and Eden. When this occurred, and who made the decision to officially refer to the area as Kaleden, seemed to be a disputed historical fact. Kevin also read that Naramata, another small town on the east side of Lake Okanagan, was named during a Ouija board session. But again, there appeared to be many versions of that story.

Of course, not all would agree that what has developed in the Okanagan Valley mirrors Eden, most especially the First Nations who were the original caretakers of this land. A culture that didn't consider that anyone could own the land any more than the sky, the Okanagan Nation lived from the head of the lakes in the northern part of the valley south to the Columbia River in Washington State. They also ranged east into the Kootenay Valley and west into the Similkameen Valley. Their true traditional territory comprised the entire Columbia River watershed.

While the Okanagan Valley south of the border in the United States is similar in weather and topography, it is vastly different in many respects. One major area of difference is that the Canadian Okanagan has a string of lakes connected by a river running from its northernmost point in Vernon to its southernmost point in Osoyoos. Besides the influence and effect these long and deep bodies of water have on agriculture, they are also one of the primary attractions for the area's tourist industry and the main component of the region's ambiance and livability. South of the border, the U.S. Okanagan region has the river system but very few lakes and is much more rugged and barren in appearance.

Although so close and so similar geographically there is an interesting paradox between the towns and communities north and south of the border that has shaped their development and character for more than a century. If you were to straddle the border with one foot in Osoyoos, British Columbia, and the other foot in Oroville, Washington, you would simultaneously be in one of the southernmost points in Canada and one of the northernmost points of the continental United States. While Osoyoos has always been one of Canada's warmest and most desirable places to live weather-wise, Oroville and that region have traditionally been viewed in the USA as a cold and northern outpost, a last vestige of wilderness compared to the more developed areas of the United States, especially those east of the Mississippi River. If you lived in the United States and wanted to move to a Sunbelt, northern Washington generally wouldn't come to mind with options such as Florida, Texas, Arizona, and New Mexico. On the other hand, if you were living in Alberta or Manitoba—or almost any province east of British Columbia—the Okanagan Valley would be a place you would consider retiring to if you won the lottery.

Kevin continued north on Highway 97, on the west side of Lake Okanagan, through the farming communities of Summerland and Peachland, and across the floating bridge in Kelowna, the largest town in the Okanagan Valley. The tree fruit and grape-growing industries were evident along both sides of the road, with fruit stands, orchards, vineyards, and packing houses the predominate features of the landscape. North of Kelowna, the topography changes somewhat and includes ranching in lowland areas where cold and frost could settle in spring and fall, negatively impacting the prospects for tree fruits and grapes. At this point, Highway 97 was now on the east side of Lake Okanagan, with the lake no longer in sight from the highway.

Just past the small town of Winfield, Kevin turned west off Highway 97, climbing the hill to Spion Kop Ranch in Okanagan

Centre. The view from almost any of the orchards and vineyards in the area is spectacular. Plantings undulate orderly down the slopes of the hillsides toward the lake, emanating a sense of place, purpose, and history similar to the beautiful agricultural landscapes of Europe but with wilderness on the fringe.

The tree fruit industry in the Okanagan Valley and in Okanagan Centre began in the late 1800s but was well established by the turn of the last century. While it was no doubt a pioneering life with many challenges, this area of the Okanagan Valley was also populated and influenced by remittance men. These black sheep of well-to-do English families came, or were oftentimes sent, to this area to establish orchards and farming operations in a young and distant country. Fortunately, most were sufficiently funded to bring many of the comforts and culture of home with them. Historical photos show early orchardists appearing more like gentry, inspecting their operations in white suits and Panama hats.

At that time, transportation through the valley by road was slow, often difficult, and limited, including no bridge spanning the lake in Kelowna to the west side. What could be counted on were the paddlewheel boats that made regularly scheduled trips up and down Lake Okanagan between Penticton at the south end of the lake to Vernon at the head of the lake. The sternwheelers would make up to twenty-eight stops on their return trip, bringing supplies to small and more isolated communities like Naramata, Westbank, Okanagan Landing, and Carrs Landing, and transported the fruit from these communities to the packinghouses.

When Kevin arrived in Okanagan Centre there was still one sternwheeler, the Fintry Queen, making limited runs along the lake during summer months as a tourist attraction. Each time Kevin saw the Fintry Queen on the lake, he would stop whatever he was doing and take in the merging of the past with the present. It was easy to imagine how exciting it must have been when the paddlewheel boats would trumpet their arrival with blasts of the whistle, welcoming everyone to the dock. For a Missouri boy like Kevin, who grew up along the Mississippi River, the Fintry Queen brought the *Adventures of Tom Sawyer* to his new home.

From the moment Kevin, and later Lorraine, arrived at Spion Kop, Peter and Anna Van der Meer greeted them with warmth and respect, making them feel welcome and an integral part of the ranch. They were invited to all family events, from picnics on the hillside or down by the lake, to Easter egg hunts, family birthdays and anniversaries, as well as Christmas dinner with all the trimmings.

Spion Kop Ranch had a strong influence on the more recent history of fruit growing in the Okanagan Valley. Peter Van der Meer was born in Holland, and his father, Garret, was an innovative horticulturalist who specialized in dwarf tree fruit production. The Van der Meers moved to Okanagan Centre in 1950, purchasing a sixty-acre bench parcel overlooking the lake. Later, the family acquired another forty acres overlooking the lake in Carrs Landing, about six miles north of Okanagan Centre. Peter and Anna also purchased another ten-acre parcel about a mile from the home ranch. While the home ranch on Goldie Road was defined and described by various alphabetically identified blocks of orchards and vineyards, the two other parcels were just called Carrs Landing and Upper Spion Kop.

In the beginning, these designations didn't mean that much to Kevin or Lorraine, other than they defined areas of the operations that they needed to understand in order to perform the right task at the right place. Both of them learned that these areas of the ranch had been specifically matched with different tree fruits or grape varieties relative to a combination of factors that included soil type, slope, and air drainage. In many cases, certain areas had different clones or strains of the same fruit variety. They also might have the same clone of a fruit variety grafted onto a different clone of rootstock to limit growth size or more closely match a specific soil type. The selection process was also influenced by the planting density of the trees and vines, as well as the trellising, or support system required. The objective was to simplify and bring efficiency to all aspects of production while maximizing harvest potential.

There are strains of Red Delicious apples that have a deep-red, almost purple coloring that, over time, became more popular with customers than the paler red strains. The darker variety was grafted onto a rootstock clone that limited the height of the tree to a specific size. Some of the fruit and rootstock combinations were not self-supporting and needed a post or espalier structure for support. Many of these systems had evolved from experimentation in Europe and from the tweaking the Van der Meers made when adapting their knowledge and experience to the growing conditions in the Okanagan. These systems have continued to evolve in fruit-growing areas around the world and are now standard for growing apples and other tree fruits in the Okanagan Valley.

One of the driving factors of this evolution was the change in consumer preference for apple varieties. Because of diminished demand for Red and Yellow Delicious and Macintosh apples, they were replaced by Granny Smith, Gala, Royal Gala, then later by Jonagold and Fuji plantings. More recently, orchardists have planted localized heritage strains of apples, as well as patent-controlled, limited-production varieties that can command higher prices and some price protection for the farmers. The high-density dwarf tree systems provided for earlier production with a higher yield over a shortened life cycle. This allowed orchardists to maximize production when demand for a specific variety is high and quickly convert to other varieties as consumer preference changes.

When Kevin and Lorraine arrived, Spion Kop Ranch was growing tree fruits using a number of different systems that included traditional free-standing trees, trees trained to grow espalier along a large trellis system, double and triple row dwarf trees, and high-density plantings, with each tree supported by its own post. All of these systems had their advantages and disadvantages. The key to a successful harvest, year to year, was to manage each system individually and correctly. The technique for pruning trellised apple trees was completely different than pruning higher density triple row apple trees, and experienced tree pruners were required to know the pruning methods and requirements for each system. It was also just one of the many things about growing tree fruits and grapes that Kevin and Lorraine knew nothing about.

Chapter 29

The Learning Curve

Lorraine arrived in Okanagan Centre about six weeks after Kevin. She first took charge of making a home of the house the Van der Meers had provided for them. The house wasn't very big but in a short time, with some of their things and a bit of paint, it felt like their place. By this time, Kevin had come to accept his daily routine of being completely overwhelmed by the variety of new tasks that needed to be accomplished in unison by a variety of people of different cultural backgrounds. Almost all of them knew more than he did about what he was asking them to do, and many of them wondered why a guy who wasn't from Canada and knew nothing about growing fruit was hired to manage them.

Most of the tasks required tools or equipment to accomplish, so there were always pruning tools that needed to be sharpened, ladders that needed to be fixed or provided to a specific block, sprayers or fertilizing equipment that had to be calibrated, tractors to be fueled and hitched to various equipment or put on a truck and hauled to the other sites. All of this assumed the tractors or farm trucks that were needed to move people and equipment were working on a given day.

Partway through any day, everything could change if the weather did, or if a specific piece of equipment broke down requiring attention to the next priority on the ever-expanding to-do list. There was nothing like a flat on a fluid-filled rear tractor tire to change the plan of the day. When that happened, Kevin needed to deal with arranging to get the tire off the tractor and repaired, possibly from a tractor in the middle of a row that was not easily accessible, all in the course of not getting done what he had hoped to accomplish that day. While Kevin tried to remember to look at and appreciate the beautiful surroundings he was working in throughout the day, too often he was frustrated. He was working at a growing list of what needed to be done or fixed or hadn't been done and therefore needed to be done tomorrow, with the syncopated notion of lost time ticking by like a metronome in his head.

It didn't take long for Lorraine to spruce up the little house. Knowing even less about farming than Kevin had learned in a few months, Lorraine decided she wanted to work on the ranch. In the beginning, Peter was good at finding jobs that Lorraine could do and not become frustrated with. Her first job was at cherry blossom time and involved cutting bouquets of cherry blossoms and stationing them near the beehives in buckets of water to increase the chances of cross-pollination. Before long, Lorraine became an essential part of surviving the first year of farming, helping Kevin move people and small equipment to the different areas of the farm and making numerous trips to town for repair parts and supplies that they always seemed to need.

By summertime, she was managing the cherry harvest and installing miles of pipe for a new irrigation system. By fall, she was driving tractors and hauling bins full of apples and wine grapes out of the orchard and vineyard blocks on the ranch.

As the days grew longer, so did the workdays. In the middle of summer, it still wasn't completely dark by nine thirty in the evening, and daylight pulled back the covers on a new day before 5:00 a.m. The crews were usually gone by five or six o'clock and even earlier when it was extremely hot. Often, Kevin and Lorraine were able to get a swim in the lake together before dinner. After dinner, they both went in one of the trucks to change the sprinklers around the ranch for the night set. As tired as they were on many evenings, they loved being in the orchard or vineyard in the evening.

After changing the sprinklers from one block to another, they would look for plugged sprinklers to make sure all of the trees and vines were being watered. When they found a plugged one, they would take turns running up the rows in their gum boots, laughing as they dodged the water from the turning sprinklers and racing back again through the gauntlet of water to the truck.

Scents of dried grass, sage, and pine subtly began to filter in, riding on the thermals as the night air raced down from the mountains toward the lake. While pheasants and quail glided or scurried to their roosts, a cloudless sky surrendered its blueness to the sun's last glow that painted itself in a temporary but expanding brilliance behind the mountains on the west side of the lake. Almost on cue, the first planets or stars would appear in a backlit grey remnant of the day, setting the stage for the night sky to come.

There were some evenings that were so perfect that it seemed for a time it was all meant just for the two of them. They didn't feel tired, and the metronome in Kevin's head stopped ticking as they rode home along the lake, intoxicated by the multi-sensual seduction of what can be experienced in the moment but never truly described.

By the end of July, all of the cherries had been harvested, and Kevin and Lorraine were turning their attention to the beginning of the pear harvest a few weeks away. The crew wasn't as big now as it had been during cherry harvest or earlier in the year for fruit thinning. Many more pickers would be needed for the apple and grape harvest, but for the moment, the smaller, more permanent crew mowed the grass in the orchard and vineyards, kept the weeds in check and the irrigation going through its cycles. Kevin picked up empty fruit bins by the truckload from the packinghouse and mustered them where they would be needed in the weeks ahead. Some of the crew were kept busy checking and repairing the picking ladders and picking bags. Peter was teaching Kevin to keep an eye out for mildew in the vineyards. Quietly, everyone hoped there wouldn't be any hail accompanying a summer storm to spoil what appeared to be a potentially bountiful apple and grape crop.

August gave Kevin and Lorraine time to reflect on how their decision to be farmers in the early days of spring was playing out in the back half of the year. There was still so much to be done before the harvest would be completed and so much yet that they had never done before. But they now had a keen understanding that the decision to learn to farm had turned out to be a decision for a complete change in lifestyle.

Living on a farm, there is never a time when the farm isn't part of you or that you can set aside the awareness of what needs to be done. Yet they found delight and awe in little discoveries and adventures they hadn't anticipated or could not even have imagined at the start of it all. They had walked through acres of trees in blossom so beautiful that the setting could have been the backdrop for a movie or a grand wedding and with a fragrance so amazingly intense that the joy of that moment couldn't be ignored. There had been treasure hunts for wild asparagus and wild strawberries that they learned to find with hints from others who had been on these seasonal quests for years. They ate cherries, apricots, and peaches of specific varieties missed during harvest, tree ripened to perfection so sweet and juicy that finding and eating them was an event in itself.

They also met a cast of unique and interesting people, both landowners and farm workers of many different ethnic and cultural backgrounds. Each one had a life story that brought them or their families to this area and to this lifestyle for one reason or another. Many were first-generation Canadians. Growing up in the USA, Kevin and Lorraine had learned about its great melting pot. But Canada, as so well described by former Prime Minister Pierre Elliot Trudeau, was much more of a tossed salad, where ethnic diversity within a multi-cultural society was encouraged. There were nights around bonfires where shared bottles of wine made from grapes grown at Spion Kop helped birth the laughter that became the common language bridging a joyful understanding beyond what limited vocabularies and accents could convey.

The biggest change for Kevin and Lorraine was the emerging realization of what could be accomplished, tree by tree, vine by vine, year to year, in a rhythm that required attention to many details within a time frame and tempo set by the seasons.

Spion Kop didn't have a large planting of pears, so the pear harvest was a warmup for the apple harvest that was the main event. Harvesting pears was not an easy job for the pickers. The trees were standard size and required ten and twelve-foot ladders to reach the highest fruit. Added to that was the weight of the picking bags that needed to be balanced up and down the ladders.

The picking crew consisted of individuals and families that had picked pears for years, along with young people passing through the valley looking for work that had never picked pears before. The harvest was paid by piecework, a set amount for each bin. This rate could change depending on the size of the trees, steepness of the slope, and the amount of fruit on the trees. An experienced picker could make reasonable money each day knowing how to efficiently approach the tree and set the ladder. Often, the new pickers had high expectations of how much money they could make but defeated their expectations and exhausted themselves with too many trips up and down the ladder and by not setting the ladder correctly. Everyone held their breath, hoping for the best outcome when they heard or saw a picker with a full bag of pears and a ladder falling to the ground.

Chapter 30

Harvest Time

By early September, the pace of the harvest picked up dramatically, with more and more blocks of apples becoming ready for harvest. Fortunately, there was a waiting list for harvest workers at Spion Kop Ranch, which had a reputation for paying well and providing a respectful and supportive working environment for their harvest crews. The almost perfect Indian summer weather of 1971 provided the clear skies and dry weather that allowed the harvest to proceed without interruption. That also meant that Kevin and Lorraine were working seven days a week, sunup to sundown, managing the crews and doing whatever needed to be done until the last apple and grape cluster had been picked. As tired as they were as the harvest progressed, they were emboldened by discovering their capacity to work at that pace, the deeper level of partnership that developed between them, and the camaraderie and sense of teamwork they felt with the crew and the Van der Meers.

The mornings were cool as a result of nights that dropped to even ground frost temperatures as the days got shorter. Kevin and Lorraine dressed in layers of shirts, sweatshirts, and jackets, knowing by mid-morning they would be shedding some of those layers as the air, warmed by the bright fall sunshine, would, at some point in the day, allow them to work in shirtsleeves. By late afternoon, as the sun became lower in the sky, the layers of clothing were put on again as the temperature began to drop.

Both Kevin and Lorraine made sure the crew had what they needed and moved them to new rows or other picking blocks when they completed picking the section they were working on. They also hauled the full bins of apples out of the orchard to the marshalling areas where they were loaded on Spion Kop's flatbed truck and taken to the packinghouse in Winfield. Peter did most of the hauls during the day, with Kevin delivering the last couple of loads late afternoons, once the pickers were finished. The full bins of grapes from the vineyard were also brought to marshalling areas for the winery that contracted for them to pick up.

Lorraine's birthday was October 13. She had been too busy to think about her birthday and knew that Kevin didn't have a spare moment to go to Kelowna and find a present for her. About a week before, Kevin promised Lorraine that, once the harvest was finished, they would celebrate her birthday at La Bussola, one of the few fine dining restaurants in Kelowna at the time. He also randomly mentioned Lorraine's birthday and his plans to Peter when they were chatting while tying down the load on the truck. By the end of the day on Tuesday, October 12, there was only one block of apples left to pick, and Kevin and Lorraine knew that Lorraine's birthday would just happen to be the last day of harvest for 1971. They both agreed that the milestone of finishing their first season of farming was a great birthday gift.

Typically, the individuals or groups on the picking crew stopped for lunch or a break when it suited them. Just after noon on Lorraine's birthday, Kevin saw Anna and Peter arrive at the block the crew was working on. Without saying a word, Peter honked the horn and they got out of the truck. The crew all responded to the honk, stopped picking, and walked toward Peter's truck. Peter shouted to Kevin to get Lorraine off her tractor and bring her over to where everyone was gathering. To both Kevin and Lorraine's complete surprise, Peter and Anna brought a birthday cake decorated with apple trees and a tractor made of icing that was big enough to share with the entire crew.

When Lorraine arrived, the cake was sitting on the tailgate of Peter's pickup with a number "21" candle. As Peter lit the candle, Anna started singing "Happy Birthday," and all of the crew with their various accents joined in. Lorraine, though blushed by the attention, blew out the candle as Kevin sang loudly, beaming with delight. Lorraine thanked everyone, gave Anna and Peter a hug, and then turned and gave Kevin a very big kiss to the delight, clapping, and laughter of everyone gathered for the cake. Kevin was now the one blushing as he said to Lorraine, "I'd like to take credit for this, but don't thank me, I knew nothing about this. It is all Peter and Anna." Lorraine gave Peter and Anna another hug and kissed both of them on the cheek.

After the cake, everyone returned to work, and by three thirty that afternoon, the last of the picking crew had finished their bins. Lorraine collected picking bags and completed final paperwork with each person before they left, thanking them again for being part of the Spion Kop team and for helping her celebrate her birthday. Throughout the afternoon, Kevin also made sure to thank everyone before they finished and extend invitations to come back for next season.

Shortly after the last of the picking finished the day and the season, Peter stopped by and suggested Lorraine take the rest of the day off and enjoy what was left of her birthday. Kevin completed the last haul of the day to the packinghouse and arrived home around 6:00 p.m. to find Lorraine relaxed from a long bath and looking like she never worked on a tractor that day. As he took off his boots, Lorraine rushed over to Kevin, embraced him, and said, "This has been the best birthday ever, Kevin, and guess what; it's about to get better. Anna dropped off a bottle of Champagne and an amazing meat and cheese platter for my birthday, so clean yourself up, cowboy, and let's get the party started."

It took the rest of the week to get the remaining bins from the harvest to the packinghouse and to collect and store all the picking ladders. At Peter's insistence, Kevin and Lorraine finished work early on Friday with the promise of a well-earned three-day weekend. Kevin made reservations at La Bussola for Saturday night. On Saturday afternoon, Peter stopped by the house and asked if he could speak to Kevin outside. Lorraine wasn't sure why he wanted to speak to Kevin without her. Once outside, Peter said to Kevin, "Hear you're taking Lorraine to La Bussola for her birthday, so Anna and I want to contribute to your special night."

"Thanks, Peter, but that's not necessary. You and Anna already gave us the champagne and surprised us with the cake in the orchard."

Peter smiled, put a $100 bill in Kevin's hand, and said to Kevin, "Just think of this as the first installment of your harvest bonus. As soon as we get the accounting sorted out, you will both have a lot more than this coming your way. Anna and I are so pleased that you and Lorraine came to Spion Kop, and we hope you will stay with us for many years. You might want to consider making an honest woman out of Lorraine before she gets away. And Kevin, don't be cheap with the wine tonight. Just tell them you want the Chianti that Peter always orders. Enjoy, Kevin. You deserve everything that you have earned."

Kevin waited until they were at La Bussola to tell Lorraine about the contribution from Peter and Anna and his conversation with Peter. Lorraine was thrilled but, in a way, not surprised. She had experienced Peter and Anna's warmth and generosity since the day she arrived. In the glow of the evening and the Chianti, she told Kevin that she couldn't remember a time in her life that she was as happy as she was at that moment. "I feel exactly the same," said Kevin. "Let's do something about that to make it better."

"What do you suggest, Kevin?"

"Not really prepared for this," said Kevin, his blue eyes radiating smiles from his heart. Without hesitation, and in the middle of La Bussola, Kevin dropped to his knee in front of Lorraine and took her hand. "I don't have a ring at the moment, but I have a twenty-carat love for you that will last forever. Will you marry me, Lorraine?"

"I don't care about a ring, Kevin. I only care about you," said Lorraine, holding back tears and too excited to be embarrassed by the public proposal. "And yes, I will, Kevin." She pulled Kevin off the floor and into a kiss to the applause and cheers of everyone in the room, including the wait staff. Their waiter appeared and asked them what they wanted, compliments of the house. "Tiramisu, please," said Lorraine.

"And two Mandarine Napoleons in snifters," chimed in Kevin.

As they lingered over their Mandarine Napoleons, Kevin smiled at Lorraine and asked her, "If that bonus Peter mentioned is big enough, what do you think about a honeymoon camping and surfing our way through Baja to Cabo San Lucas?"

"You should know the answer to that question by now, Kev," she said with a gentle smile. "I'm always ready for an adventure with you. Let's do it!"

With no Uber in 1971 and no taxis in Kelowna willing drive to Okanagan Centre, the only option for getting home from La Bussola was the farm truck they drove to the restaurant. Definitely tipsy from the evening, Kevin drove them home as carefully as he could on the back road to Okanagan Centre in the truck with no seatbelts.

Chapter 31

Reality Sandwich

Inspired by their plans to get married and honeymoon in Baja, Kevin and Lorraine bought a used four-wheel drive Dodge panel truck for their adventure with a portion of the harvest bonus. Within a month, they had converted the rear portion of the truck into a bed and storage area for the food and camping gear they would take with them. They also bought and studied books about visiting Mexico and driving the Baja Peninsula.

On U.S. Thanksgiving, Thursday, November 25, 1971, Kevin and Lorraine were married at 11:30 a.m. at the courthouse in Vernon, British Columbia. There were no rings to exchange, and the only other people in attendance were Peter and Anna. Kevin and Lorraine exchanged brief vows that brought small tears to the corner of Lorraine's eyes. After they were pronounced husband and wife, they sealed their marriage with a long kiss while Peter and Anna clapped for their happiness.

As one of their wedding gifts, Peter and Anna took them all to lunch at Jamieson Booker's Eating Establishment, a quaint restaurant in Vernon known for its classic menu and great food. There was no wedding cake, but the Van der Meers made sure a house-made Black Forest cake arrived at the table with a bride and groom figurine on top of the cake. On the ride home with the Van der Meers, Kevin and Lorraine sat close together in the backseat and held hands. In spite of the simplicity of the ceremony, they both felt more special than they had even imagined.

On the morning of December 15, with light snow beginning to fall, Kevin and Lorraine began their adventure to drive from Okanagan Centre to the tip of Baja. From Portland, they took the road to the Oregon Coast and then spent the night in Depot Bay. The next morning, walking back from breakfast, they discovered an artisan jeweler and purchased a set of wedding rings that were inspired by ocean waves. That evening, they stayed at a cabin on the ocean with a fireplace in Gold River, Oregon, and exchanged their vows once again while drinking champagne in front of a well-stoked fire. Over the next two months, they would spend Christmas with Lorraine's parents, camp and surf at remote beaches that they were directed to by other Baja adventurers, stop at a roadside, ramshackle, lean-to structure and eat chicken and beans cooked over a wood fire, buy seafood direct from the boats on both the Sea of Cortez and Pacific side, witness hundreds of whales gathered at Scammon's Lagoon giving birth and finding a mate, and dance, completely alone, beneath an exploding, star-filled sky on New Year's Eve 1971, on the cliff just above the Arch at Cabo San Lucas.

When Kevin and Lorraine crossed the border back into Canada the end of February, they were happy to be home and ready to take on year two of farming at Spion Kop. The days in late February and early March were still cool, but many of them were sunny, giving a promise of spring. Most of their first month back at Spion Kop was spent pruning apples and grapes. As each day grew longer and a bit warmer, they noticed the snow retreating from the orchard and vineyard floors and that they could, once again, take off some of their layers of clothes in the early afternoon.

On Friday, March 26, Kevin and Lorraine finished pruning a small block of Riesling vines and decided to call it a day. Before heading home, they drove to the post office in Okanagan Centre to get the mail from their box. Kevin parked across the street by the beach and went in for the mail. When he came back to the truck, Lorraine noticed his expression seemed more serious and he was holding a manila-colored envelope that she knew immediately was from the Selective Service.

Kevin slid onto the seat and ripped the envelope open, putting the letter between them so they could both read at the same time. It was not the news they wanted to learn. They had hoped that the review of the new medical information presented by Dr. Harnel would disqualify Kevin from the draft. Instead, Kevin was instructed to report to the induction station in St. Louis for a second and final physical, and to be prepared to immediately be inducted into the U.S. Army if he passed. They sat together in silence for a moment and looked out at the lake. Finally Kevin said to Lorraine, "We knew this was a possibility, but how are you feeling about it?"

"Wish it was the other way, Kevin," said Lorraine. "But it's not, and we both knew this was a possibility. We just need to be thankful that we have a home in Canada and are doing what we love with Spion Kop. Let's see how it all plays out, but I don't want you to even think about going to St. Louis for a physical. We're here, it's good, and it's done for now, and I don't care what anyone thinks. Just think of all you have done to make it possible for us to have a home here in British Columbia—and don't you ever forget all the chaos in the United States that brought us here in the first place. In my heart, I feel our decision will come to shape our lives in ways we can't even comprehend at the moment. Let's close the door behind us for now and truly live here."

Lorraine's strength and conviction about the moment was like a shot of adrenaline for Kevin, and he reached over and hugged her. They held hands for a few minutes and continued to watch the lake while letting the finality of their news wash over them. Finally, Kevin said, "Let's go home, sweetheart. We've got a weekend to get on with."

Chapter 32

Watergate

A number of times since they'd first met, Kevin said to Lorraine that it is the "out of the blue," completely unexpected phone call or event that becomes the crossroad for major changes in life. According to Kevin, these were surprises from the universe so profound, and sometimes, seemingly random, that you could not have imagined them or the path forward they suggested, even if you had meditated in the wilderness for two weeks straight. And so it would become.

On the afternoon of June 18, 1972, Kevin was moving one of the tractors to the Carrs Landing orchard block on the flatbed truck, listening to the CBC news on the radio. Near the end of the news report, there was a story about five individuals being arrested and charged for burglary after they were caught breaking into the Democratic National Headquarters at the Watergate office complex in Washington DC. Over the next two years, these arrests would evolve into one of the biggest political scandals in the history of the United States, but on that day in June, it only caught Kevin's attention because it was a U.S. news story on the CBC. By the time he had unloaded the tractor and returned to Spion Kop, he had forgotten about it.

For Kevin and Lorraine, 1972 at Spion Kop Ranch was a fully involved but more relaxed and confident repeat of 1971. Both of them knew more about what to anticipate at each stage of the harvest season, allowing them to take more responsibility with less guidance from Peter and Anna. They also continued to develop their synergy for cooperatively managing the Spion Kop operations and positively interacting with the others working at Spion Kop.

On a beautiful but busy September day in 1972, Kevin and Lorraine were working with the picking crew at Carrs Landing harvesting Macintosh apples. Just before noon, they were both surprised to see a Royal Canadian Mounted Police car drive up the long dusty orchard road and park at the top of the orchard where they were marshalling the apple bins. Lorraine had just dropped off a full apple bin when the RCMP officer arrived and got out of his car. Clearly wondering why the RCMP had come to Carrs Landing, she drove the tractor over to where he was standing and got off to meet him. When the officer told Lorraine he was looking for Kevin Fischer, she kept her poise, but inside, worry overwhelmed her. "Kevin's here," said Lorraine. "That's him coming up the drive on the tractor."

When Kevin pulled up, turned off the tractor and was climbing down, Lorraine said to Kevin, "The officer is looking for you for some reason, Kevin."

"How can I help you, sir?" asked Kevin.

"My name is Constable Jackson. I'm looking for Kevin Fischer. Is that you?"

"Yes, sir," answered Kevin.

"There's no real problem, Kevin," said Constable Jackson. "Just need to ask you a few questions. The RCMP were contacted by the FBI in the States, who indicated you did not show up for your induction into the U.S. military earlier this year, and they stated that they haven't heard from you since. They assume you got the notice and wonder if you are intending to come back to the USA. Our understanding is, unless you return and report for induction soon, you will be criminally charged. Of course, we have no jurisdiction related to this case, and you have no problem with the RCMP or anyone in Canada. I can assure you that the government of Canada will not become involved in any way or try to deport you. We were just requested to ask you your intentions."

"I don't have too much to say," said Kevin. "I did get the notice and decided not to go. My intention, if they need to know, is that

I am living in Canada and have no intention of returning to the United States anytime soon."

"That is all I need," said Constable Jackson. "I apologize for interrupting your day. Take care, and enjoy living in this beautiful valley."

As Constable Jackson got into his car and headed back down the orchard road, Lorraine, who had been listening but not saying a word, moved closer to Kevin and took his hand. "Guess that's that," said Lorraine.

"Guess that's that," replied Kevin.

To celebrate the end of the harvest in 1972 and Lorraine's birthday, Kevin and Lorraine once again went to La Bussola and shared the same bottle of wine that they had in 1971. It was great to already know that their harvest bonus was going to be larger than the year before. What they weren't going to be able to do was to leave Canada and vacation anywhere warm. They knew of other draft dodgers and deserters that had taken direct flights to Mexico or other locations, so they didn't need to stop over and enter the United States. But they also knew that there had been occasions where, because of weather or mechanical problems, these direct flights had been diverted to a U.S. airport, resulting in arrests for anyone with an outstanding warrant. The U.S. also seemed to have ever-changing treaties and agreements with countries that obligated these countries to detain and deport individuals wanted for draft evasion or desertion.

The first full winter in Canada was more challenging for Kevin and Lorraine than they had anticipated. From harvest through Christmas, it all seemed very new and exciting except for the disappointment of Richard Nixon handily beating George McGovern in the U.S. presidential election. They had plenty of wood put up for their woodstove, and with part of the harvest bonus, they bought a hot tub. Peter and Anna gave them each a pair of cross-country skis. They enjoyed taking their four-wheel drive truck up the mountain to the powder snow wilderness, but as warm as they dressed for the weather, they were always cold in an hour or so.

Peter and Anna invited Kevin and Lorraine to all of their holiday festivities, including Christmas dinner and New Year's Eve, but by the middle of January, a winter funk began to set in. Temperatures were colder than they had been the winter before, and there was more snow that year, but what depressed them more than anything was the low valley cloud. As a result of temperature variations between the air and the water on the large and deep Lake Okanagan, a thick blanket of low-hanging cloud would all but blot out the sun of the very short winter days. By 8:30 a.m., it was technically light outside, but it was a marshmallow world of light, shadowed in grey mist and fog. The sounds of life were dampened by a thick cloud layer which settled in halfway between the mountain peaks and the surface of the lake. By three-thirty in the afternoon, the day, which was never really very light, was signaling its quick return to darkness.

With their harvest bonus, they also bought a slightly bigger black-and-white television set, but they were still only able to reliably receive a few Canadian channels. On certain days, with a tinfoil-wrapped antenna pointed in the right direction, they could receive U.S. stations from Washington State. What began to occupy the news, and Kevin's attention, was the evolving story of the Watergate burglary.

By the end of February 1973, days with more bright sunshine were returning. Kevin and Lorraine were once again working their way out of layers of clothes in the afternoons while pruning in the vineyard. The damp and earthy early smells of spring seemed to herald the new sequence of the seasons and the end of winter.

One evening in March, Kevin's mother called long-distance to say that the FBI came to their home that day asking questions about Kevin and to let them know he had been indicted for draft evasion. The agents encouraged Kevin's parents to contact him immediately and tell him he had one last chance to turn himself in for induction into the army. Kevin thanked his mom and tried to comfort her while also saying, very simply and calmly, that he and Lorraine were doing fine in Canada and they had no intention of returning to the United States. The call ended with Kevin's mother in tears. His father came on the phone to sternly state to Kevin how deeply his actions have hurt his mother and his grandparents and shamed the entire family.

Two weeks later, Kevin received a letter from home addressed in his father's handwriting. When he opened the envelope, the only thing in it was a newspaper clipping from the St. Louis Post Dispatch with the story about Kevin being indicted by the U.S. government for draft evasion. The story ended with the fact that Kevin was believed to be living in Canada and could face up to five years in federal prison if he returned or was apprehended.

In May of 1973, the Watergate drama had progressed to live television, with the Senate Watergate Committee hearings breaking new Watergate-related facts and tidbits almost every day. Farming at Spion Kop occupied most of Kevin's time during 1973, but everything Watergate seemed to occupy the rest of his mind, in front of or away from the TV.

With the end of the harvest of 1973, Kevin and Lorraine knew that winter was once again just around the corner. As a tradition, they celebrated Lorraine's birthday and the harvest at La Bussola. They looked forward to skiing up in the mountains and to long nights in their hot tub.

Winter melted into spring and spring blossomed into summer. With all that had to be accomplished in time with the season that keeps pace only with itself, all too quickly, the cherries were ready for harvest. A month later, after many long and hot days harvesting and delivering the cherries to the packinghouse, Kevin and Lorraine were ready for a summer break. They planned to spend five days camping and swimming along the lakes in the South Okanagan, ending up at John and Kathrin's in Grand Forks, British Columbia.

The speed at which Watergate had revealed itself during 1973 became the catalyst for Kevin to begin corresponding with John again more frequently. John, who was managing a potato farming operation in Grand Forks, welcomed the increased contact and wrote Kevin long and opinionated letters each week that challenged Kevin to dig deeper into the dark mysteries and intentions of the U.S. shadow government. Some of what John said puzzled and frustrated Kevin since, even if all of what John was telling him was true, what was he supposed to do about it? But just hearing from John and swimming in his energy again was worth his conundrums that some-times stayed with him for days at a time.

With no real agenda and perfect Okanagan summer weather, it took four days before they arrived in Grand Forks. In early August, Grand Forks is often hotter than the Okanagan, but with no lake. Grand Forks does have the Granby and Kettle Rivers, with beau-tiful clear cool swimming holes. Other than changing sprinklers in the potatoes, John took a couple days off while Kevin and Lorraine were visiting. Lorraine could get on with almost anyone and took Kathrin's intentionally directed moodiness in stride. John and Kevin couldn't stop talking and laughing the entire time they were together again. They discussed some of the topics in John's letters, but mostly, they enjoyed the familiarity of their shared immigrant adventure, swimming in the river, and playing guitars while drinking beer and wine in the evenings.

Too soon for Kevin, it was time to head home. The weather forecast for August 8, 1974, indicated temperatures climbing to over 100 degrees. Kevin and Lorraine didn't want to drive in the heat and knew, if they took the shortest route back to Spion Kop through Rock Creek, it should only take about four hours. In August, it wouldn't be dark until after 9:00 p.m., so they decided to spend the day at the river with John and Kathrin and leave for home around 5:00 p.m. Saying goodbye to John after not seeing him for so long was difficult for Kevin, but their time together had renewed their relationship and reminded both of them what they cared for and respected in each other. Though Lorraine knew she would never be close with Kathrin, who often made her uncomfortable, she was happy to see Kevin so relaxed and carefree during his time with John.

Once they left Grand Forks, there was no point in trying to listen to the radio. There would be nothing but static on the AM channel until they reached Kelowna. They stopped for fish and chips at a café in Rock Creek and then continued home around 6:30 p.m. A half an hour out of Kelowna, Kevin tried the radio and was able to briefly pick up CBC, but it was fading in and out. Just before 9:00 p.m., Kelowna was in sight in the valley below and the radio was coming in clearly. The lead story on the CBC nine o'clock news reported that, in a televised speech to the nation that evening, President Richard Nixon announced he would resign his presidency the following day. Like most of the people around the world, Kevin and Lorraine had no idea that Nixon was going to give up his fight and resign. They looked at each other and both kept saying, "Oh my God, I can't believe it. Wow! Wow!"

Kevin pulled into an overlook on Highway 33 and parked the truck. They both got out of the car, hugged each other, and jumped up and down with energized delight. And as darkness began to descend on the valley below, they danced together to the sounds of the summer night in the light of the moon that was rising in the east.

Chapter 33

Seeking Resolution

Kevin and Lorraine's elation about Nixon's resignation morphed quickly into questions about what this would mean for the United States and possibly for them. As it turned out, they didn't need to wait long. Exactly one month later, on September 8, 1974, while once again listening to CBC radio in their truck, they learned that newly appointed President Gerald Ford granted Richard Nixon a full and unconditional pardon for any crimes he may have committed against the United States while president. Reactions to President Ford's pardon of Richard Nixon were divided along the same political fault lines that had fractured the country for years, with the voices of opposition to the pardon growing daily.

On September 16, 1974, in what he would call "an act of mercy to bind the nation's wounds and to heal the scars of divisiveness," President Ford proclaimed a conditional amnesty for men who had evaded the draft during the Vietnam War and for those who deserted their duty while serving in the U.S. military. The conditions of the amnesty involved reaffirming allegiance to the United States of America and serving for up to two years working in a qualified public service job.

This second proclamation, within eight days, did not initially provide the reconciliation President Ford had hoped for. The amnesty was welcomed by many of those who were outraged by Nixon's pardon but disliked by most that continued to support Richard Nixon and the Vietnam War. Caught somewhere outside of that polarity were the men and women who had served in Vietnam and the families of those who died or were injured. This group of Americans had a reference point for the war that couldn't be fully comprehended by the others, including Kevin and Lorraine.

Throughout the harvest of 1974, Kevin and Lorraine's minds were occupied by the amnesty and what it could mean for them. In the evenings, they would discuss their options, which vacillated between staying where they were and enjoying the life they had made together and leaving as soon as harvest was over to enroll in the amnesty program. Because they were working long hours each day and seven days a week, they didn't have time to research the details of the program and what the decision the return to the United States would actually and practically mean.

On a day in October, when all harvest activity was cancelled by rain, Kevin called his draft board in Webster Groves, Missouri, to get the details about the program he was unable to determine in Canada. By the end of the phone call, he learned that the first step for a draft evader living in Canada was to send them a letter stating his intention to return to the United States and enroll in the Reconciliation Service Program. Upon approval, Kevin would be issued a letter that allowed him to cross the border into the USA and report to the office of the United States Attorney's Office within ten days after entering the United States. He also learned that he could do his service anywhere within the United States as long as he could find a job that met the program's qualifications. If Kevin could not find a job that met the program qualifications, he would be assigned one by the Selective Service.

Kevin and Lorraine now had a better understanding of how to enroll in the program and how the program worked. What was far less clear was what this would all mean in terms of where they would live, what would Kevin's job be like, where would Lorraine work, and how they would feel if they left Spion Kop Ranch.

Two weeks after the phone call, the harvest was finished, but they had not made up their mind about returning to the United States for the amnesty program. There had been days when this question became their complete focus. There were other days when neither one of them spoke about it. As had become their tradition, Kevin and Lorraine went to La Bussola to celebrate the harvest, their bonus, and Lorraine's birthday. Kevin hoped they could find their way to a carefree celebration like the previous years at La Bussola and avoided bringing up the subject of the amnesty program for the first part of the evening. In spite of the wine they shared, no spontaneous laughter had occurred between them, and Kevin noticed that Lorraine seemed to be avoiding any lingering eye contact. As the main course was served with a smile, a silence that magnified the sounds of their cutlery surrounded their evening. Halfway through her cannelloni, Lorraine looked Kevin directly in the eye and said, "What are we going to do, Kevin?"

"I don't know, Lorraine, I truly don't know," said Kevin. "I want to resolve the situation so we can come and go in the United States if we want to or take our winter trips to warmer climates, but it's so hard to imagine giving up the life we have built at Spion Kop to end up in jobs or even a town or city we know nothing about. All the uncertainty makes me sick inside, and I almost wish we didn't have this choice."

Lorraine reached across the table and took Kevin's hand. "I feel exactly the same way, Kevin. Some days I just try not to think about it and pretend it's just another day in our life at Spion Kop, but it's not. There is so much at stake here. I think we should start making a list of pros and cons and with a bit of time and prayer, we can figure it out. It's only for a couple of years, and after that, we can do what we want. Maybe we'll even be able to come back to Spion Kop. We are adventurers, Kevin, and we'll figure it out. But tonight, let's just remember why we are together, and how much we love each other. That's what matters."

Kevin smiled, and with a tear trickling out of his eye, he agreed. "You're right, Lorraine, that's all that really counts. How about that tiramisu and our Mandarine Napoleons?"

Chapter 34

Northern Lights

When Kevin opened his eyes on the morning after their evening at La Bussola, he saw Lorraine with her head on her pillow, looking into his eyes and smiling. "Good morning, Kevin," she said softly. "What do you think about our decision last night?"

"I still think it's the right choice," said Kevin. "What about you?"

"When I woke up and saw you sleeping next to me, I knew with complete certainty that going back to the United States and getting this behind us is the right thing to do," said Lorraine. "We just need to get focused on everything we need to do and then make it happen like we always do."

Reaching over, Kevin cradled Lorraine in his arms. "You continue to amaze me, sweetheart," said Kevin. "Let's get up and at it and start making our lists."

Lorraine pulled Kevin in for a kiss. "Sounds like a plan, Kev," whispered Lorraine. Why don't you go and stoke the fire and then come back to bed for a bit and we'll warm up."

Later that same day, Kevin called Peter and invited him and Anna to dinner on Sunday evening. When the Van der Meers arrived on Sunday, Kevin and Lorraine still didn't know exactly how to break the news. But as it so often does, all of that took care of itself. Kevin poured everyone a glass of wine, and together, they toasted to another successful harvest. Shortly after, Kevin's anxiousness overwhelmed his sense of caution about the matter at hand. Taking a deep breath, he briefly looked over at Lorraine and then just calmly stated, "Lorraine and I have some news to share with you both."

"Bet you're going to tell us you're headed back to the States for that amnesty program," said Anna.

"How did you know?" exclaimed Kevin.

"Peter and I have been talking about this for a couple of weeks now," replied Anna. "Given the choices, and knowing you two as we do, we figured this is what you would likely decide. We think it's the right decision for you both."

"Don't give a second thought to Spion Kop," chimed in Peter. "We'll be here to welcome you with open arms if you decide to come back when all of this is behind you."

"And we will be back," said Lorraine with a tear running down her cheek. "You guys are so amazing, and this is home."

"Okay, enough of that smoke blowing and schmaltzy stuff," said Peter with a chuckle. "Let's toast to reconciliation and your new adventures and then get into that great food you two always make."

Later that evening, lying in bed next to Lorraine and listening to the fire crackling, Kevin felt very contented and secure about Peter and Anna's support for their decision and the offer to return to Spion Kop. Just before he drifted off to sleep, he wondered how John would take the news. Remembering their conversation at Smitty's about getting drafted a few years earlier, he was pretty sure he knew. As it turned out, Kevin received John's answer in the mail before he even posed the question.

John's letter to Kevin was short and to the point.

> Kevin,
>
> Glad to see that ass clown Nixon go down in flames. Hope he burns in hell with Spiro Agnew and the other war criminals that are responsible for the millions that have been killed or maimed in the Vietnam War. I hope to fuck you are not considering going back to the US for that half-baked amnesty program. But if I know you, it's eating you up inside.

Just remember this, my friend. You are not
the one who needs fucking amnesty or absolu-
tion. You decided not to go kill innocent people just because your government told you it was
necessary for reasons that they could never or
would never clarify. Be glad you are in Canada,
Kevin. You may think the war is over, but the
same greed, evil, and propaganda that perpetrated and prolonged the Vietnam War will raise
its very ugly head again before you know it.
Nobody's really changed their mind. Hard hats
will still beat up hippies, and the majority of the
US thinks the kids at Kent State that were murdered by the government deserved it. And guess
how many fucking churches supported the war
and the "killing of those yellow bastards"?

As I said to you before, Kevin, Canada is
not a consolation prize, it's the grand prize, and
you get to live here and be part of maybe the best
democratic experiment happening in the world
today. Are you going to give all of that up and
go back to all you know is wrong with your tail
between your legs? I hope not, Kevin. But if you
are you know where I stand, and don't look to me
to support your decision.

Love ya,
John

There was nothing John said in his letter that really surprised
Kevin, but it left him with a profound sadness and sense of guilt.
He shared the letter with Lorraine, who wasn't surprised either, but
she did wonder out loud why John was so full of rage and seemed
to have no middle ground of understanding. Kevin knew there was
no point in trying to change John's opinion and that John would
not be interested in the reason for his decision. His letter to John
was also short.

John,

Got your letter, and there is nothing you said that I don't really agree with. However, as we have talked about before, I don't think everything about the US is evil or fucked-up. The very fact that the country rose up and demanded an end to the war is proof that things can change, that voices of the people can be heard and that democracy does work. Democracy is not always pretty, and because all sides must be heard, concession is required for democracy to succeed. I am proud of a system that was able to expose and remove a corrupt president, and even though it took way too much time, a system that allowed, at street level, the people of the United States to stop an unjust war and end the killing.

Lorraine and I are hoping to return to Canada, but life is longer than we can imagine at the moment, and we want to keep our options open for all of the possibilities that life may present. So many people have been hurt and scarred by the war. Words have been said and deeds have been done that shouldn't have been. Reconciliation can lead to understanding and to healing. I want to be part of that reconciliation and healing, and hope I can find closure and new direction in doing so.

I don't expect you to agree with me and I know you won't, but I care for you deeply and hope we can stop by and see you on our way back to the US. Our opinions matter, but our friendship matters most to me.

Love you, John,
Kevin

Two weeks after Kevin mailed his letter to John, he got a very short note back from John.

> Kevin,
>   Let me know when you are coming. I look forward to seeing you before you cross over.
>   John

By mid-December of 1974, Kevin had made all the arrangements with the draft board for returning to the United States in early January. By Christmas, Kevin and Lorraine were packed up and ready to go. Most of their furniture had been sold, and during the last ten days before they left, their remaining furniture consisted of a mattress on the floor, a small table with two chairs, and a tiny Christmas tree with a few lights and an eclectic set of ornaments that they intended to take with them when they left.

Peter and Anna invited Kevin and Lorraine to Christmas dinner. They had a great evening, and everyone was joyful, but a sense of finality hung quietly in the air, presenting itself more clearly as Peter and Anna's door closed behind them when they said goodbye. It was cold outside when they walked home from Peter and Anna's under a moonless but star-filled, magnificent sky. Holding gloved hands, they walked through squeaking snow without saying anything until Lorraine saw the first green ghosting of the Northern Lights over Spion Kop Mountain. "Wow, Kevin, look, Northern Lights over Spion Kop!" she shouted with excitement. By the time Kevin turned his gaze to Spion Kop, the upward arching, here again-gone again, light cloud surprises were peek-a-booing over a wider horizon. The topography of Spion Kop was bathed in a glowing and growing white light, so bright that it seemed to be coming from a city of a million people in the wilderness where it didn't exist.

"Is this a sign, Kevin?" wondered Lorraine.

"Of something, Lorraine, that's for sure," said Kevin. "Of something."

Chapter 35

Crossing Over

O n the cold and clear, blue-sky morning of December 29, 1974, Kevin and Lorraine said goodbye to Spion Kop Ranch and drove to Grand Forks, British Columbia, to visit John and Kathrin before crossing back to the United States. The drive to Grand Forks was beautiful. The entire route was covered in glistening snow and looked like a picture-perfect travel poster, but all of the main roads were open and snow-free.

Kevin wasn't sure what John's reception or mood would be like, but the plan was to stay with John and Kathrin over New Year's and cross over into the United States on January 2. When they arrived in Grand Forks, both John and Kathrin welcomed them inside, where the wood stove was keeping the house wonderfully warm. John and Kevin immediately started the laughter they usually shared just being together while Lorraine was invited by Kathrin to come help her in the kitchen with the dinner she was preparing. Over the next few days, John never dwelled on Kevin's return to the United States other than wondering where they were planning on staying and what kind of job Kevin hoped to find in the program. Mostly, they played their guitars and sang the songs they loved to sing together.

On New Year's Eve, just after midnight, John brought out the absinthe and offered it to everyone. Only Kevin and John imbibed. Lorraine and Kathrin went to bed, and over the next couple of hours, John and Kevin's discussion became more serious. Very little of what they talked about challenged Kevin for returning to the United States, but by association, all that John remembered and was troubled about by his time in Vietnam and the U.S. government's deception rekindled the feelings of guilt that Kevin had worked so hard to put aside.

Finally there was a small silence that signaled there was nothing left to say and that sleep was the appropriate choice. Kevin rose from his chair to say good night to John. For a minute, John just stared deeply into Kevin's eyes through absinthe lenses and then moved closer and gave Kevin a strong hug. Opening from the hug, John once again looked deeply into Kevin's eyes and said, "Take care, my friend, and have a good life. And don't be afraid of the consequences of awakening and enlightenment."

Kevin's mind was swirling from the absinthe, and he wasn't sure what John meant or why he was telling him to have a good life. The first thing that came out of his mouth was, "I'll see you soon, John; you take care of Canada until I get back." Without saying anything else, John headed to bed. Throughout New Year's Day, John never mentioned what they had discussed the night before or said anything negative about Kevin's return to the United States. For both Kevin and John it was a magical day. They played music together, ate the many leftovers from the night before, and in the early afternoon, went for a long walk along the partially frozen but flowing river.

January 2, 1975 was another blue-sky snow-covered day. After breakfast and goodbyes, Kevin and Lorraine were on their way in their four-wheel drive Dodge Power Wagon to the border crossing at Danville, Washington. At the time, Danville was a very remote port of entry along a mostly unguarded and unfenced borderline between the sparsely populated interior regions of British Colombia and Washington State.

Kevin and Lorraine became very nervous when they saw a very small border building with a hand-operated gate appear in the distance on a remote and tree-lined section of British Colombia Highway 41. Kevin was driving, and Lorraine held the envelope with all of the paperwork they believed they needed. This included the letter from Selective Service giving Kevin passage to St. Louis, Missouri, since his U.S. passport had been revoked in July of 1973. They made the decision to cross into the U.S. at the Danville crossing, since it was the only point of entry close to Grand Forks, British Columbia. As they slowed for the border, they now wondered if this was the right decision and how they would explain their purpose for coming back to the United States.

There were no cars ahead or behind them when Kevin stopped the truck in front of the closed gate and the sliding window of the small building. Kevin rolled down his window and the border patrol guard slid his open.

"Good morning," said the border guard. "What's your purpose for coming to the US today?"

"Good morning, sir," said Kevin. "We are both US citizens, but I am coming back to the United States for the amnesty program established by President Ford." As he said President Ford's name, he happened to notice his picture on the wall directly behind the border guard.

"I'm not sure I understand, son, exactly what you mean," said he guard. "Just back up, park your truck, and come inside."

As Kevin was pulling into the parking space, he noticed another border patrol guard come out of the small building, clearly walking in the direction of their truck. He also noticed the border guard had a pistol in his holster. Kevin and Lorraine got out of the truck and greeted the border guard with the pistol, who only told them to leave the truck unlocked and go inside. Once inside the building, they then realized how small it was, containing only a little area with two desks behind a counter, a stool under the sliding window they had pulled up to, and what seemed to be a door to a bathroom.

The border guard they spoke to at the sliding window, who they could now see was also packing a pistol, had gotten off the stool and was now facing them over the counter.

"Now let me try and understand this, son," said the border guard. "You are coming back to the United States for the draft dodger program President Ford recently announced?"

"Yes, sir," said Kevin.

"And what do you have to do with all of this, young lady?" the border guard inquired with a smile.

"We are married," said Lorraine. "Wherever Kevin goes, I go."

"Guess you should be glad that's not jail," chuckled the border guard, to which Lorraine didn't say anything.

"Let me see that paperwork you're holding," said the border guard. "Does anyone know you are coming into the United States, or did you just show up?"

"Yes, sir," said Kevin. "The letter from the Selective Service indicates I can cross into the United States and go directly to the U.S. Attorney's office in St. Louis. I don't have a passport because it was revoked not too long after I was indicted, but my wife does. It's all in the envelope."

The border guard behind the counter was reading the letter from the Selective Service when the border guard who had been going through Kevin and Lorraine's truck came in the building.

"The truck looks okay, Jim," he said. "No problem there."

Without saying anything, the border guard behind the counter went over to a radiophone and contacted someone, since there was no telephone service at the Danville crossing. Between "over," he explained the situation he had at the border crossing and then gave the person on the other end of the phone Kevin's full name and social security number; "Over."

There was a long period of silence before the person on the other end of the radiophone came on again. When he did, he repeated Kevin's full name and social security number, along with his height, weight, hair, and eye color. He also stated that Kevin had been indicted and was wanted for draft evasion. After another pause, he indicated that they had no record of Kevin's correspondence with the draft board in Missouri, but that if Kevin had the original letter on Selective Service letterhead, they should let him in. "Over."

The border guard behind the counter thanked whomever he was talking with—"over and out"— handed the paperwork back to Lorraine, and said, "You're free to go, and good luck to you both."

Kevin and Lorraine thanked both of the guards and then, just before leaving, Kevin said to the guard behind the counter, "What's it like living in Washington right on the border?"

"I don't live here, son," replied the guard. "I live on the Canadian side, where you just came from. I'm a U.S. citizen and love the USA, but I like living in Canada."

With a very puzzled look on his face, Kevin said thank you again to both of the border patrol guards and then walked back to the truck with Lorraine, both very relieved that this first step of their journey seemed to be working out. The border guard who had inspected their truck lifted the gate, and for the first time since his Army physical, Kevin crossed the border into the United States. The sun was still shining, and they had four-wheel drive, but it was January, and they had no idea what kind of weather they would encounter on their journey. Fortunately, the weather and old truck gods were with them. Five days and 3,300 miles later, they pulled into the driveway of Kevin's parents' house.

Chapter 36

Home Again

Kevin and Lorraine found a warm welcome when they arrived at Kevin's parents' home in Kirkwood, Missouri. Both Kevin's mother and father were very happy and proud that Kevin had come back to the United States to enter the amnesty program. It was the first time either one of his parents had met Lorraine, and they were taken by her immediately. They assured Kevin and Lorraine that they were welcome to stay with them for as long as they wanted while they sorted out the amnesty program.

One evening during dinner, Kevin's father briefly brought up the war in Vietnam. For a few moments Kevin, Lorraine, and Kevin's mother didn't know where the conversation was headed. Their concerns quickly vanished when Kevin's father spoke directly to Kevin and told him that over the past five years, his opinion about the war had changed dramatically. He wanted Kevin to know that, while he did still not fully agree with Kevin's decision to go to Canada to avoid the draft, he now understood and respected the moral objections that fostered his decision.

"Thanks, Dad," said Kevin as Lorraine gently squeezed his hand below the table. "That means more to me than you may realize."

Kevin's mother used her napkin to gently wipe the side of her mouth and then tried, inconspicuously, to dab the corners of her eye where tears were trying to flow.

On the drive from British Columbia to Missouri, Kevin and Lorraine had many hours to talk about what lay ahead and all the uncertainty. Lorraine remembered the American Friends Service Committee that they'd met on campus and suggested that Kevin should contact them for any details on the amnesty program they might have before going the meet with the U.S. Attorney's office. Kevin agreed and on Monday, January 6, the first day after they arrived in Kirkwood, he found the number of the American Friends Service Committee in St. Louis and gave them a call. When his call was answered, Kevin briefly explained his situation and was transferred to a young lawyer that was working in the American Friends Service Committee offices named Michael Foster. Kevin explained to Michael that he was going turn himself in to the U.S. Attorney's office later in the week and was seeking any advice he might have. In a very reassuring voice, Michael invited Kevin to come meet with him later that afternoon to review the details of his situation.

The meeting with Michael Foster was scheduled for 3:00 p.m. at the American Friends Service Committee office in downtown St. Louis. When they drove past the office looking for a place to park, they were shocked to see that all of the street-facing windows and the entry door were scarred by what looked like bullet holes in the glass. What remained of the sign on the door when deciphered through the holes in the glass indicated the American Friends Service Committee, so they parked the truck at the first space available and walked back to the office. When they tried to open the entrance door to the office, it was locked, so Kevin knocked on it carefully between the bullet holes. Very quickly, they saw someone approach the door from the other side and heard it being unlocked. It was Michael Foster, who greeted them and said, "Hi, I'm Michael Foster, you must be Kevin."

"Good to meet you," said Kevin. "This is my wife, Lorraine."

"Wonderful to meet you too, Lorraine," replied Michael. "Come and sit over by my desk, I want to hear your story." Michael locked the entry door behind them. Kevin and Lorraine sat across from Michael, who was sitting behind an old oak desk.

"Michael, I've got to ask," said Kevin. "Are those bullet holes in the window and door?"

"Unfortunately," replied Michael. "I do legal work with the Institute for Peace and Justice, and now, as a result of our move to the

American Friends offices, I am doing more work that comes through American Friends. Neither one of our organizations are very popular with ultra-right-wing elements in St. Louis. Someone drove by and sprayed the windows with an automatic rifle Saturday night. Fortunately, no one was in the office, but we definitely got the message. The police think it was the American Nazi Party, but it's not likely anyone will be able to prove that."

"That's really frightening," said Lorraine. "Is it safe for us to be sitting here?"

"I don't think they are going to come by again during the day," said Michael. "But if it would make you feel better, we can move to the conference table at the back of the office."

"Let's do that please," said Kevin. "It will make it easier to show you the files I have anyway."

After moving to the conference table, Kevin told his long story to Michael from the draft lottery forward, documenting each step of the way with letters and notices from the folder he brought with him. When Kevin finished, Michael was quiet for a moment, looking at the stack of paperwork now in front of him. Finally, he looked up and said, "Wow. That is quite a journey, Kevin. If I understand what you are telling me, you were ordered to report for induction after passing your first physical, but because of new information provided by your doctor and the letter from the senator, your induction was postponed for further review. Then you were ordered to report for another physical on the premise that, if you passed that physical, you would be immediately inducted into the Army. Which also means you never had the second physical that would have determined if you were physically eligible to be drafted."

"That's pretty much it," said Kevin.

"Hmm," murmured Michael. "That's going to be an interesting story to present to the U.S. Attorney, unless you just plan on signing the amnesty agreement."

"What choice do I have?" asked Kevin.

"I'm not really sure yet," replied Michael. "I've got to do a bit of research and give it some thought. But at this point, I don't think there can be any harm in briefly presenting a legal argument that calls into question if you should have been indicted without having taken the physical that would have determined your eligibility to be drafted. In the end, you can always sign the agreement, but your argument might reduce the amount of time you need to spend in the program if you do need to sign the agreement. Since your appointment with the U.S. Attorney is on Friday, we have a few days to prepare. Can you come back on Wednesday after I do some research so we can get our plan together?"

"Sure, Wednesday will work," said Kevin. "But I need to know how much all of this is going to cost, because we don't have lots."

"How about five dollars for a retainer fee," said Michael, "and then you won't need to worry about that anymore."

"Okay," said Kevin. "But that doesn't sound like much money. I can pay you now if you like."

"Money's not the issue, Kevin. Peace and justice are priceless. How about you bring the five with you when you come Wednesday."

"Deal," said Kevin. "And thank you so much, man."

Kevin and Lorraine were very relieved to be leaving the American Friends' office riddled with bullet holes. What Michael had presented to them wasn't what they had expected. They really had just wanted a lawyer to go the U.S. Attorney meeting so Kevin would know what he was signing in the agreement. Now it looked as though they would be presenting an argument to the U.S. Attorney about Kevin's need to be in the amnesty program at all. If he wasn't going to go into the program, then what would they do? How would this all be concluded? After a long and endlessly looping discussion on the ride home, Lorraine suggested they try to set the questions that they couldn't answer aside until they met with Michael again on Wednesday. Kevin agreed but also suggested that his parents didn't need to know anything about this at the moment other than the positive news that a lawyer would accompany them to meet with the U.S. Attorney.

On Wednesday morning, Kevin and Lorraine met Michael again at the American Friends office. It was comforting to see that the windows and the door had already been repaired. Michael enthusiastically told Kevin and Lorraine that the research he had done suggested that Kevin's case was much more complicated and interesting than he had imagined. He now believed that Kevin's draft lottery pool, and a delayed renewal of the Selective Service Act, might positively thread into a body of information that could support a case that Kevin should have never been drafted in the first place. He cautioned that this was just a theory based upon some quick research he had done in the Selective Service case studies he found in the American Friends library. The strategy Michael suggested to Kevin and Lorraine was to present the same complicated facts and supporting documents that had caused him to question Kevin's case to the U.S. Attorney on Friday and see how he reacted. Any further legal action that they might decide to take related to Michael's new theory would all be downstream from the outcome of their meeting with the U.S. Attorney. For now, they would just stick with the facts at hand.

On Friday morning, January 10, 1975, Kevin, Lorraine, and Michael walked into the United States Attorney's office for their 10:00 a.m. appointment. In spite of assurances from Michael, Kevin and Lorraine weren't sure what kind of reception they would receive, since Kevin had an outstanding warrant for his arrest and had avoided prosecution by living in Canada. Beyond the smile and cordiality they encountered at the reception desk, the only question they were asked initially was if they wanted coffee or tea.

From the reception desk they were taken straight to the conference room. After less than five minutes, Terrance Earl Lowry, the Assistant United States Attorney for the Eastern District of Missouri, entered the conference room on crutches wearing a full leg cast, along with his administrative assistant, and introduced himself. He shook hands with Kevin, as well as Michael, and acknowledged Lorraine with a smile and a nod. Michael presented Terrence Lowry with his business card and indicated he would be representing Kevin.

"What happened to your leg," asked Kevin.

"Took a bad fall while skiing in Colorado," said Attorney Lowry. "Shouldn't have made that last black diamond run."

"Ouch," said Lorraine. "So sorry."

"That's water under the bridge now; or maybe I should say snow down the mountain," joked Attorney Lowry. "Nothing serious really. They say it will heal just fine."

Over the next thirty minutes, Michael summarized the timeline and facts of Kevin's Selective Service story, accentuating some of the facts in legal jargon that Kevin and Lorraine didn't fully understand. By the end of Michael's presentation, Assistant Attorney Lowry was shaking his head and scratching his chin, seemingly pondering the same conundrum of circumstances that came to mind the first time Michael listened to the story. After a few follow-up questions to Kevin, Assistant Attorney Lowry paused briefly, formed a pyramid with the ten fingers of his hands, and after spreading his fingers apart and pressing his hands toward each other in and out four or five times, calmly commented, "This is quite a unique situation, and at this moment, I am not sure just how to handle it. My instinct is, given all the circumstances involved, Kevin's situation can possibly be resolved without the amnesty program. However, I need to follow up on some of the facts and documents you presented before we can make a decision. Give me the rest of today and Monday for that and let's all get back together next Tuesday morning at 10:00 a.m. Will that work for everyone?"

Michael and Kevin agreed, shook hands again with Attorney Lowry, and as quickly as that, the meeting was over. Leaving the office, they waited until the door on the elevator closed before they spoke.

"What does all that mean?" Kevin asked Michael.

"Sort of what we were hoping for," said Michael. "Your case has some twists and turns and doesn't fit neatly in their box. It seems that Lowry is very sympathetic to your situation and is trying to find a way to set it aside without you needing to even go through the program, which would be incredible, since then, all charges would be dropped and that would be the end of it."

"Really?" said Lorraine excitedly.

"Really," said Michael. "We can be hopeful, but let's not count chickens yet."

"So true," said Kevin. "I've had my hopes up before, and nothing has gone as expected. Guess we'll see next week."

Back outside on the street, it was cold, so they didn't linger long. Lorraine gave Michael a big hug and told him how much they appreciated all he was doing for them. Kevin told Michael, "Ditto for me, man. Fingers crossed we'll see you here on Tuesday. Have a great weekend."

The next three days were anything but easy for Kevin and Lorraine. They told Kevin's parents everything went well at the first meeting with the Assistant U.S. Attorney but no more than that. They spent some time on Saturday and Sunday with Kevin's friends from high school and people they both knew from Mizzou. Most of them wanted to know what it was like living in Canada and seemed to support their decision to go there. But there were unintended awkward moments in a few of their conversations when they learned of people either Kevin knew or they both knew that had been killed in Vietnam since they last saw them. At a bar on Saturday evening, they also ran into a few people that were now back home from Vietnam. None of them challenged Kevin about going to Canada. But later in the evening, after more beer and liquor had been consumed, Kevin had a conversation with a very intoxicated high school friend who had recently returned from Vietnam that journeyed to dark places, similar to some of Kevin's discussions with John. Kevin didn't sleep much that night, as the interconnectedness of his current situation and the conversations of that evening shouted their annoying presence.

At nine forty-five on Tuesday morning, Kevin and Lorraine met Michael in front of the elevator that would take them to Assistant Attorney Lowry's office.

"Morning, Michael," said Kevin. "Guess this is it."

"We'll see, Kevin," said Michael. "But whatever happens today, we still have options. I spent a lot of time over the weekend looking into your case, and I firmly believe now that you were not eligible to be drafted, for more than one reason. That doesn't matter today, and let's hope for the best, but if it doesn't go as we hope, it's not over, believe me. For now, let's just focus on the meeting."

Once again, everyone was friendly and polite when they entered the U.S. Attorney's offices, and they were taken straight to the conference room. Less than a minute later, Attorney Lowry and his administrative assistant came into the room. The expression on his face seemed more serious than when they last saw him. After greeting all of them, Assistant Attorney Lowry said to Kevin, "Do you remember writing a letter to a Lieutenant Colonel MacDermott at the Missouri State Headquarters of the Selective Service?"

"I think he was the guy that I wrote to and suggested I was willing to spend two years in any kind of service to others but that I was not willing to go to war and kill people," said Kevin.

"That's the one," said Assistant Attorney Lowry, "and he is still some kind of pissed off about that letter. When I suggested we set aside this case with you altogether, he just about blew a gasket. Pardon my French, but he wants your ass. All that said, you can still enter the amnesty program and there is nothing he can do about it."

"Assistant Attorney Lowry, can I have a brief word with my client alone please?" stated Michael.

"No problem, let me know when you're ready," said Attorney Lowry.

Once they were alone, Michael explained to Kevin and Lorraine that he was still confident that, in the end, he could get Kevin's charges dismissed, but that would take time. For the moment, Michael strongly suggested that Kevin sign the Agreement for Alternate Service and look for a job that met the program's requirements. Once he was in the program, Michael would continue with his case.

"That makes sense," said Kevin, "but how much is that going to cost?"

"Don't worry, Kevin," replied Michael with a chuckle. "I already got your retainer last week."

"Wow, Michael," sighed Lorraine, "that is so wonderfully generous. You have helped us so much already. Thank you, thank you, thank you!"

Michael left the conference room and let them know Kevin was ready, and Attorney Lowry and his administrative assistant returned with the agreement. After Michael's quick review of the final document, Kevin signed the two-year Agreement for Alternative Service dated January 14, 1975. With that behind him, all he needed to do now was find a job that qualified for the program sometime during the next ninety days.

Chapter 37

Rain on the Windshield Headed South

During the remainder of January, Kevin met with Michael a number of times to help clarify the facts that Michael needed to prepare Kevin's case challenging his draft notice and indictment. Michael's intention was to file the paperwork by the middle of February, ahead of the ninety-day deadline for Kevin to find a program-qualified job.

Kevin also spent part of each day going through the help wanted section of the newspaper searching for jobs that could meet the amnesty program's qualifications. With no success in finding a job in the newspaper, he expanded his efforts by applying for jobs at a number of hospitals in the St. Louis area. The frustration of searching for a job he didn't really want in the first place, combined with the cold and gloomy winter weather and living at his parents' house, had Kevin more depressed than he had been since his first Christmas alone in Vancouver.

Lorraine shared many of these same feelings as the financial realities of living in St. Louis for at least two years on minimum-wage jobs began to settle in. To make matters worse, the United States had been in an economic recession since 1973. Because of the OPEC-imposed oil embargo in response to the U.S. government's support of Israel during the Yom Kippur War, the price of oil had quadrupled, causing higher prices for gas and frequent severe oil shortages across the country. Though they both knew about the U.S. economic downturn and the oil crisis before returning to the United

States, they had been mostly unaffected by its effects while living in Canada. Now, it was front and center in their lives, as it was with all Americans at the time.

On an unusually cold February Friday, exactly one month from that day Kevin signed the amnesty agreement, Kevin and Lorraine went to Michael's office to finalize the United States of America v. Kevin P. Fischer injunction he intended to file in Federal Court. After their meeting, Kevin and Lorraine stopped at Luigi's Pizza because they were hungry and to delay returning back to Kevin's parents' house. Sipping on a beer and waiting for their pizza, Lorraine asked Kevin, "If you could be anywhere in the world right now, Kev, where would that be?"

"I'm not exactly sure," said Kevin. "But I know it would be warm. Most likely somewhere that Jimmy Buffett sings about. I sure liked Florida when I was there on spring break."

"Then let's go," said Lorraine decisively.

"What are you talking about?" said Kevin in a slightly irritated voice. "How the hell can we do that with the little bit of money we have and all we are facing?"

"I'm not talking about a holiday," said Lorraine. "I mean packing up the truck and moving to Florida to find a job that qualifies there. At least we can be warm and by the ocean while all of this plays out. How can it be any worse than living in St. Louis?"

"Man, that's a crazy but very tempting idea," said Kevin, now in a better mood. "Are you serious?"

"One hundred percent," replied Lorraine. "I feel an adventure coming on."

"Pinky swear," said Kevin, extending his right hand.

"Pinky swear," said Lorraine, wrapping her little finger around Kevin's.

On March 1, fifteen days after Lorraine gave birth to their new adventure, they left St. Louis for Florida in their truck, listening to Jimmy Buffett's *A1A* album on the cassette player. Their goal was to drive straight through to Destin, Florida, and then figure it all out from there.

By the time they arrived in Destin fifteen hours later, the heater in the truck was off and the windows were down. They ate breakfast with a beach view at the Holiday Inn in Destin. Over eggs with biscuits and gravy, they were captivated by the white sugar sand dunes and beach that showcased the vibrant watercolors of the Gulf of Mexico.

After breakfast, they went for a walk along the beach. Almost immediately, they saw a pod of dolphins that seemed to be keeping pace with them along the beach. Not too far from the Holiday Inn, and just about the time their walk reminded them that they hadn't slept in almost thirty hours, they found a small but slightly funky-looking beachfront motel with off-season pricing. Sure that the dolphins were a sign that they had found their new home on the first stop, they rented a room for the night, both had a shower, and then slept until 3:00 p.m. That evening, they ate oysters on the half shell at the bar of a waterside restaurant, and Lorraine had her first ever hushpuppy. In the glow of everything there is to love about "Old Florida," they fell asleep in each other's arms, hopeful that tomorrow Kevin could find a job.

In the morning, they drove to Panama City to see if there were any job openings at the hospital that they knew would meet the job qualifications for the amnesty program. From the reception desk, Kevin was directed to Human Resources, where they gave him an application to fill out. When he turned in the completed application, he asked the HR receptionist if he could talk to someone to explain the circumstances surrounding the type of job he was looking for. When the receptionist asked Kevin to explain that to her, he did.

After listening to Kevin's explanation, she still looked confused, and told him she had never heard about the hospital being involved in any kind of program like that. She told Kevin to wait, and he saw her go into the HR director's office. Kevin heard her try to explain his situation, telling the director that Kevin needed some type of special job for Vietnam draft dodgers. Kevin couldn't hear the director's response but saw him shake his head. When the receptionist returned, she stated rather coldly to Kevin, "I'm sorry, but we don't have any of those kind of jobs at this hospital."

When Kevin returned to the hospital lobby, Lorraine could see he was upset.

"What's wrong, Kevin?" asked Lorraine.

"It'll be okay, Lorraine," said Kevin. "I just forgot how close this part of Florida is to Alabama. I don't think we'd be very welcome here."

"What now?" asked Lorraine.

"Let's drive further south, to Sarasota," said Kevin. "I read an article in the paper once that said you could grow three gardens in one year in Southwest Florida. With all the retirees, I think there will be many more hospitals in that area."

Kevin and Lorraine wanted to stay off of the interstate and follow the Gulf along the coastline as much as possible and took Route 19 South to Yankeetown, Florida, where they found a reasonably priced motel for the night. After sleeping in the following morning, they arrived in Tampa around noon to very congested traffic on U.S. Route 41, the only road to Southwest Florida at that time. With big-city traffic and congestion, it was not the Florida they were looking for, and not much was said between the two of them as they endured their very slow stop-and-go ride.

Traffic was lighter by the time they got to Bradenton, but even in Sarasota, it was far busier along Route 41 than they ever would have imagined. But it was a sunny and glorious 78-degree day. Windows were down and their spirits were rising once again when they noticed Sarasota Memorial Hospital come into view. When Kevin requested a job application, he didn't mention anything about his special circumstances. After completing the application, he was sent to the assistant director of Human Resources. She politely told Kevin she liked his qualifications, but that there were no openings in the Dietary Department at that time. She followed by telling Kevin she expected there would be some openings that he was qualified for within a few weeks and inquired if Kevin had a phone number to reach him. Kevin told her that he had just arrived and didn't have a phone, but he would check back every week.

Lorraine took this news as a positive development. She suggested Kevin should look for a job at a restaurant until an opening at a hospital became available, since there were almost two months remaining for him to find a qualified job. Lorraine hoped that once Kevin secured a restaurant job, they would be able to afford an apartment and then she could look for work also.

Leaving the hospital, they headed south again on 41. They noticed many restaurants, but when they saw the parking lot full at the Oyster Bar, Kevin pulled into the parking lot and said, "This place looks promising."

Lorraine waited in the truck while Kevin went inside the restaurant to ask about a job. After waiting at the counter for someone to talk to him, he was told it was still lunch rush and he would need to come back at 4:00 p.m. to see the manager. With over an hour to kill, Kevin and Lorraine drove to Siesta Key, took their shoes off, and walked along its beautiful white sand beach that clearly reminded them why they came to Florida in the first place.

Just before 4:00 p.m. they arrived back at the Oyster Bar. Once again, Lorraine stayed in the truck and Kevin went in to inquire about a job. Kevin had been waiting for ten minutes when the manager came out of the kitchen and introduced himself to Kevin and told him to follow him to his office. Kevin explained his restaurant experience to the manager, who seemed to be listening closely and sincerely interested.

"Sounds impressive," said the manager, "but I don't have an opening at the moment. I do have someone leaving in about ten days. How do I get in touch with you?"

"I just arrived in Florida two days ago and don't have a phone number," said Kevin. "I can check back with you though."

"Sure, that will work," replied the manager, handing Kevin his business card.

"If you don't mind me asking," said Kevin. "What is your pay scale for a cook?"

"All depends on experience," said the manager. "If you're as good as you suggest, we could start you at ninety cents an hour, and if it works out, you'd be up to a buck real quick."

"Thanks," said Kevin, staying as upbeat as possible. "That will help me budget for an apartment. I'll check back with you next week."

"Rent's expensive in Sarasota," stated the manager. "You might want to look further south, in Osprey or Nokomis."

"Thanks for that tip," said Kevin. "Talk to you soon."

Back at the truck, Lorraine asked how it went.

"Looks like he might have a job opening soon," said Kevin, "for fucking ninety cents an hour. How the hell are we going to live on that?"

"C'mon, Kevin," Lorraine said encouragingly. "Let's not give up just yet. I will be able to work too. If we had it all figured out, it wouldn't be an adventure."

"You're right, Lorraine, I know, but I just feel so discouraged," sighed Kevin. "Okay, I can rally. The manager said that rent is cheaper further south. Let's go have a look."

They drove further south on Route 41, passing Osprey and Nokomis, the two places the manager mentioned. While it was pleasant in a way, there was no real sense of the Gulf of Mexico as there was on Siesta Key, so they didn't bother stopping. Just before Venice, at Roberts Bay, and just for a brief moment, they could smell saltwater in the air. Too quickly, the view and the sense of the water were gone again. The main route turned slightly east and away from the water at the junction of Business 41, presenting a hodgepodge of strip malls that no urban planner would ever want to admit to.

Kevin wasn't sure where to go now and pulled into one of the strip mall parking lots to study their now crinkled map of Florida. He noticed that, just a couple of miles south of where they were, Business 41 rejoined Route 41. A few miles after that was a junction for State Road 776 that went to Englewood. On the map, it appeared that Englewood was surrounded by water, with much of it on Lemon Bay or the Gulf of Mexico. "Next stop, Englewood," said Kevin.

Not long after tuning onto 776, still in Venice, they noticed there were no more commercial buildings, only single-family houses and undeveloped land. Just as Venice transitioned, with nothing more than a sign, to Englewood, Lorraine saw another sign for Manasota Beach.

"Turn right here, Kevin," she said excitedly. "Let's go watch the sunset."

Kevin turned west on Manasota Beach Road, and then it only got better. Most of the homes were on large-sized lots with either undeveloped lots or large tracts of vacant land in its natural state between the houses. Less than a mile later, they were crossing a drawbridge over the intercoastal waterway, with the Gulf of Mexico glimmering in sight, a stone's throw away. There were only three other cars in the parking lot that overlooked the Gulf. The beach park consisted of a few picnic tables underneath rustic pavilions, one set of restrooms, and a simple but narrow boardwalk between the sea-oat-covered dunes and the open beach.

At the end of the boardwalk, they noticed a couple with their beach gear waiting their turn to get on the path back to the parking lot.

"Thanks for waiting," said Kevin to the couple.

"Not a problem," said the man. "We are on beach time and in no hurry at all."

"Do you live here full-time or are you just here on holiday?" asked Lorraine.

"We're snow birds," the couple unintentionally said in unison and then laughed. "We're here every winter, but we'll head back to Michigan soon after Easter, depending on spring weather up north."

"Cool," said Kevin. "Hey, how far can you walk on this beach?"

"Long way," said the man. "I think you can walk north to Venice, about twelve miles, and south to Stump Pass would be five or six miles or so. Either way, it's pretty much the way it's been for the last forty years except for a new beachfront house once in a while. If this is your first time in the area, and you want to see an even better beach, just follow the Key road to Middle Beach a few miles south of here. Part of the road isn't paved yet around Middle Beach, but most of the time, there's no problem getting through unless it's right after a big storm."

"Wow, thanks so much for the tip," said Kevin. "I think we'll go there now and catch the sunset at Middle Beach."

Just beyond the boundaries of the park, Manasota Beach Road is covered, for almost the entire way to Middle Beach, by a canopy of live oaks, banyan trees, cabbage palms, and native pine trees intertwined with a variety vines, some of them big enough for Tarzan to have a swing. The houses on the intercoastal side of the key are closer to the road because of the narrow strip of land that exists between the road and the intercoastal waterway. On the Gulf side, most of the houses are set back from the road and closer to the Gulf, hidden from sight by the canopy and the un-landscaped natural growth.

Less than a half-mile before Middle Beach, the pavement turned into a packed sand road, washboarded by the dried remnants of rivulets created by a recent downpour, making its own pathway to the Gulf. Soon after the road ran out of pavement and became sand, the canopy opened up, showcasing the first view of the Gulf of Mexico Kevin and Lorraine had seen since they left the parking lot at Manasota Beach. There was no sign indicating Middle Beach, but there was a rough-cleared gravel-and-sand area across the road from the beach that appeared to be the informal parking lot.

When Kevin and Lorraine pulled into the parking area, there were no other vehicles, and there was no one on the beach. The only picnic table sat underneath a small grouping of cabbage palms, providing shade for the table in the heat of the day. Sitting on the table near the water's edge, Kevin and Lorraine watched a sunset that, long after it went below the horizon, glowed with ever-spreading colors within the mountains of cloud formations out in the Gulf. As the day dimmed its way to night, they drove further south along the Key to Englewood Beach in the last remnants of the light show.

A few miles south of Middle Beach, the canopy ends where Sarasota County does, and Charlotte County begins. In Charlotte County, low-profile condos and motels, as well as beachfront trailer parks, had been established for many years. But compared to Siesta Key or Venice Beach, Englewood Beach was still very underdeveloped Florida. Just before the Circle K and the left turn that takes you off the Key and back to 776, they stopped at the Lock and Key restaurant hoping for seafood. Truly Old Florida, the walls, as well as the ceilings that were hung with large fans, were made of pecky cypress. Other than the walls, most of the building was enclosed in screen to allow the Gulf breezes in and to keep the bugs out.

When Kevin asked the waitress what was good, she answered, "Everyone seems to like the clam chowder."

"Two bowls of chowder and two Michelobs it is, then," said Kevin.

The beer was cold, and the chowder was as good as promised. After all they had seen and done that day, it was wonderful to ponder the events and their future in an unassuming restaurant across the street from the Gulf. Without a doubt, Englewood was the best place they had been to in Florida since Destin.

"What's next, Kevin?" asked Lorraine.

"Not sure really," said Kevin. "I think we just need to find a place to sleep and see what the morning brings. It seems like this area is very laid-back, with lots of open spaces, so maybe we can find a quiet place to park and sleep in the truck."

"I'm up for that if we can find the right spot," said Lorraine.

After leaving the Lock and Key, they drove off the Key over the Tom Adams Bridge and then turned back north on 776. It was dark now and difficult to find anywhere that looked like a safe place to park the truck for the night. Before they knew it, they were back at Manasota Beach Road that they had taken to Manasota Key earlier in the evening. Instead of turning left toward the beach, Kevin turned right on a gravel road that quickly turned into undeveloped land on both sides. Less than a mile in, Kevin saw a wide spot on the left-hand side of the road big enough pull off. After an eight-point turn, the truck was facing in the other direction and he parked just off the road. With the dome lights on, they made up their bed in the back of the truck on top of the boxes that were filled with all that they owned. Kevin locked the doors, turned off the lights, and lay down next to Lorraine with the rear sliding windows of the truck open on each side.

All too soon, the mosquitoes and no-see-ums found them, so they closed the windows and swatted all of the bugs they could find inside the truck. Without the windows open, the truck became warm and stuffy. Lorraine finally fell asleep and Kevin could hear her soft breathing. Many swirling thoughts later, Kevin dozed off, only to be awakened by a knock on the window and a flashlight beam staring him in the face.

"Sarasota County Sheriff. Please step out of the truck. I need to see some ID," stated the deputy.

"What? I mean, yes, sir," mumbled Kevin.

Startled, Lorraine spoke loudly, "What's going on, Kevin?."

"It's okay," said Kevin. "Sir, I'll be right out. Can she stay inside?"

"Yes," replied the deputy, still shining the flashlight into the window. "You can bring her ID or she can pass it out the window."

Outside of the truck, Kevin gave the deputy his driver's license and Lorraine passed hers out of the rear side window. Kevin explained that this was their first day in Englewood and they didn't have a place to stay and were trying to save money for the rent. The deputy indicated he understood and sympathized with their situation but explained that what they were doing was illegal in Sarasota County. He shined the flashlight back into the truck on Lorraine and asked her, "Is everything all right with you, ma'am?"

"Yes, sir, officer," said Lorraine.

"Let's do this," said the deputy. "Y'all can stay here the rest of tonight, but only tonight. Make sure y'all are gone in the morning."

"Yes, sir," said Kevin. "We will, and thank you for your understanding."

Without saying anything else, the deputy walked back to his car and drove away.

Kevin and Lorraine closed the windows again and tried to kill all the mosquitoes inside the truck before laying back down on top of their bed of blankets. Sweating, looking at the ceiling of the truck, they both wanted the sleep that didn't want to come. The discoveries of the day, which included the echoes of "ninety cents an hour," emboldened their worries about the future, casting a wide net of doubt on the decision to make their stand in Florida. Something about the all-that-was-going-to-be just wasn't anymore.

Chapter 38

Apple Fritters and Toes in the Sand

At 6:00 a.m., after very little sleep, they were both awake and ready to get out of the hot and sticky truck. Kevin remembered a little donut shop they passed the day before and suggested they get donuts and coffee and welcome the morning at the beach. Heading south on 776, they found Abby's Donut Nook about a mile before the turnoff to Englewood Beach, all lit up and serving customers.

A tiny free-standing wood-sided building, Abby's looked like a giant-sized children's playhouse with a single entrance door framed between two cottage-style windows. Inside, there were a few stools in front of a counter, with just enough room for other customers to stand behind them and shout out their order for the donuts that were displayed on the open shelves on the wall between the counter and the small kitchen where they made the donuts. Waiting their turn to order, Kevin asked one of the customers at the counter what his favorite donut was.

"They're all good," replied the man at the counter. "But if this is your first time at Abby's, you've got to try the apple fritter. It's an experience."

A few minutes later, Kevin and Lorraine were on their way to Englewood Beach with two large coffees and a bag of warm apple fritters. The sun was just beginning to announce itself in a glow of pink as they crossed the Tom Adams Bridge over the Intercoastal Waterway. Groups of pelicans were already winging their way to their fishing grounds and Lorraine shouted, "Dolphins, Kevin!" as two of them surfaced for a moment by the fishing pier below the bridge.

Instead of going to Englewood Beach, they went about a mile farther south on Manasota Key to Stump Pass Beach, an undeveloped beach preserve the waitress at the Lock and Key told them about the night before. Where the road ended and Stump Pass Beach began was an unpaved area big enough for three vehicles to park, and all three spaces were still open. From the small parking area, a spit of land about one-third of a mile wide stretched almost two miles further south between an open inlet on the Lemon Bay side, the locals called Ski Alley, and the Gulf of Mexico on the west side. Except for a narrow path that came and went on the Ski Alley side and the broad beach on the Gulf side, the land was covered in cabbage palms and an ever expanding, and invasive, forest of Australian pines. More than people, Stump Pass Beach was home to raccoons, a few bobcats, eagles, osprey, gopher tortoises, a variety of snakes and lizards, as well as a huge population of mosquitoes and no-see-ums all coexisting with piles of some of the most beautiful seashells that can be found in Florida.

Kevin and Lorraine took their coffee, apple fritters, and a blanket to the beach on the Gulf side where they discovered they were the only people there to experience the magic of that morning. After their coffee and fritters, they walked to the pass and back and the magic continued. With no other people on the beach, they saw more dolphins than they had ever seen at one time and squadrons of pelicans skimming over the water and then rising quickly in an arch to dive into the twinkling Gulf for their breakfast. They witnessed an eagle in a dogfight with an osprey for the fish the osprey possessed at the moment, in the backdrop of a brilliant and cloudless blue sky. Below, and oblivious to the sky battle, little sanderlings scampered between incoming and outgoing small waves, frantically searching for multicolored coquinas trying to burrow into the white sand as it retreated with the water.

When they reached the pass, a manta ray leapt completely out of the water for a reason only it could know, just before they saw two manatees riding into Lemon Bay on the incoming tide. Remembering to look down from all that was getting their attention in the water, they were delighted by the discovery of another beautiful shell on the beach that they didn't know the name of. In not much more than an hour, they had forgotten about the muggy and sleepless night in their truck and fallen in love with Englewood, Abby's apple fritters and all.

Energized by their morning, Kevin and Lorraine were determined to make their situation work in Englewood, and they knew that meant finding a job that met the amnesty program's criteria. Lorraine suggested they look in the Englewood newspaper but also drive to Venice and buy a newspaper that would likely have more ads for job openings. They stopped at the Circle K and purchased the Englewood Sun and, back at the truck, turned straight to the classifieds. Very quickly, they determined there were no program-qualified jobs, and no jobs at all that Kevin was qualified for. It was a quick and unpleasant reminder of how bad the economy was in Florida. Their determined elation from the morning at the beach was silently fading away and was definitely evident in the expression on Kevin's face.

"Let's head to Venice, Kev," said Lorraine. "I just have a feeling we're going to find something in the paper there."

"We're off," said Kevin with a smile.

When they got to Venice Island, they bought a Venice Gondolier at a convenience store but agreed not to read it until they were at the beach. Lorraine believed that looking for a job in the classifieds while sitting in front of all that had so deeply captivated them earlier in the day would be the catalyst for making what they wanted happen.

They parked the truck at Venice Beach and walked to a picnic table that faced the Gulf. With Lorraine looking over his shoulder, Kevin went straight to the classifieds and found the section for Restaurant/Hotel. He saw an ad for a dishwasher and one for a cook at Waffle House, but nothing that looked promising or that would work for the amnesty program.

"Shit," said Kevin, "I really wanted this to work out. Maybe it's just not meant to be. I'm tired, I need a bath, and we are no closer to figuring this out than we were yesterday. As much as I don't want to, going back to Kirkwood and living with my parents might be the best answer. It's only for two years."

"Let me see the paper, Kevin," said Lorraine very determinedly. "Maybe you missed something."

"Help yourself," said Kevin.

Lorraine went to the beginning of the Help Wanted section instead of looking first at Restaurant/Hotel. Just after Professional she saw Medical. The fourth ad down between an ad for Maintenance Man and one for Phlebotomist, Lorraine saw an ad for Cook—Dietary Department.

"Here it is, Kevin, listen to this!" said Lorraine very excitedly.

"Cook required for busy hospital kitchen. Must be a self-starter and experienced in all areas of food preparation. Weekends required. Salary dependent on experience. Contact James Addison at Venice Island Hospital—485-0713.

"C'mon, Kev, there's a pay phone back at the parking lot."

Kevin dug into his pocket and found a dime as they walked quickly to the pay phone. Looking directly at the Gulf, he deposited the dime and dialed the number. Just as he heard the phone begin to ring at the other end of the line, he saw a pelican diving headfirst into the water and then surface with his beak pointed to the sky. Then, with a wriggle of his gullet, he swallowed his catch and twitched his tail feathers.

After the operator answered, Kevin was quickly connected to Mr. Addison. As confidently as possible, Kevin said he was calling about the job and wanted to get more information. Mr. Addison was very friendly, explained the position, and asked about Kevin's experience. After Kevin stated his training and experience, Mr. Addison invited him to come to the hospital for an interview that afternoon.

Kevin hung up the pay phone with a smile, and as he returned his attention to his surroundings, he noticed another pelican dive into the Gulf for a fish.

"Sounded positive, Kev, tell me, tell me, tell me!" pleaded Lorraine, grabbing Kevin with both her hands on his shoulders.

"It was positive, and I'm sure the job at the hospital will qualify, but he doesn't know the amnesty part of the story yet. Hopefully, he will understand."

"Well, he's more likely to if we get you cleaned up a bit. Time to hit the showers for both of us."

They got soap and shampoo from the truck and cleaned up as best as they could in the beach shower with their bathing suits on. Kevin shaved at the sink in the men's bathroom and then changed into clean pair of pants and shirt. Right near the hospital, they found a small diner and split a fish platter for lunch, since they hadn't eaten since their apple fritters in the morning.

At the hospital, they entered the lobby together. Kevin explained to the receptionist that he was here to see Mr. Addison in Dietary. The receptionist called Dietary and then told Kevin that Mr. Addison would be out shortly to see him. A few minutes later, Mr. Addison appeared in the lobby and introduced himself to Kevin. Kevin couldn't be sure, but Mr. Addison looked like he was in his early thirties. They shook hands and then Kevin introduced Mr. Addison to Lorraine.

"Good to meet you, Lorraine," said Mr. Addison with a sincere smile. "From my discussion with Kevin this morning, it looks like we can use this boy. I won't keep him too long."

"Absolutely no hurry," replied Lorraine. "Keep him as long as you like. We're just grateful for the opportunity."

When they got to Mr. Addison's office, they talked about Kevin's culinary experience in greater detail but also his management experience with Spion Kop Ranch.

"What took you to Canada, Kevin, and what brings you to Florida?" Mr. Addison inquired.

"That's the part that I didn't want to mention on the phone, Mr. Addison," said Kevin. "I came back to the States to become part of the amnesty program announced by President Ford. I need to find a job that qualifies for the program. I know the job at this hospital does, and I know I can do a very good job for you over the next two years, but I'm not sure how you feel about the program."

"Were you a deserter?"

"No, sir. More like a mix-up about my draft status and a physical that got a bit out of hand. Anyway, I didn't report for induction when I was supposed to."

"Oh, you were a draft dodger then," Mr. Addison said with a smile that Kevin didn't know how to interpret.

"I don't use that term, but I guess that's what many people call it."

"Not a problem, really. I was a Green Beret myself and did two stints in Nam. Saw a lot of stuff and a lot of people get hurt. Did what we needed to do and I'm proud of that, but I never did figure out why we were really there. Maybe you looked at it from a different set of glasses and a few years later than I first took a look. Used to just be my country, right or wrong, but I don't think that covers it anymore. What kind of paperwork do I need to fill out for you?"

"For the job, you mean?"

"Yes, for the job and the amnesty program. You want the job, don't you?" chuckled Mr. Addison.

"Yes, sir, I do. Very much, sir, thank you. I have the papers in the truck."

"Then it's yours," said Mr. Addison, extending his hand to Kevin. "Get me that paperwork you have, and I'll sort that all out. The only question now is, when do you want to start? Right away, or do the two of you want to get some beach time and a tan first?"

"A bit of beach time would be great, sir. We fell in love with Stump Pass in Englewood."

"Okay, get me the paperwork before you go today and then report back here a week from tomorrow at 9:00 a.m. I suggest you trim your hair a bit before you start, if you get my drift."

"Yes, sir, I will, and thank you again, sir. You don't know how much it means to Lorraine and me."

"Just glad I can help put the war and all that Nixon stuff behind us like President Ford wants. And by the way, rent is cheaper in Englewood than Venice, so you're on the right track."

"I forgot to ask you, sir. How much does the job pay?"

"I'm going to stretch for you, Kevin, because I think you can do what you say. I can start you at $1.15 per hour, but if all works out as I expect it will, I will bump you to $1.30 at the end of thirty days. How does that sound?"

"Sounds good, sir, thank you."

When Kevin came back to the lobby, Lorraine could tell by the smile on his face that he couldn't contain that he got the job.

"Do those smiling blue eyes mean we're all good, Kevin?"

"Damn good," Kevin said just a little too loud for the lobby. "And bonus, I don't start for a week, so we can find a place to rent and just hang out at the beach until then."

Lorraine gave Kevin a hug and whispered in his ear, "Guess it's a good thing I had a second look at the newspaper you were so pissed off at."

"Good thing for sure," replied Kevin, looking in Lorraine's eyes. "You're good at helping me see what I have missed. Not sure I could live without you."

"Not sure you could either. And try not to forget that."

Chapter 39

Thistle Dew

Now with a job that qualified for the amnesty program, the next thing on their list was to find a reasonably priced place to rent in Englewood. Lorraine remembered seeing a Cottage for Rent sign on 776 when they were driving to Venice and suggested they check that out first. Heading south, just after the turnoff for Manasota Beach Road and right before the Honeybee Nursery, Lorraine spotted the sign.

"There it is, Kev, just ahead on the left."

Kevin slowed down, and with no traffic in sight, turned left onto a narrow gravel-and-sand driveway that was covered in a canopy of mostly native trees and foliage. Less than one hundred yards later they ba-bumped over a small, narrow wooden bridge spanning a creek bed that was dry for the moment. Just after the bridge, the property opened up to a group of three small cement block cottages, two of them duplexes. Along with the main house that was set back from the cottages for privacy, the twelve-acre property was showcased by a neatly mowed Florida lawn, typically consisting of a random combination of grass and weeds, native oaks, cabbage, queen and coconut palms, hibiscus, bougainvillea and plumeria in multiple colors, as well as citrus trees, figs, and papaya, all surrounded by palmettos and native Florida jungle.

Kevin drove past the cottages and parked in front of the main house, a rancher made of concrete blocks and cypress with a massive stone fireplace chimney rising above the peaked roofline. There was no electric doorbell. Instead, there was a small brass bell attached to the wall next to the door that entered into the Florida room, along with a small wooden hammer hanging by a leather shoe string decorated with small seashells, placed just close enough to the bell to ring it with the hammer. Shortly after Kevin rang the bell, a dark-tanned leathered-skinned salty dog-of-a-man wearing only shorts and slip-on sneakers walked from the main house through the Florida room and opened the door.

"How do you like our doorbell?" he chuckled.

"Love it," said Lorraine with a big smile.

"Bet you're here about the cottage."

"Yes, sir," said Kevin. "Is it still available?"

"Sure is, let me show it to you. By the way, my name is Fred, Fred Degenhardt."

"I'm Kevin Fischer and this is my wife, Lorraine. Good to meet you."

"Good to meet both of you also."

It was only a short walk to the cottage for rent, but Lorraine and Kevin were captivated by all of the flowers and trees full of fruit they passed along the way.

Opening the door, Fred winked at Kevin and Lorraine and chuckled in a way they were already getting fond of. "You're in luck today, the cottage for rent is the only standalone cottage I have. Nothing wrong with the duplexes of course, but this one offers a bit more privacy."

The cottage was thirty feet long by twenty feet wide, with louvered window doors on the front and one side, along with windows on all sides designed to let the breezes blow through the cottage. Inside, there was a living space with a couch, coffee table, two chairs, and small table, a kitchenette with stove and refrigerator, one bedroom, and a compact but adequate bathroom with a shower. The inside walls were cement blocks painted off-white, the floors were covered in a slightly yellowed linoleum.

"This is it. Not very big, but it has everything you need, including furniture and dishes, for only seventy-five dollars a month."

"Is there air conditioning?" asked Kevin a bit sheepishly.

"No air conditioning or heat, but I'll bring you a couple of space heaters if it's going to get cold again next winter. We're past that now. Tell you what; if you are going to stay for at least a year, I will build a small screen porch on the front of the cottage. That will be cooler in the summer, and you can even sleep there if you want to."

Kevin looked at Lorraine and Lorraine spoke first. "We'll take it, and we'll be staying at least one year, and more likely, a couple of years, so we'd love that screen porch."

Extending his hand to Lorraine, Fred smiled, chuckled again, and said, "Deal, and welcome to Thistle Dew. Now, why don't you two come over to my place, meet my Elaine, and let's have a cocktail."

The first thing Kevin and Lorraine noticed when they entered Fred's through the Florida room was a workbench at the far end of the room piled with conch shells and seashells in all sizes and surrounded by stacks of boxes all full of more shells.

"Wow!" said Kevin. "What do you do with all those shells?"

"I make stuff and sell it. Not as much as before, since I'm kind of retired, but I've made my living for years traveling through the Caribbean finding handbags, artwork, and knickknacks I could import and sell back here in Florida. Along the way, I saw some very creative uses for shells, and I've used them to decorate just about anything, including a bottle opener I'll show you in the kitchen."

They found Elaine in the kitchen, who greeted Fred with a smile and a kiss even though he hadn't been gone very long.

"These kids are our new tenants, darling—meet Kevin and Lorraine."

"Welcome," said Elaine. "I hope you will like it here."

"I know we will," replied Lorraine. "It is so beautiful and close to the beach. I hope we can buy some of the fruit from you too."

"That's one of the perks that comes with living at Thistle Dew," said Fred. "Now, will you have beer, wine, or a rum drink?"

Over the next ninety minutes, Kevin and Lorraine learned that both Fred and Elaine lost their first spouses to cancer, and the two of them had only been married for a few years. They also discovered that Fred was a passionate environmentalist who, along with others in Englewood and the surrounding Gulf islands, had been in an almost continuous legal battle with General Development Corporation and other developers that wanted high-density development along the pristine beaches. One of those battles resulted in blocking a bridge a developer wanted to build from Englewood to Stump Pass and onto Palm Island, with the victory allowing Stump Pass to become a park. But Fred seemed to be most proud that their efforts limited the building density and building height of the coastal areas from Englewood to Boca Grande.

"Is that why Englewood looks so different from Sarasota and even Venice?" asked Lorraine.

"That's why," said Fred as his face turned serious. "And we've got to keep it that way because those bastards have their hands in every pocket in Tallahassee and too many of our county commissioners. They're just waiting for their moment, even if that takes years."

"It is so uniquely and naturally beautiful in Englewood," sighed Kevin. "It's hard to imagine why anyone would want to ruin it."

"They just don't think that way, Kevin. It's all about the money!"

Elaine took Fred's hand and squeezed it. "It's okay for now, Fred, so let's not let this discussion raise your blood pressure."

"You're right, darling. We'll need to take these kids on the boat to Little Gasparilla Island so they can see what natural Florida is really all about. For now, let's have one more drink before you move your things into the cottage."

The rest of the week before starting work at the hospital, Kevin and Lorraine explored as many beaches as they could around Englewood. They had a few more fritters from Abby's and bought shrimp off the boat in Placida that they cooked on the grill that came with the cottage. Near the end of the week, they paid the bridge toll and made their first trip to Boca Grande. Before the bridge, they stopped at Eldred's Marina for a Coke and were amazed by the number of people their age living at Eldred's on boats or cobbled-together float houses.

Just over the bridge, on the intercoastal side of road, was a very basic campground, with undesignated spaces amongst the Australian pines, big enough for tents and small trailers and perfect for anyone that wanted to fish or swim. A quarter-mile beyond the campground, on the Gulf side of the road that faces Little Gasparilla Pass, there was a road to a property development that fell victim to the economic downturn to become a cul-de-sac to nowhere, though it provided easy access to that part of the beach. From there, almost all the way to the Johann Fust Community Library on Tenth Street, there were only a handful of houses. Past the library, and just before town on the Gulf side of the road, the grand mansions of the island sat peacefully behind walls covered in purple bougainvillea. Shortly after mansion row, the Gasparilla Inn, with its manicured golf course, came into sight, just before the stop sign that designated the beginning of the little village of Boca Grande.

There weren't many businesses in Boca Grande at the time, but there was a U.S. Post Office, Hudson's Grocery, Fugates little department store, Seale Real Estate, the Pink Elephant and the Temptation restaurants, referred to by the locals as the "Pink" and the "Temp," as well as the "Temp's" package liquor and wine store. These businesses conveniently provided most of the essentials the small population of permanent and winter residents required without going off island. In a striking but odd contrast, these simple but well-cared-for businesses and the Gasparilla Inn shared the downtown area Boca Grande with a historic but extremely derelict train station, partially boarded up to keep people and critters out and with the glass from the broken windows still laying on the ground around the station.

It was still season on Boca Grande, and the Gasparilla Inn was full, so there was a quiet bustle of activity in town. Kevin parked the truck across the street from Hudson's Grocery and they walked through the village on Park Avenue down to where they got their first look at Banyan Street, aptly named for the magnificent tree canopy created by the banyan trees on both sides of the street. On Banyan they walked left toward the intercoastal waters in a path that would eventually take them by the Pink Elephant and the Gasparilla Inn back to the truck.

When they got to the Pink Elephant, Kevin insisted they needed to go inside and see what it was all about. Unlike the grandeur of the Gasparilla Inn, the Pink Elephant was a simple eating and drinking establishment almost fully screened with no air conditioning catering to the eclectic population of fisherman, laborers, day trippers, guests of the Inn, and the residents of the mansions, that for the most part peacefully coexisted on the island.

Walking into the Pink, it was darker inside than either Kevin or Lorraine expected. It was almost lunchtime, so the Pink was filling up, but it was evident that some of the fishermen at the bar had been drinking for a bit already, and possibly, some of them for days. The menu was Old Florida, and when the waitress came to the table, they ordered two Michelobs, two cups of clam chowder, and an oyster basket to split.

After they ordered, Kevin said to the waitress, "This is a very cool restaurant, but it seems so different than the inn across the street."

"It is," she replied. "But in another way, it is a place where everyone on the island can come and just be themselves regardless of who they are or how much money they have or don't. You might not know who they are, but working here, I see millionaires and mullet fishermen sharing a table and conversation. Gets a bit crazy on Friday and Saturday night and there's dust ups once in a while, but all's usually forgiven before they leave or the next day. Very much like Key West here but smaller, and not many people know about it yet. We love it that way."

"Do you live on Boca Grande?" asked Kevin.

"Yep, we live down at the south end near the big oil tanks in one of the old houses. Lots of other freaks live in that area of the island, along with the few blacks that work on the dock. You should check it out if you want to see the real Boca Grande. And if you want to party, the best place on the island is the Laugh-a-Lot. If you drive down to the south end past the lighthouse, you'll see it. It's right on the Gulf. Really, you should go there one night. Everyone's mellow and very cool."

"Thanks, we'll check it out for sure. What's your name?"

"Karen, and my old man's name is Jamie. We're all going to the Laugh-a-Lot tomorrow night. You should join us. If you get too wasted and don't want to drive home, you can crash on one of our screen porch beds. Really, you should come. They're having a great band, it's going to be a full moon, so it will get crazy.

"We just might take you up on that. Thanks for the invite, Karen."

"No problem, I better go put your order in."

After lunch, Kevin and Lorraine drove south to see the parts of the island Karen had mentioned. They saw the Laugh-a-Lot, two lighthouses, and at the very end, the large oil storage tanks and the dock where the ships came in with the oil. Right before the oil tanks were the houses Karen mentioned but they weren't sure at the time which one she lived in. The old southern-style houses were a bit run down, but there was a unique charm about them that brought to mind questions about the history of Boca Grande. When they stopped at the big lighthouse on the way back home, they realized how captivated they were with Boca Grande and the sense of peaceful quiet distance from everything except exactly where they were at that moment on an island in the Gulf of Mexico.

They decided not to go to the Laugh-a-Lot as Karen suggested, since Kevin's first day of work was the following morning. But in the months to come, Kevin and Lorraine spent as much time as they could on Boca Grande and became good friends with Karen and Jamie and other saltwater free spirits and fishermen that lived on the island.

Chapter 40

Out of the Blue

Kevin's first day of work at the hospital was a Saturday and Mr. Addison's day off. After Kevin finished with the paperwork at Human Resources, he was introduced to Chuck Morris, one of the three Dietary Department supervisors. Supervisors were required on all Dietary Department shifts, but on the weekends, when Mr. Addison was off, they had full charge of the kitchen. Within the first few minutes after they met, Chuck let Kevin know he was recently retired from the U.S. Air Force and took the job to supplement his income. Kevin wondered why Chuck shared this fact so quickly and what Mr. Addison might have shared with Chuck and others about his situation. To Kevin's relief, Chuck didn't say anything further that day about his military service and seemed genuinely interested in helping Kevin get oriented to the job.

The first person Chuck introduced Kevin to was Mrs. Gaynell Palmeter, the head cook. She was a short, stout, but solid woman and appeared to Kevin to be at least sixty years old. Mrs. Palmeter was born and raised in Arcadia, Florida, but now lived outside of Venice, Florida, with her husband on the Myakka River. She had been working in the Dietary Department of the hospital for over twenty years. Though Mr. Addison and the supervisors were technically her superiors, it was Gaynell Palmeter that really ran the kitchen. The majority of the other Dietary Department staff were also women, all who respected Mrs. Palmeter and, to some degree, feared her scolding and potential wrath.

"Good to meet you, Kevin," said Mrs. Palmeter with a smile. "We've heard so much about you. Glad you finally decided to give up sun tanning and come to work."

"Pleased to meet you, Mrs. Palmeter. Where would you like me to start?"

"How about those pots in the sink. Seems like the girls made more of a mess than usual this morning at breakfast. Do you think you can handle that?"

"Yes, ma'am."

Kevin wasn't sure what to think about Mrs. Palmeter's comment about hearing so much about him. He wondered if what she learned about him had anything to do with being assigned to wash pots. He wondered what others might know. It was hard to put those thoughts aside as he washed the dirty pots from breakfast. Before he was finished, the women began to bring more pots that had been used for lunch preparation. He saw Chuck walk by a few times, but other than looking his way, Chuck never said a thing to Kevin. By the end of his first day at the hospital, Kevin had washed pots, worked on the dishwasher line after lunch, cleaned and mopped the walk-in refrigerator and freezer, and taken out all of the trash. He made sure he checked in with Mrs. Palmeter before he clocked out, who only said to him, "See you tomorrow, son."

When he reported to work the following day, he went to say good morning to Chuck, who was seated behind the supervisor's desk in one of the offices. Chuck looked up from the desk and said hello, but then told Kevin to see Mrs. Palmeter.

"Seems like you did a good job on those breakfast pots yesterday, Kevin. Why don't you have another go at them today?"

"Yes, ma'am."

On Monday, after Kevin punched in, he went to Mr. Addison's office to say hello.

"How were your first couple days, Kevin? Are they putting your talents to good use?"

"Well, they seemed to be pleased with how well I can wash pots and load the dishwasher."

"Is that all they had you do for two days, Kevin?"

"That and a bit of mopping and taking out the garbage."

"Well, that's just not the plan, Kevin. I told Chuck to let Mrs. Palmeter know how much experience you have. Tell you what, I will introduce you to Dolly Marchand, one of the other supervisors, and make sure she knows how capable you are around the stove."

"Thanks, Mr. Addison. That would be great. But I don't want to cause a fuss, and maybe they just want to see that I am willing to work."

"Maybe so, Kevin, but I have plans for your talents, so hang in there and let me see how I can grease the gears a little, if you get my drift."

"Yes, sir, I think I do.

Over the next few weeks, Mr. Addison and Dolly Marchand carefully and tactfully integrated Kevin in the cooking hierarchy of the kitchen, starting with suggesting that Kevin work on the luncheon for the hospital board of directors and key benefactors. Kevin developed a menu with Mr. Addison that was gourmet by hospital standards, and on the day of the luncheon, prepared all of the main items himself. The day after the luncheon, Mr. Addison found Kevin in the kitchen and asked him to come to his office. Kevin followed Mr. Addison, and once he sat down in front of Mr. Addison's desk, Mr. Addison closed the door.

"Congratulations, Kevin, all the board members can talk about this morning is the lunch you prepared for them yesterday. They all want to know who that boy is. I think this is working out exactly as I had hoped, and now we need to move to phase two."

"Thank you, sir, but I'm not sure exactly what you mean."

"Kevin, have you taken a look at the food that arrives at the back door of this kitchen?"

"Yes, sir, it looks good to me. I am always amazed at the quality of the fresh seafood, and the roasts and chops look every bit as good as the meat that came into some of the best restaurants I have worked for."

"Bingo, Kevin, that's my point. Quality food arrives at the back door, but by the time Mrs. Palmeter and the women have cooked it too early and it sits in the steam table for hours, it's not that great anymore. Just as bad, if not worse, is that the food they are preparing for the employee cafeteria is boring and, many days, downright awful. We are not very popular with the employees, who complain to administration on a regular basis about how bad the food is. I've tried to change that, but until now, I didn't have the way to do it. With you on board, I now think we can.

"I want to strike while the iron is hot, Kevin. The board loves what we did yesterday, and I think they are willing to spend a bit more money to make the food in the cafeteria better. I am going to suggest to them that, if they will let me hire another couple of people with a level of cooking skills close to yours, we can make dramatic improvements to the cafeteria food first and, eventually, to the food that goes up on the floors. I think they will also approve paying for you to go to school at night to get an associate degree in Hospital Foodservice Management. But while you're doing that, I want you to manage the new team for the cafeteria. What do you think, Kevin?"

"Wow, I never expected this, but it's exciting. Just like you said, we have quality food coming in the back door and we have all of the equipment we need to prepare it as well as any good restaurant. I think it's exciting, but I'm not sure how Mrs. Palmeter will handle all this."

"Not to worry, Kevin, that's my job. I want to build both of our reputations on this project. And I will make sure the board authorizes a good raise for you. I don't want you telling anyone, even the supervisors. This is our project, and I think it can really impact the hospital in a positive way."

"Thank you, Mr. Addison. You have my one hundred percent support, and I won't let you down. I do have one favor to ask though. Could you put in a good word for Lorraine in administration? They have her resume and she is well qualified, but we haven't heard back from them. She wants to work weekends like I do so we can have our days off together. That should be a plus for them having someone that wants to work every weekend."

"Consider it done, Kevin. I think you better get back to the kitchen before they wonder what we are up to. And not a peep about this to anyone."

"Yes, sir, and again, thank you, sir."

Within a week, Lorraine was hired in administration and had Mondays and Tuesdays off like Kevin. The board approved everything Mr. Addison requested, including Kevin's raise, and Kevin enrolled in the Hospital Food Service program at the University of South Florida in Sarasota, paid for by the hospital. Two months later, Kevin and Mr. Addison had completely changed the quality and variety of the food in the employee cafeteria. Their first step was to introduce a salad bar with a large selection of items and homemade salad dressings. They revised the menu, with new items being offered each week and created special celebration days that included Hump Day Pizza, Steak Fridays, and fresh from the Gulf seafood platters. Kevin was the secret weapon Mr. Addison hoped for, and the Dietary Department went from zero to hero. In the eyes of the board of directors, the hospital administrator and other department heads, Mr. Addison was a superstar, though all of them seemed to know the role that Kevin played and greeted him by name when they saw him.

The respect generated by the changes in the employee cafeteria flowed back to all the dietary department employees, who now seemed to care for and respect Kevin. Even Mrs. Palmeter seemed to be excited and not threatened by the changes and new positive energy in the kitchen environment. When Kevin suggested a new recipe or technique or taught someone in the kitchen how to prepare it, Mrs. Palmeter reacted as if Kevin's skills and teaching ability were an extension of her own. If there were concerns about a "draft dodger" working at the hospital in the beginning, all of those concerns had evaporated, even with the "good ole boys" in maintenance.

When Mr. Addison filed his monthly reports with Selective Service, he made sure they knew that Kevin was the poster boy for the amnesty program. Kevin also had to report in by phone each month to the Selective Service office in Webster Groves, Missouri. His call was always transferred to the administrative assistant, Clair Worthington. For the first few months when he called, Mrs. Worthington seemed stoically professional and matter of fact. Their brief conversations consisted of a few basic questions about possible change in address or violations and arrests, after which she would tell

Kevin she expected his call, without exception, the following month. More recently, Mrs. Worthington was more friendly with Kevin and, at times, almost chatty.

"We hear good things about you, Mr. Fischer," she told him at the end of one call. "How is school going?" she said to him on another. On his most recent call, Mrs. Worthington asked him about the weather in Florida and then closed the call by saying, "Just keep up the good work, young man. The time in the program will go by before you know it."

On almost every day off, Kevin and Lorraine spent at least part of it at the beach. Fred and Elaine took them on the boat to Little Gasparilla Island a number of times, but their favorite days and nights were spent on Boca Grande with a growing group of friends. They became regulars at the Pink and Miller's Marina and were now completely familiar with long nights of dancing at the Laugh-a-lot and sleepovers on the screen porch at Karen and Jamie's. Jamie's good friend, Mark Fritch, was born and raised on Boca Grande. Mark's father and grandfather were nautical pilots that guided the big ships through Boca Grande Pass to the docks. Mark was studying to become a pilot and worked with his father whenever he brought a ship in. Jaime was a deck hand for many of these trips and helped to secure the ships lines once it was at the dock. On a few occasions, when Kevin was with Jaime and Mark, he mentioned he would like to help on one of the trips if there was ever an opportunity to do so. Mark assured him if they needed someone to fill in, they would give him a call at the hospital or leave a message with Fred.

On Sunday, February 15, 1976, almost thirteen months after Kevin and Lorraine arrived in Englewood, Kevin received a call from Michael, letting him know that he had presented Kevin's case in Federal Court on Friday and that the judge was expected to rule on the case next week. When he hung up the phone, Kevin felt anxious about the potential outcome, but he also realized how long it had been since he had given the case any thought. In a fleeting moment of clarity, he pondered if that was because he was more contented living in Englewood and working at the hospital than he had expected to be. Before he could think about that possibility any further, he was called to the dietary office for another phone call. He expected the call to be from Michael again, who must have forgotten to tell him something on the first call. Instead, he was surprised that it was Mark, asking him if he was available to help bring in an oil tanker that evening. With no hesitation, Kevin said he would be there.

At 8:00 p.m., Mark's father, Mark, Jaime, and Kevin pulled away from the pilot boat dock, passing by Miller's Marina on the way to Boca Grande Pass. It was a full moon night, but in a sky free of artificial light intrusion, Kevin beheld the most beautiful and brilliant southern skies he had ever seen. Shortly after going through the pass they could see the lights of Jean Paul Getty II bobbing in the Gulf. Two miles later, they came off-plane, slowly and carefully approaching the ship. Mark was at the wheel of the pilot boat, and his father was advising him about the best approach to the ship. The Gulf was relatively calm, but even the small swells accentuated the movement of the ship and its relationship in size to the pilot boat. About twenty feet from the starboard side, Mark turned the pilot boat parallel to the ship when it was at the bottom end of the swell. Now the pilot boat and the ship were rising and falling together in the small swells moving east toward the shoreline of Boca Grande. The crew on the Jean Paul Getty II threw a rope ladder over the side that uncoiled its way down the hull of the ship to about five feet above the waterline. With each rise and fall of the Gulf, the ship moved closer to the pilot boat, going deeper into the bottom of the swell than the boat, bringing the bottom of the rope ladder to the height of the pilot boat's deck rail. With the ship only feet away from the boat, Mark's father climbed up on the deck rail. At the bottom of the next swell, he leapt from the deck rail to the rope ladder and climbed quickly up the ladder, just as Mark gunned the engines on the pilot boat to peel quickly away from the ship. For Kevin, it was a heart racing level of precision and danger he hadn't imagined would be part of the experience. With adrenaline pumping in all their veins, the pilot boat headed to the oil dock while Mark's father guided the ship in.

When the ship arrived, it was Kevin's job to tie some of the big lines to the pylons. There were multiple lines to tie, requiring

Kevin to jump from one pylon to another one for the next line. The dock was well lit and illuminated the water around the dock. To Kevin's surprise, there were a number of hammerhead sharks circling through the dock area hoping the light would attract fish. It was another aspect of the adventure Kevin hadn't considered.

Once the ship was secure, they left the oil docks at the south end of the Island and slowly motored back to the pilot boat dock on the canal just past Miller's Marina. Back on shore, beers were popped and Mark's father patted Kevin on the back.

"Good job, Kevin. You'll be a Cracker before you know it."

"Thanks, Mr. Fritch, I really have grown to love Florida more than I ever imagined. Lorraine and I love Boca Grande most of all."

"Lots to love, boy. That's why the Fritches have been here for so long, and I doubt Mark will ever leave the island either. It just gets into your blood. And don't forget what the old-timers say—once you get Boca sand in your toenails, you'll always come back."

On the drive home, with all the windows open on a February night, Kevin knew that he couldn't feel much better or more alive than he did at that moment. If the moment could be compared, it was in many ways like everything the best moments of his life had ever been, or the drive home from Carrs Landing while the sun was going down after changing sprinklers in the orchard on a warm summer night, or dancing under the stars with Lorraine above the Arch at Cabo San Lucas on New Year's Eve. But he smiled as he remembered that to compare the moment was to rob the moment of its magic and take him away from the moment itself. Bringing his attention back to his joy, he saw a shooting star blaze its way across the sky over the Gulf.

"I don't know what's next," Kevin stated to no one. "But some-how, all this will have to be part of my life."

By Wednesday, when Kevin and Lorraine returned to work, they hadn't heard from Michael, but with no phone, and no answer-ing machine at Fred's, they knew that he might have tried to reach them. Just after 9:00 a.m., Mr. Addison's secretary told Kevin he had a call. When he picked up the phone, he expected to hear Michael's voice. Instead, it was Clair Worthington.

"Kevin, this is Mrs. Worthington from the Selective Service office in Webster Groves." With her voice now slightly trembling she carried on, "I've called to give you some news. We were informed late yesterday that a federal judge ruled in your favor, and your case has been dismissed. We will be sending you and Mr. Addison a letter stating that you have been released from the amnesty program and are free to do whatever you like."

"That's great news, but I'm not sure exactly what to say, Mrs. Worthington. Do I need to do anything else or sign any papers?"

"You don't need to do anything else, Kevin, but on a personal note, I want to wish you all the best for the rest of your life. I think I understand why you did what you did, and I'm glad, in the end, it has worked out for you."

"Thank you for saying that, Mrs. Worthington. That means a great deal to me. Thank you for your support along the way. Goodbye now."

"Goodbye, Kevin, and good luck."

Kevin hung up the phone and, without asking permission from anyone, left the kitchen and, in a fast walk, went straight to the administration office to see Lorraine. When he came into the office, their eyes met and his smile gave him away.

"Really, Kevin?"

"Really, sweetheart!"

Chapter 41

Vineyard Logic

Kevin's unexpected and immediate release from the amnesty program brought about a dramatic shift in perception for him and Lorraine about why they were in Englewood and a dilemma they hadn't considered. It was the vision of returning to the Okanagan Valley after completing the amnesty program that provided the courage they needed to enter the program in the first place and had sustained their resolve for more than a year. What they hadn't expected at the outset was how much they would grow to love the west coast of Florida.

When he learned about Kevin's release from the amnesty program, Mr. Addison told Kevin he was very pleased it all worked out so well. He also assured Kevin that his job and the opportunities that lay ahead were still available to him. Lorraine was given similar assurances by the hospital administrator.

When they shared the news with Fred and Elaine, it was evident they were genuinely pleased for Kevin and Lorraine, but almost immediately, they asked them what they were going to do.

"We're just not sure yet," said Kevin. "We've got to give it some thought."

It was the same question asked by all of their friends on Boca Grande, and they answered the questions with the same response, because they just didn't know. For more than a week, Kevin and Lorraine discussed their options and vacillated between staying in Florida and building a life in Englewood or returning to work with

Peter and Anna in Okanagan Centre. One evening, a passionate discussion about the pros and cons of each choice seemed to bring them to an overwhelming conclusion that they should return to Canada. The next morning, while sharing apple fritters at 19th Street Beach on Boca Grande, they changed their mind and wondered how they could ever leave their slice of paradise.

A few days later, when they seemed to be less certain about remaining in Florida, Lorraine proposed a new way of looking at their decision.

"Maybe we're coming at this the wrong way, Kev. I don't think it's really about if we want to stay in Florida or go back to British Columbia. I think the question is, what do we want to do, what are we most passionate about?"

"Okay, but I thought that's what we've been talking about. You know for a fact that I'm not too passionate about being cold in the winter."

"Very funny, Kevin, but that's not what I mean. Ever since we've been together, our decisions needed to be based upon what was confronting us that we had no real control over, or the consequences of decisions we made that limited what we could or couldn't do. For the first time, there is nothing standing in our way from doing anything. If we decide to go back to Canada, the decision will be one hundred percent, because that is what we want to do. The same goes for staying in Florida. We could go to Europe, New Zealand, or even Hawaii, but there should a reason or a passion for something that steers the decision. I think the real logic we should use is, what do we want to do? Not just now, but what do we want to be doing in five years."

There was an extended pause before Kevin said anything.

"I have never really considered the decision from that perspective. Mostly, I've thinking about what I like about Florida verses the Okanagan, but I haven't really wrapped my head around what I would be doing in Florida in five years. I suppose managing a kitchen in a hospital or a restaurant, which I do enjoy, but it's so much different than managing a vineyard."

"Exactly, Kevin, and I don't see me working with you in your kitchen. I do know our lives and purpose on the vineyard will be more intertwined and flow with the pace of the seasons. It will also be much easier to get ahead with free housing, free medical, and higher pay than Florida wages."

"I think you are really on to something, Lorraine. Peter talked to me about using vineyard logic a few times. He'd say that each season is a learning experience and different from the next. No matter how much you plan, it's the things you can't control like the rain, hail, wind, and cold, even the birds that play the game with you. Peter said the wines are part of the game too. The wines reflect not only the terroir of the vineyard and how it is tended, but also the difference in the weather from year to year. He told me once that, over time, I would become grounded by the vineyard and develop an intimacy with the land, the wildlife that shares the space, the lake, and the surrounding mountains."

"Look at you, Kevin. Your blue eyes are flashing with passion as you tell me this. It's been a while since I've seen your baby blues look like that."

"I guess I do get very passionate, and when I think about being in the vineyard in five years, I have a clear picture of enjoying more of the same but different. I can't say that about running a kitchen operation. Maybe we can even get involved in wine making at some point."

"I'm sure we can if we want to. They say in Canada, you can become a big fish in a small pond."

"And the biggest fish in that pond at the moment is Pierre Trudeau, who gave us shelter and allowed our conscientious choices that brought us to now."

"Is that our decision, Kev?"

"If I use Peter's vineyard logic, I'm ready to roll north if you are."

"Let's call Peter and Anna."

Later that day, with a stack of quarters in hand, they called Peter and Anna who were extremely happy to learn Kevin was released from the amnesty program and that Kevin and Lorraine would be back at Spion Kop by April 1. With the remaining quarters he had, Kevin called John and told him the news. Kevin promised to stop in Grand Forks on the way to Spion Kop and get caught up. John let

Kevin know that he was happy Kevin was coming back to Canada, but with his tell-it-like-it-is nature and post-combat view of the USA, he warned Kevin to get his ass back up to Canada as quickly as possible before the United States started another war somewhere. Shortly before the operator came on-line to say that he had thirty more seconds on the payphone, Kevin was telling John he thought, that with the lessons learned from the Vietnam War, it would be a long time, if ever, before the United States would initiate another war or put soldiers in a combat zone. The rest of that discussion would need to wait until Kevin and John were together again in Grand Forks, but he suspected John might not agree with him.

Over the next few days, Kevin and Lorraine gave their notices at the hospital and shared their decision to go back to Canada with Fred and Elaine and their friends in Boca Grande. Everyone they spoke to supported their adventurous decision to return to British Colombia and manage a vineyard operation. Some the people at the hospital still found it difficult to believe that you could grow grapes in Canada. Most of the people they told their plans to knew that Canada was north of the USA, but not many knew where British Colombia was located. Kevin would always tell them it was north of Washington, to which many replied that it must be really cold and snowy.

Kevin and Lorraine's last day of work at the hospital was Sunday, March 14. Fred and Elaine hosted a going away party for them at Thistle Dew that evening and invited all their closest friends. The guests brought a wide variety of beer, wine, and libations, along with food to share, and even a bit of weed for those so inclined. The pot-luck assortment of food included all the dishes they loved in Florida, chilled, Gulf, pink shrimp, stone crab claws, oysters and clams on the half shell, and oysters for roasting, smoked mullet dip, grouper fingers, and grouper cheeks, pulled pork, hushpuppies, coleslaw, potato salad, and black-eyed peas. As the evening progressed, guitars and other instruments appeared as musicians traded songs around the fire pit. When it was Kevin's turn, he played and sang *Nothing but a Breeze*, written by Jessie Winchester, who spent a few years in Canada under the similar circumstances to Kevin. By the time he finished the first verse, it was hard for Lorraine to hold back her tears. By the end, she was sobbing, though not everyone was sure why.

> Life is just too short for some folks
> For other folks it just drags on
> Some folks like the taste of smoky whiskey
> Others figure tea's too strong
> I'm the type of guy who wants to ride down the middle
> I don't like all this bouncing back and forth
> Me, I want to live with my feet in Dixie
> And my head in the cool blue north
> In a small suburban garden
> Not a single neighbor knows our name
> I know the woman wishes we would move some place
> Where the houses aren't all the same
> Jesse, will you would take me where the grass is greener
> Though I couldn't really say where that may be
> Some place high on a mountain top
> Or down by the deep blue sea
> And there we'll do just as we please
> It ain't, nothing but a breeze

Soon after the song, Lorraine announced she was calling it a night and made the rounds for hugs, kisses, and goodbyes. Not long after, everyone began to leave, and Kevin got his hugs and goodbyes. After helping clean up what needed to be done that night, he went back to the cottage and slipped into bed with Lorraine.

"Hi, Kevin. It was a great night, wasn't it?"

"Magical, but I wasn't sure if you were feeling all right. I didn't see you drink anything."

"Just didn't feel like it."

"What was all that sobbing about during the Jessie Winchester song?"

"Just a bit emotional lately, and my mixed emotions seem to be getting out of hand.

"I'm fine. Let's go to sleep. We've got lots to do before we leave in two days."

By 7:00 a.m., Tuesday morning, the truck was all packed, but before they left, they shared coffee and final goodbyes with Fred and Elaine. Soon after, they headed up the driveway and heard the ba-bump of Thistle Dew's little wooden bridge for the last time. Nine hours later, and an hour before sunset, they were checked in at same little beachfront motel in Destin where they spent their first night in Florida more the fourteen months earlier.

"Not long till the sunset, Kevin. Let's go out on our porch and take it all in."

"Do you want a beer or glass of wine, sweetheart?"

"No, I'm good, Kev."

"Are you feeling okay?"

"I'm fine, Kevin, come sit and let's just enjoy our last night on the Gulf."

It was a glorious sunset that seemed to glow on forever and one that was worthy of a green flash. If there was one though, they didn't see it. Pelicans skimmed inches above the Gulf, dove for last fish, and winged their way back to their night roost. A small pod of dolphins swam through the last of the sunbeams, seeming as if they were enjoying the sunset too. Kevin and Lorraine were transfixed by all that they loved about Florida, now playing out in front of them but soon to be coming to an end.

"Are you still happy with our vineyard logic decision, sweetheart?"

"Couldn't be happier, Kev. I've been waiting for this moment to tell you something."

"What, is something wrong?"

"Nothing's wrong, Kevin. The last week of work, I got an appointment with Dr. Carlson. I wanted him to check something out."

"And?"

"And he said I was fine. Well, really, he said, we were fine, because there is going to be a new Canadian about seven months from now."

"You mean you're having a baby?"

"No, we are having a baby."

They both stood up to embrace at the same time, in a blue grey mist quickly fading to night. A warm wind blew softly through their hair as they danced without speaking beneath a starlit southern sky.

"I'm so happy about the baby, and I love you so much."

"I love you too, Kevin, very, very much. Tell me about the Canadian geese again."

"Oh, you mean TMFL. They mate for life, sweetheart. They always mate for life."

About the Author

Searching for an alternative to the political and social unrest in the United States, Kenn immigrated to Canada in 1970 and spent over twenty years in British Columbia's Okanagan Valley managing large vineyard and orchard operations. Kenn, along with his wife and best friend Linda, currently live a Gulf Coast lifestyle in Placida, Florida.

Kenn is a business adventurer, "entrepreneur," pragmatic optimist, hopeless romantic, father of five children, grandfather of a growing number of grandchildren, musician, songwriter, poet, trained chef, wine grower, surfer, and a global ambassador of good ideas. Wary of both half-truths and spreadsheets, Kenn tries to follow Robert Mondavi's philosophy of "balance in all things with glorious exceptions." As such, he is a part-time vegetarian and has carefully saved five minutes of his fifteen minutes of fame for this book.

CPSIA information can be obtained
at www.ICGtesting.com
Printed in the USA
FSHW011537210519
58295FS